IT'S JUST CHEMISTRY

RITA H ROWE

It's Just Chemistry

This novel is a work of fiction. All names, characters, businesses, places, events and incidents in this book are either the product of the author's imagination or used in a fictitious manner. Any resemblance to actual persons, living or dead, or actual events is coincidental.

It's Just Chemistry

For my husband,
the absolute love of my life,
my first,
my last,
my absolutely everything.

It's Just Chemistry

Prologue

What is it about your first love? Is it because it's something that only happens once in your life? Is everything that comes after not as important or is it because that feeling can never be replicated? The first look, the first touch, the first kiss. Maybe not the first kiss you've had but the kiss of the first person you ever loved. Twenty years later, you can still picture it. Maybe it's the perspective—years tend to change things. Everything back then seems so romantic, so touched by magic. But whatever it was, or is in your head, it is imprinted, and the years may come and go, your true love may come and light up your life and sweep you away into forever, but you still can remember the first one that touched your heart.

Chapter One

1989

"Why don't you write me love letters?"

"I'm a seventeen-year-old boy," Danny said with a laugh.

Fiona frowned. "But what if I wrote you one?"

"Then I would read it," he replied, bending over and kissing her on the tip of her nose.

"And would you reply?"

"Of course, I would."

"Okay," she said and nuzzled her face into the crook of his neck.

*

Dear Danny, I'm so happy you asked me to be your girlfriend.

Fiona bit the end of her pencil and twisted her mouth. She turned around onto her back and thumped her fists on the mattress in frustration. It sounded so childish, like a crush, nowhere near how she felt, but what did she want to say to him, really? That she loved him? She wasn't sure she did yet. She pulled at a lock of hair that spilled around her shoulders and smiled. He always told her he loved her hair and twirled his fingers through the thick dark curls when he kissed her.

"Danny Devoy." She let the name linger on her lips, and her mouth involuntarily turned up in a smile, a flush of warmth invading her belly and she relished it for a moment, closing her eyes to savour the memory of the last time she saw him, when he held her so close, kissed her deeply, just two hours before. An ache raced through her chest, and she swallowed. It would be two days before she saw him again, heard his voice, felt his fingers entwined in hers, and she sighed.

She turned back to the matter at hand. What to write. It had been less than two months since they'd been together, and before that, Fiona barely knew he existed even though he had been at the same high school with her for two years and was part of the in-crowd.

She certainly was not part of *that* crowd, with their pretty clothes, stylish hair, and pictures of *A-ha* on their folders and bags. Most of her clothes came from the local *Target,* and she tried to make do with what she had — her cute face, her thin body, and the way she walked, an air of nonchalance, pretending not to care what people thought of her.

She cared.

Having arrived from Italy four years before and heading straight into the craziness of high school, Fiona Macrone was utterly unaware of how evil high schoolers were. They teased, and they tortured, things she wasn't accustomed to. At first, it was her olive skin, and when they heard her accent, that was fodder for the bullies. At least she had an Anglo-sounding name, passed down to her from a distant Irish cousin, or else that would have added to the insults. Her surname was already converted to macaroni the moment she set foot into the classroom on her first day of school in Melbourne.

For a twelve-year-old going into this jungle by day and coming home to a different sort of jungle at night that was her family life, Fiona had to adjust who she was and who she was supposed to be—a bit like a chameleon. When she thought about it later, this might have been where it all began, the start of what she was destined to become.

This foreign land into which she and her elder brother Alfredo, or Alfie as everyone called him, were thrust was a blow from the fairly innocuous childhood where school was pleasant, kids were fun, and they lived in a place they actually liked living. A place where neighbours peeled potatoes as they watched the neighbourhood children play with marbles and chase each other in the street, where schools were a little nest of activity, students trying to outdo each other by putting their hands up first, where that same competitiveness was forgotten once they were in the yard at playtime.

Maybe it was the timing. Perhaps if Fiona had gone to high school in Italy, things might have been the same—nasty kids exist everywhere, she guessed. A child on the cusp of adolescence, thrown into a world of competitive beasts, doesn't stand a chance, and Fiona watched in silence the way the popular girls tossed their hair this way and that, the way they laughed with their chins raised and their mouths puckered. She resented them for their style and their automatic place in a society that looked down on newcomers, and Fiona felt the heat in her rise, knowing that she could match them at anything, yet she had to change who she was to be a part of that society. But she learned quickly, practising her Aussie lilt, watching, learning how to fit in, how to mask who she was, how to become one of them, much to the point that she didn't know who she was, not for a very long time.

Alfie didn't fare well, turning into a recluse six months after they arrived, preferring the company of comics and novels. Fiona watched with fascination as it turned him into an enigma, a wildly interesting boy with flowing black hair and dark brown eyes, who sat by himself engrossed in his books while other kids at school, including girls in her year level, two years younger than him, flirted, whispered and gossiped about him. He stopped caring about fitting in, and for them, he was a mystery they wanted to solve, so for a while, a very short while, Fiona became their source of information, and for those few months, she enjoyed what popularity was. She liked it — a lot. But soon, the mystery faded, and no one cared, and she was on her own again.

"God, you're ugly," the freckle-faced Tori said one day in class, looking at Fiona with disgust. She sat with her more poised friend, Carrie, who turned to Fiona with a smirk and went back to drawing love hearts on the picture of George Michael plastered on the front of her diary.

Fiona was taken aback, shocked, humiliated, and thankful the olive colour of her skin disguised all of the above. She turned to the board on which the teacher was furiously writing. She wanted to say many things back. Like, *oh, have you looked in a mirror lately,* or *you're the ugliest one,* nothing intelligent enough to warrant anything but more insults, so she kept her mouth shut, her ears burning and her pride broken.

"I know you can hear me," Tori hissed, and a nudge from Carrie stopped her from pushing further.

It went on, and whenever they felt the urge to pick on someone, Fiona was it. She knew she wasn't the only one, but she still felt the sting whenever somebody levelled one of their insults at her.

Fiona was an astute student, observing, learning, and knowing what she had to do to become the person she was not. She woke up early every morning, settled her wild hair, perfected her look by borrowing her mother's eyeliner and lip gloss, lost her accent, and by grade nine, the insults waned. She also refined her air of detachment, and once their words had no effect, or so they thought, the bullies, for the most part, left her alone. She had a couple of friends, good friends, smart friends, kind friends, and she was slowly gaining the approval and acceptance she so sorely craved. She was pleased with her success. Her first foray into acting had begun.

"Fionaaaa," her father called, and Fiona jumped, that voice so familiar, and yet he always managed to give her a fright when it came out of nowhere. She loved her father, short, sturdy, strong. With a temper and a booming voice that would leave the bravest of men scurrying, he was a gentle man with Fiona, always trying to teach her something about life. But boys. No talk of boys. No talking to boys. If a boy, any boy, was in any level of proximity to his daughter, Ricardo puffed out his chest, holding his breath as he did, and his eyes would narrow dangerously. It was all that was needed to scare Fiona and the boy that might have just happened to walk too close to her or call out a hello from a distance. Fiona dreaded the parent-teacher interview evenings, which Ricardo insisted on attending, and Fiona would keep her head down, aiming straight for her teachers, not daring to acknowledge any of her peers.

Fiona tucked her notepad under her pillow and scrambled off her bed. Nothing was coming to her, nothing meaningful anyway. As she moved past her window, she noticed the droplets of rain hitting the pane, and she rolled her eyes, but a smile broke out on her face. When the rain came down, especially after a warm day, Ricardo wanted to dance in it. It was their ritual for as long as she could remember. At times, her mother, with an exaggerated sigh, paused her housework to join them. Even the reluctant Alfie would get pulled out of his room, and in the backyard, they would close their eyes and wave their hands about until their skin was soaked. "Coming, Papa," she called back, skipping out of her room.

Chapter Two

What do I write? Danny thought to himself as he sat on the edge of his seat watching the World Cup qualifier on television, leaning forward, a pencil in his hand, hovering over a blank piece of paper. Just then, a shout from the crowd and Danny dropped the pencil, jumped up and pumped his fist in the air. "Yeah! Go, boys," he yelled at the TV. He sat down again and picked up the pencil and the piece of paper, looked at them for a second and pushed them towards the end of the table. He couldn't focus on it now, as much as he wanted to make Fiona happy. He would finish the match and get back to it. Besides, watching the match was research, he justified. He was going to be one of them, and the more he watched and played, the closer he would get to his dream.

He let himself smile as he thought about her. Fiona was his dream, had been for a long time, and he finally got her to notice him. He grinned to himself, shifting aside his light brown hair with his fingers and sighed. It was important to her. He pulled back the piece of paper and leaned it on his sports magazine. He picked up the pencil and began writing.

Dearest Fiona,
I miss you when I'm not with you, like right now. I wish we could see each other whenever we want. Maybe one day

*we will be able to tell your dad about us, and he will like me.
I want to call you, but I know I can't. I keep wishing you
could call me. Every time the phone rings, I wish it was you.
I can't wait to see you on Monday.*
Love, Danny.

He wondered if it were too short a letter, but he
didn't know what else to say. He told her how he felt
in person — it was so much easier. But she wanted this,
and he wanted to make her happy, to see her smile,
those big brown eyes light up as they did when they
set eyes on him.

"You home?" his mother's voice called from the
front door and Danny jumped. He hadn't heard her car
pull up in the driveway and he quickly scrunched the
paper into the pocket of his jeans and strode to the
door to help Grace, who had just returned from her
shopping trip. He took the bags from her, and she
smiled in relief. "Thanks, honey," she said, returning
to the car to grab more.

Danny felt guilty for not going with her to help
with the shopping, but she always shopped so early in
the morning on Saturdays, and he couldn't rouse
himself out of bed before nine on the weekend. But she
never complained, and yet again, he cursed his father
under his breath for leaving them, leaving him the
man of the house.

It had been two years since he'd all but disappeared
from their lives, finding love in the arms of his
secretary. *Such a cliché*, his mother said often. They'd
barely seen him before he abandoned them, leaving for
work just after the sun rose and not returning until

Danny and his mother readied themselves for bed. His advertising company, *Devoy Media*, was always his first and true love, and Danny and his mother always played second fiddle to his father's growing empire. When Danny was old enough to understand, he realised his parents were not in love with each other, and even though it almost came as a relief when he finally left them for good, he resented his father for not making them the most important things in his life.

His mind often went back to when he was younger, when his father took him into the office where he played on the carpeted floor with his plastic dinosaurs while his father worked at his oversized teak desk. Danny would reach over on his tip toes to look above the desk, where his father would lean back on his leather armchair, speaking on the phone in a booming voice to his employees and sometimes sweet-talking clients. People rushed in and out of his office, dropping papers on his desk, picking up papers from his desk, bringing him coffee, sometimes a snack for Danny, usually a tray of croissants, which he didn't really like but ate to make them happy. He felt small, insignificant in comparison to his father, but his eyes would shine as his father barked orders, sometimes so angrily that Danny would shrink back to the floor in fear. His father's secretary, Rebecca, would occasionally pop in, giving Danny's head a tousle as she walked past. He remembered the way she giggled when she spoke to his father. He thought she had the loveliest laugh, a little tinkle that poured from her mouth.

"Hi, Danny Boy," she always crooned to him as she walked past, and Danny would beam with pleasure. He liked Rebecca, her pretty blue eyes shiny under a coat of blue eyeshadow, her pink lipstick always so perfect, Danny thought it was the real colour of her lips.

When Danny was twelve, his mother had dropped him off at his father's firm after school on her way to an appointment. Tired after a long day, he sauntered in, his backpack dragging on the floor behind him. Rebecca was not at her desk, so he began to open the door of his father's office, but as he turned the doorknob, that tinkle wafted out. He knew right then something was wrong and that he shouldn't go in. His heart beating fast, he put his backpack on Rebecca's desk and sat straight-backed in her chair. He couldn't go home. It was too far to walk, and he couldn't catch a bus by himself. He looked at the phone on Rebecca's desk and realised he couldn't even call home. His mother wasn't there. He looked around at the other workers, some of whom looked at him with sympathy, one asking if he wanted a soft drink. He shook his head in silence, his lips pursed, his mind unsettled. As he waited, a slow fury began to burn his chest, and he clenched his teeth. He knew what was happening in that room shouldn't be happening, but he was at a loss as to what to do about it.

Twenty minutes, he sat, rigid, waiting for her to emerge from his father's office. When she did, giggling and patting down her hair, he glared at her with all the anger he could muster, his arms crossed in vehemence. She stopped short at the sight of him, and her face sobered. She cleared her throat. A jealous rage engulfed him, and he got off the chair, picked up his backpack and strutted past her, aiming a kick at her shins.

"Danny," he heard his father yell as Danny dashed out of the office, letting hot tears roll down his face. He wished he could run home, be away from here, from his father, from that woman. He hurled his backpack on the sidewalk and sat down beside it, that tinkling laugh hammering in his head.

He didn't know how much later his father had come out but by then Danny had still not calmed down. "Let's go home," said his father and Danny gritted his teeth, picked up his backpack and followed him to the car. Nobody said a word about the incident on the way home. Or ever. His father didn't try to defend or hide what he had done, and Danny had never gone back there.

When his father left them, he wasn't sure how to feel but he soon realised that his mother still loved his father, even after he'd gone and taken up with the one with the tinkling laugh. Grace would sit on the back porch in the evenings looking at the stars, a glass of wine in her hand and the glimmer of tears in her eyes. Danny watched her sometimes through the window, feeling helpless and angry. He wished his parents could have worked it out, that they had tried harder to love each other. They must have done so at some stage, enough to marry each other and have him. When did that go? When did his father look for comfort in the arms of other women?

He thought about the way he felt for Fiona. It blinded him sometimes. It gave him an ache in his belly when he wasn't with her, at times, felt nauseous when he knew he was not going to see her for a couple of days. No, he knew he would never lose what he felt for her. It may only have been a couple of months that they had been together but he knew he already loved her, that he would always love her. He'd lost his seventeen-year-old heart to her and couldn't think of a moment in his future where she didn't exist.

Chapter Three

Fiona had never felt what she was feeling when she was with Danny. She couldn't quite describe it. It wasn't just how he kissed her, which was with such abandon, her insides twisted with fury. It was like she wanted to somehow get so close to him she was a part of him. When his mouth was on hers, she let herself sink into him and finally understood how it felt to need something so bad, like a thirst that was finally being quenched.

She remembered her first kiss two years earlier and wanted to balk at just the thought of it. "Wanna kiss?" Andrew, a tall lopsided boy with a tilted head, caught Fiona on her way out of school. Like every other teenage girl, she imagined being in love, kissing the boy on the other side of the classroom. For Fiona, it was Andrew's best friend, Toby, a quiet boy who didn't have time for anyone but looked at her occasionally, going red as he did. But he'd never made a move, and she was giving up hope that he liked her back.

She looked behind Andrew and saw Toby leaning casually on the fence, trying not to look their way. He frowned, and Fiona felt powerful. He was jealous! Surely if she went off with Andrew, Toby would realise how much he wanted to be with her and maybe ask her out.

Fiona had learned about lust and jealousy all her life. Her parents had taught her that lesson at a very early age. Many a fist was thrown at a guy who looked too closely at her mother, and too many cries were heard when her father talked too cosily to another woman. And much love was made in the aftermath of those jealous rages. But she knew her parents loved each other — to the detriment of their children. Fiona and Alfie were not neglected, not in the slightest, but were often embarrassed by their parents' open affection towards each other, especially after a spat, when their father would grab their mother by the buttocks and place her on the kitchen counter, quite unconcerned that they were in full view of their impressionable children. But Alfie and Fiona would just roll their eyes and walk out of the room. Fiona silently hoped that one day she could feel that way about someone and swoon when a boy finally kissed her.

Andrew was not the boy that made her swoon.

"Here?" Fiona asked Andrew, looking around at the hordes of students exiting the gates as quickly as they could, and she tried to ignore the drip of saliva that was beginning to seep from the side of his mouth. This was going to be her first kiss, and she certainly didn't want to do it in front of a crowd of kids. In fact, she didn't want to kiss Andrew at all, but she was curious. Everyone her age had done it, or so they said, and she just wanted to know what it felt like. Seeing it in movies and reading about it in books makes one curious, and she couldn't help but wonder about those smouldering scenes where the girl goes weak at the ankles or bends a knee in pleasure when held passionately by a man.

"I can walk you home," Andrew said, and Fiona hitched her backpack on her shoulders and followed him, sneaking a glimpse at Toby, who tossed them a look of annoyance and slunk the other way. She smiled. It worked, and she was glad that Toby had noticed, but now she was stuck with Andrew, who didn't even take her hand. Her heart began to beat a little faster; she was nervous. She would have to kiss this guy. She swallowed, feeling her armpits moisten but she set her jaw. This was going to be a first for her. How would she perform? How would she stack up against the girls he'd kissed before? She sneaked a look at him from the corner of her eyes and, by the anxious look on his face, surmised he must not have kissed that many girls, but that still didn't quell her apprehension.

The crowd of kids going home thinned out, and soon they walked alone towards her house. She couldn't let him anywhere near her place. If her father were to see her walking with a boy, she would be in terrible trouble, and he would probably have Andrew's private parts cut off. But how was she to get this kiss before she reached home?

She paused in front of a church, which seemed deserted. "I live just up there," she said, pointing to her house, where she could see the tail end of her father's car parked in the driveway.

He jumped as if she had interrupted his thoughts, and he stopped and nibbled on his thumbnail. "Come with me," he said and grabbed her hand, pulling her around the back of the church.

She was about to protest when his big lips were on hers, and although taken aback, she tried to let herself be taken with the moment, lifting her face to his, expecting him to tenderly graze her lips with his, to feel his hand slide over her neck, the other around her waist, and she raised her arms entwining them around his neck.

But suddenly, his tongue was in her mouth, pushing, shoving, like a jackhammer, and she reared her head back, but he moved forward with her. She could barely breathe and jerked her head away from him. He was smiling. Clearly, he was enjoying this more than she was. He leaned forward, and after a few more bursts from his mouth, she wrenched her lips from him, trying to slyly wipe the blob of spittle he left on the side of her face.

"Do you want to do more?" he asked.

"What?" She screwed up her face in indignation.

"You know, more than kissing."

"No!"

"Are you frigid?" A word she'd heard over and over again, afraid that she was labelled one herself. Hence the situation she was in.

"No. I just don't want to."

"Wanna kiss again?"

"I have to get home," she said and picked up the bag that she'd dropped when he'd tugged her to him.

"Okay. See ya." And off he went, leaving Fiona gaping after him as he ambled away, a silly grin on his face.

She leaned on the fence and ran her fingers over her scraped lips—her first kiss. She didn't see fireworks. She didn't fall in love with Andrew. It wasn't anything like it was in the movies or her beloved books. She walked home, trying to find any sort of romance in what just happened, trying to replay every second in that boy's arms. But she couldn't even remember if he took her in them. It was a letdown, but she tried not to remember it like that, and when she got home, she ignored the raised voices coming from her parents' room, a fight that would be resolved with a bout of passion, no doubt, and went to her own, plonking herself on the bed. Despite it all, she smiled to herself. She had just had her first kiss.

One could never remember the second kiss they had. At least it was that way for Fiona. Toby never made a move after that day, and Andrew, well, she never spoke to him again.

Chapter Four

It was at the beginning of year eleven when Fiona thought her heart had been taken.

His name was Thomas, and when she saw him on the first day of school, she knew she was going to fall for him. He was new, a curiosity to everyone, with looks that rivalled Brad Pitt, and when he strutted into Fiona's English class, her eyes widened and her heart, she could swear literally, skipped a beat. She remembered that quite clearly. He knew the effect he was having by the way he slid his books on the table and slouched into his seat, a crooked grin on his face. Nudges by her best friend, Victoria, brought Fiona back and looking around, Fiona could see he had the same effect on everyone else in the classroom.

"Cute, hey?" Victoria tapped her pen on her bottom lip, her eyebrow raised in admiration.

"Uh-huh," Fiona replied with what she thought was nonchalance, and slyly looked his way again.

Thomas let his gaze roam around the curious class until they caught Fiona's, and before she could look away, he grinned, showing a neat white set of teeth. She smiled back shyly, and feeling prickles on her skin, she rubbed at her arms and looked to the front of the room. But when she deliberately slid her pencil off her desk and bent down to retrieve it, she sneaked a glance at him. There he was, staring at her, a flirty grin on his face, and Fiona felt her cheeks flush. He chuckled, and she looked away, embarrassed.

By the end of the day, Thomas had crossed her path many times, always curling the side of his mouth when his eyes caught hers. At the end of the day, as Fiona waited at the lockers for Victoria to pack her books into her backpack, he strolled past and stopped right in front of her.

"Hi," he said. "I'm Thomas."

"Fiona," she replied and caught herself in time from putting her hand out to shake his.

"See you tomorrow," he said with a wink and swaggered away.

"He likes you!" Victoria cried, slamming her locker door shut.

"No, he doesn't," Fiona said, but her heart was already thumping, and she opened her diary to check if she had English the next day. She did and hugged at her diary in pleasure. She went home excited, his smile etched in her brain, and she couldn't wait for the next day to arrive to see if she'd just imagined it or if he actually did like her.

With the cool looks of James Dean and the gift of the gab, Thomas had already inserted himself into the group of ultra-cool kids, and Fiona, although taken with him, knew those kids didn't mix with hers. Nevertheless, he took every opportunity to bump into her, to go out of his way to smile at her, and the next few days were spent sneaking looks at each other, awkward greetings of *hi* and *hey* and *what did Ms Gayle say to do for homework?*

Fiona thought this was it, that she had fallen in love at the tender age of seventeen. She daydreamed about Thomas taking her in his arms as she looked into his green eyes, running her fingers through his tinted, mulleted hair.

"What's up with you?" Victoria asked, nudging her as Fiona bit on her pencil and dreamily looked out of the window into the sunny day while she drew little hearts on her test paper.

"Huh?" Victoria had almost a sixth sense regarding Fiona, who had yet to reveal how she felt about Thomas.

"Your test," Victoria hissed.

"Oh, yeah." Fiona looked at her paper, which was barely written on. She shrugged. It was only a pre-test, and it was easy. She put Thomas out of her mind and finished the test before everyone else was done. Then she leaned her chin in her hand and gazed out the window again, wishing she had English today.

"So, are you going to tell me about your crush?" Victoria asked when they had left the classroom.

Fiona sighed. She wanted to talk about Thomas, but it seemed premature, and as so far, there was no real conversation, no move by him to make his intentions known. She hoped Thomas would do something, ask her to eat lunch with him maybe, and was irritated that they had to live in a world where the boy always had to make a move while the girl patiently waited for him to do it. "Thomas," she said, and Victoria nodded knowingly, a satisfied smirk on her face.

By lunchtime the next day, no move was forthcoming, and Fiona stood glumly at the canteen window with Victoria, staring at him over the tables where he sat with his friends. Suddenly, one of his friends, Danny, got up and walked straight over to Fiona with an air of confidence, but when he got to her, he hesitated, and a nervous smile crossed his face.

"Do you like Thomas?" he asked, looking at the floor. Danny was a nice kid, but he had only been in the school for a couple of years, and Fiona had never really spoken to him before, just a *hi* here and there when they bumped into each other.

"Um, does he like me?" she asked, sticking out her chin.

"Yeah."

"Then I like him, too," she replied, her heart singing, and even as a seventeen-year-old, she realised how childish this exchange was, but she didn't care.

Danny frowned for a second, then turned on his heel and returned to the table where he delivered the message to a waiting Thomas, who turned Fiona's way and winked.

* * * *

Danny couldn't exactly remember the moment he noticed her, but suddenly she was there, everywhere, in his classes, in his head, in his dreams. And the moment Danny decided it was time she noticed him, along came Thomas. Thomas, with his coolness, rugged exterior, and way with everyone. People were drawn to him, and even though Danny liked the guy, he was envious of how he spoke so easily to everyone and fit in without even trying.

Danny never had such luck. He had to earn his way into his group as a newcomer two years before. But he had something to offer, a house that was so close to the school where his friends often gathered and used on occasion to truant from school. It also helped that by the time he had arrived at Freemont High, he was good at soccer and was immediately cast as the star of the school team. He didn't want to play for the school. He was already in one of the lead clubs that had selected him for interstate matches, and his training, three times a week, left him with little time to train at school. However, the school's coach assured him that his playing for the school would not impede on training for the club, and Danny, knowing this would put him in good stead at his new school socially, accepted.

It did, and before long, he was hailed the team's captain, which automatically drew to him a new band of mates. He bonded immediately with Jeff, a tall, lanky guy who couldn't aim properly but was so amiable he kept the team's rapport up and brought a camaraderie that was desperately needed in a team that, before Danny arrived, lost almost every match they played. Jeff and Danny were different in nature but found things in common, music, comics and playing pool at Jeff's place, and Jeff introduced Danny to his flock of friends, most of which were like-minded guys, light-hearted, playful, people Danny enjoyed being with.

But Thomas. As much as Danny liked Thomas, his attraction to Fiona came as a surprise. It shouldn't have, he realised. Even though Fiona was not part of the popular group, she was beautiful. Most of his friends watched as she walked past, Danny trying not to ogle her along with them. But the way she walked, poised, her chin in the air, a smile or a laugh always on her face, he understood the attraction, and he sat directly behind her in history so he could admire her without her noticing while he worked on getting up the nerve to approach her.

Danny had girlfriends before, his first kiss happening on a camp in year eight with a girl whose name he couldn't remember, which boosted his confidence, and he even courted a couple of girls, romances that fizzled quickly. They never kept his interest long enough, and his busy routine didn't give him much time to think about it.

But he had noticed Fiona towards the end of the last year. It was at the school play, where he sometimes hung around on a free evening with Jeff, who helped out with backstage work. There she was, long flowing wavy hair, almost black, brown eyes, big and expressive, and after she had performed her part, which was second lead, she bounced off the stage with an excitement that was so infectious, he couldn't take his eyes off her.

"Oh, sorry, Danny," she said, touching his arm when she flounced past and ran straight into him.

"It's okay," he called after her as she kept moving, and he was tickled that she knew his name.

Those were the only words that had ever been exchanged between Fiona and Danny, but she had never left his mind, and whenever he tried to talk to her, he found his throat dry, and before he could say anything, she was gone. He didn't talk to anyone about it, not even Jeff, who showed no serious interest in girls, only as objects to admire and fool around with at parties or behind the gym. But his mother, although still walking in a mild haze, he knew he could talk to, and one evening, after two months of nervousness, he decided he had to play it right with Fiona. She wasn't any girl he could have for a couple of months and discard at the drop of a hat. The more he observed her, the more he overheard snippets of her conversations with other people, the more he knew this one would be important to him.

"I like this girl, Mum," he said after dinner, when Grace was settling on the back porch with a glass of wine and a book.

"Oh, Danny," she said with a burst of excitement, closing her book with a thump. "Come sit with me. Tell me about her." She patted the chair beside her.

Danny placed himself on it and pursed his lips. Maybe this wasn't such a good idea. What teenage boy talked to their mother about stuff like this? But his mother was different, always asking about his interests, about whether he had set eyes on a girl. He'd even brought Tina home once to meet his mother, but he didn't know why he bothered. He had already been getting bored with her. He surmised he just wanted to see how it worked, and Grace went out of her way to make the girl feel comfortable. But once Tina's parents picked her up, Grace refused to comment. "I don't know her well, so I can't say, but she's pretty." He hoped Grace would have more to say about Fiona, something better than that, if the time ever came...

"She's...well, her name is Fiona," he said now, momentarily pausing.

"And she's..." Grace prodded.

"She's beautiful," he said with a burst of breath.

Grace reared her head back and widened her eyes, her face beaming. "Wow, okay. This is new."

"I can't stop thinking about her. I want to ask her out, but I don't think she even knows who I am."

"Then introduce yourself. This is not new to you, Danny."

"But it's different."

"So, she's beautiful. What else?"

"She's a bit quiet, but when she's on the stage, she just shines." Danny could feel his heart surge even as he said it, picturing her singing her solo, the song of which he couldn't remember. "And she's a good girl. You know, she doesn't hang out with a bad crowd. Not sporty, but smart, always has a book with her. I think she's religious. I heard her say she went to church every Sunday."

"So what's the problem?"

"The problem is I haven't had the guts to talk to her yet, and it's been two months, and I can't get her out of my mind. And also, the summer holidays are coming up, and if I don't get the courage, I won't do it and..." He shook his head.

"Honey," Grace said. "Just talk to her. Don't overdo it. Just make conversation. Become friends."

"That's the problem. Our groups don't hang out together, so it's hard."

"Well, bump into her, I don't know, at your lockers, maybe? Get in her way. Make her notice you. You've never had a problem talking to girls before."

"Yeah, but this one is different."

"You've got this, Danny," Grace said with a confidence Danny didn't feel.

Danny knew time was running out, but he thought it might have been best that he was unable to see Fiona for the six weeks of summer vacation. He was so scared of her rejecting him, and he preferred not to take the chance. Perhaps he would realise it was just a silly phase and would be over her when school began. Maybe he would find another girl in the meantime, someone who knew he existed. But it was not to be. Danny found that even though he spent most of his spare time with the boys, going to the movies, hanging out at the Freemont shopping centre, Fiona's face invaded his brain, but by the end of the holidays, he felt better. If he could go six weeks without seeing her and be fine, he could get over his silly attraction to a girl he barely knew. Yes, he would leave her alone.

Yet, on the first day of school, as she walked into the gates with that smile on her face, his insides twisted and he felt an acute yearning for her. He gritted his teeth in annoyance with himself. He was tougher than this. But as the day went on, she was everywhere, and he knew he would have to do something about it. He would have to face rejection if that were what it came to, but it was better than never knowing if he had a chance with her. He would take his mother's advice, go slow and become friends with her first, and he was still trying to figure out how to do that. He had never had a problem being friends with a girl before, but whenever he thought about approaching *this* girl, his heart beat out of control, his palms became clammy, and he couldn't do it.

She was in one of his classes, history again, and he thought about how he could *accidentally* sit next to her. He began to bump into her more often, rushing to Jeff's locker, which happened to be beside Fiona's, and waiting for her to reach hers. Fiona always had a friendly smile for him, and he was encouraged. He was gaining ground on his confidence with her, and he knew the time was coming for him to see if she could be interested in him. He was just going to ask her out straight off the bat. That would be the only way, he had decided.

And then came Thomas, instilling himself into their group and, taking a liking to Danny, followed him everywhere. Danny was okay with that until the day Thomas mentioned Fiona.

"Do you know her?" Thomas had said one lunchtime as he slouched in his seat, nodding as Fiona walked past and slowed to a stop, gazing in their direction, her smile now shy, uncertain.

Danny's heart jumped when he saw to whom Thomas was referring. He tried to remain casual. "No, I don't, really."

"She's cute."

"Yeah, I guess." Danny swallowed the lump that was beginning to lodge itself in his throat.

"Has she got a boyfriend?"

"No, I don't think so." Danny hoped the following sentence would not be the one it was.

"I think she likes me. I don't know for sure."

"Why don't you ask her?" Danny tried not to frown.

"Could you?" Thomas sat forward with eagerness.

"Why me?" Danny jerked back and glared at Thomas.

"Because I don't want to get rejected," Thomas said with a laugh and punched Danny on the arm.

Danny looked towards Fiona, who was still looking their way, and it suddenly dawned on him that she wasn't looking at him. She was looking at Thomas. "I'll ask her," Danny said, hoping against hope that Fiona would laugh and tell Danny that it was not Thomas who she was looking at, it was him.

Chapter Five

When Fiona thought back on her time with Thomas, she remembered that she knew she had fallen for him and could understand why, with the dashing looks of a rock star, the teasing voice in which he spoke to her, the cool, flirtatious words he said and his infectious smile that he donned whenever he looked at her. She remembered kissing him and knew she liked it, the boy could kiss, but she was not clear on where and when. She remembered her excitement when Danny asked if she liked Thomas, and she was heartbroken when Thomas dumped her two weeks later, why she didn't know. She guessed he outgrew her, or perhaps she was a challenge, and once he'd won her over, he didn't want her anymore. Or maybe it was that he realised that she wasn't popular enough for the likes of him. Whatever it was, Fiona was broken hearted and hankered for him months after their tryst, and even though Thomas didn't want to be her boyfriend, he still flirted with her and chatted with her, keeping her hopes alive.

"Give up already," Victoria said a little shortly one afternoon when Fiona sat around sulking and trying to work out how to get him back.

"Vic! I love him."

"Do you really?"

"Yes. I want him back," Fiona said mournfully.

"He's a shit. He's leading you on," Victoria said.

"But he talks to me and flirts with me and…"

"Yeah, because he's a narcissist."

"That's a big word." Fiona couldn't help laughing.

"Yeah, just learned it in English," Victoria said with a chuckle.

"Well, I can't stop thinking about him."

"That's because you need someone else to think about."

"You make it sound like I'm boy crazy."

"No, but you need something else to focus on. The play is coming up. Are you going to audition?"

"Yeah. It's a weird one this year. One of the teachers wrote it. Many leads, so yeah. You?"

"God, no! You know that's not me. I can't sing or act. You know that. But I thought it would be fun to help with set-up and stuff. That could be cool."

"Yeah, I have to ask my parents first. They are never keen on it, and my dad, well, he's just so controlling. It's a battle every year."

"They always let you in the end."

"I guess so," Fiona said thoughtfully. Her parents had become even more volatile lately, but they were unhappy. Having been in the country for nearly five years, they still had not adapted to the lifestyle, and rather than reminisce about their life there, they argued about whose fault it was that they had come here.

"To give the children a better life," her father said, his hands waving towards Fiona and Alfie sitting on the couch watching TV. They looked at each other and rolled their eyes.

"We had a good life there," her mother shot back.

"Yes, but that's us. There are more opportunities in this country. Lila and Rosso are happy here," he said, referring to his brother and wife.

"Lila and Rosso came here ten years ago. Oh, and Lila..."

On and on it would go. Fiona and Alfie stood up in unison. The parents would get louder, and Alfie would blast his music in his room, and Fiona would do the same in hers to drown out the yelling. Their parents wouldn't even realise that their kids had left the room. Eventually, they would be in each other's arms again, and Fiona understood then that fights were their way of talking and didn't intrude on their love for each other. On one of these occasions, Fiona decided to throw in her question about the play using their distraction to her advantage. It worked. She got a hurried nod from her father, and she skedaddled quickly back to her room before he realised what he'd done.

Fiona was thrilled. When the students gathered for the first meeting before auditions, she saw that Thomas was there too, and she hoped she'd get a part that put her close to him. She was determined to win him back and hoped that when he saw her perform, he would fall for her again. When they were partnered for a dance number, she was almost giddy with excitement.

When rehearsals began, she looked forward to them twice a week after school, but although Thomas remained friendly, still flirty, he made no move to take it anywhere she wanted it to go. But she held fast to his hand as they danced together and even tried to make him jealous by flirting with the star of the play, a handsome boy with many girls on his arm. But that didn't work either.

She was devastated when she found out that he had gotten another girlfriend.

* * * *

Danny watched as Fiona fawned over Thomas and gazed at her as she drew little hearts on her paper while she stared out the window. His heart was crushed when she'd said she liked Thomas, and it broke even more when he saw them together, kissing at the front of the school, at the back of the oval. But when Thomas, who seemed to think that Danny was his confidante, told him that he was done with Fiona two weeks after they had started dating, Danny was perplexed.

"Why?" He tried to keep his emotions in check. His heart didn't dare become too excited.

"I don't stay with a girl for too long, you know."

"But you liked her. You won't stop talking about her." Danny had listened to Thomas almost every day talk about Fiona and how he wanted to go further with her, but she wasn't that type of girl. Danny had been so relieved that she wasn't.

"Yeah, she's cool, but it's time to move on."

"Well, okay. Have you told her yet?"

"No, I was…"

"Hell no! I'm not doing that for you."

"Come on, Danny."

"Clean up your own mess," Danny said. He was not going to be the one to break Fiona's heart. But his own heart was dancing. Fiona would be free again, and maybe he could help her out of her heartache. But as the months passed, he saw she still had no interest in him, and there was no subtle way of inserting himself into her life. He looked forward to the school day, eagerly awaited his history class, and settled for being an observer in her life. He began to dislike weekends, knowing he wouldn't see her, and when he went to a party, he always hoped that by some miracle, she would be there and then he would be able to make casual conversation with her rather than seeking her out to do so at school, which had become impossible for him. But she never was at any of the parties he went to, and on the odd occasion, he settled for kissing another girl, hoping it would take his mind off Fiona. Finally, he decided he would have to forget her—he would never have the guts to ask her out. He focused on his soccer and spent more and more time with his friends.

Then one evening, while walking his bull terrier, Cruz, past the school, he saw Jeff in the distance, standing by a log bench near the school gym, and he ambled over to say hello. As he neared, he saw Fiona sitting on the bench talking to Jeff. He paused, his heart thumping as usual at the sight of her, and wondered whether to approach them. It would be casual. He was saying hello to his best friend—it wasn't like he was seeking her out. It wouldn't be awkward. But as he stood there, he already felt his throat clog and his palms become clammy. Cruz pulled on the leash and gave a little yelp, and Danny lost his nerve. He pulled Cruz away in the other direction but heard Jeff call his name. His dog had made their presence known.

"Cruz," Danny muttered between gritted teeth and turned back and waved at them.

"Danny, come over here," Jeff called.

Danny walked over to them, trying to keep his eyes off Fiona, who was leaning backwards on the flats of her hands, a smile on her face. "Hey, Danny," she said and propped herself forward to pat Cruz, who scurried towards her now outstretched arms. She tousled the dog's head and leaned into his nose. Cruz licked her nose and wagged his tail wildly. "He's so cute," she said, tickling the happy dog under his chin.

"What are you guys doing here?" Danny asked, now a little concerned that Fiona and Jeff were sitting alone outside the gym. What did it mean?

"A break," Jeff said. "Mister Simons and Miss Lovery are having some creative differences." Jeff puckered his mouth and made kissing noises, and Danny couldn't help but smile.

"Where's everyone else?"

"They're practising," Fiona said, her hands still on the contented dog. "Just needed a break, needed some fresh air."

"Yeah, me too," Jeff said. "We'll have to go back soon. "Hey, come help if you want." Danny looked at Cruz and wished he hadn't brought him, but how was he to know Jeff would ask him to stay?

"Yeah, come," Fiona said, and Danny dared to look at her. Her eyes were creased strangely, sending a shiver down his spine.

"I have to take Cruz home. Maybe next time. When are you guys rehearsing next?"

"Thursday," Fiona said. "You should come. It's fun."

"Okay, maybe." He said goodbye and walked back home, a quickness in his step and a smile on his lips.

Chapter Six

Fiona needed a moment. She had just had her dance with Thomas, and they were to do it all again in half an hour. She knew it was never going to happen for them again. But she didn't feel as bad about it, knowing that he was now out of reach. She certainly wasn't going to hone in on a guy that was taken. She had more pride in herself than that. But she did hope that their relationship would peter out and maybe… No, she knew she was fooling herself. Her interest in him had been waning of late, and she was slowly tiring of his overconfident stance and self-importance. Maybe it was just the idea of him, a guy who finally caught her attention.

She sat on the log bench, the evening sun already dipping, winter closing in fast. It was cool, and she wished she'd brought her coat. Jeff hadn't come out with her, nor had Wilma or Jason, her friends she usually hung out with at rehearsals. Jeff was a nice guy, funny, easy going, and fun to chat with, but his friend, Danny. She considered him. He seemed more reserved and distant, and Fiona sometimes wondered if he just didn't like her. He seemed to behave as any ordinary teenage boy would when he was around his friends. She caught him staring at her sometimes, and he was awkward as hell when he was near her. But since he'd been hanging around the gym at rehearsals, he was trying to converse with her, and there was something about him…

"Fiona."

She turned to see Danny heading her way. He had been joining her and Jeff when they took a break together, and although slightly awkward still, there was something about him…

"Hey, Danny," she replied with a smile. "Here, sit with me." Perhaps he needed some encouragement. She noticed the shy, almost fearful way he sidled across the bench. Fiona looked at the gap between them, more than a metre apart and suppressed a smile.

"Good day today?" he asked.

"Yeah, not much for me to do now. Not my scene," she said.

"The dance was good."

"Yeah, but…"

"Tom?"

She looked at him sideways and suddenly realised he was the one who had kind of brought her and Thomas together. She shrugged.

"You still like him?"

She shrugged again. "I know he has a girlfriend now. So what difference does that make? Besides…" She hesitated. Why was she about to open up to this boy?

"He liked you a lot," Danny said, looking at his shoes.

"But now, not so much," she said, managing a little laugh and peered at him.

"Do you love him?" He turned and looked her in the eye. She was surprised that he had asked such a personal question. "Sorry, I just meant…"

"No, I'm not in love with him," she said with an air of indignance. "Maybe I'm just pissed off that he broke up with me," she said and was taken aback at her candour.

"There are other guys who would kill to go out with you," he said, looking down at the ground again and pushing a clump of grass with his shoe.

"Right." She sniffed. "Who?"

"Heaps."

"Name one," she challenged.

"There's Jason." Fiona screwed up her nose. Jason had been asking her out almost every day for the last two months, and although he was cute, he had become more of a friend. She certainly felt no attraction to him. "And what about Pete?" Pete was a playboy, so not her type.

"I can't think about anyone else right now anyway. I don't have time for boys." Fiona smirked, and a few moments of uncomfortable silence ensued, Fiona watching Danny move his foot back and forth against the ground.

"I used to like you," Danny said, and Fiona's head jerked up.

"What?"

He blushed and looked away. "At the start of the year."

"Really?" An unexpected thrill ran through her.

"You know, the day I asked you if you liked Tom, I planned to ask you out." His voice was hesitant, yet he didn't seem to be holding back.

"Why didn't you?"

"That was the day Tom told me he liked you. He wanted to see if you liked him too. And he was my friend." He chuckled nervously. "And I also hoped you would say you didn't like him back." A shy laugh escaped his mouth.

Fiona was silent for a moment, letting what he said sink in. She barely knew Danny existed until that day. All she knew of him was he had arrived at the school a couple of years before that and quickly situated himself among the jocks, and he had quickly become known for his prowess on the soccer field. Apart from that, she hadn't really noticed him as their paths didn't cross or ever needed to cross until now. And he wanted to talk about Thomas?

"Fiona?"

She looked up into his face and, for the first time, noticed his eyes, so blue she felt like she could swim in them. The way he clutched the wooden log they were sitting on with his chest inclined forward showed her a sensitive boy of seventeen, in love with her. "I'm sorry," she said, not knowing what else to say.

"No need," he said. "I think I got over it." He laughed, a forced, nervous laugh.

"Oh, good," she replied, wondering if she felt relief or disappointment. She returned to rehearsal and found herself thinking of those eyes, getting lost in them, and wishing she had more time to spend with him. When Thomas grabbed her hand and spun her around the stage, she barely noticed, and when he tried to flirt with her, as he usually did, she began to wonder how she felt so much for him at one point. Instead, she spent most of the dances looking past his shoulder, searching the stage for Danny to see if he was looking her way, for some sign that he still cared. Yes, there he was, watching, his eyes narrowed, his lips pursed, and she felt her heart flutter. Her mind was awhirl, confused, untrusting of how she felt.

What was it about this boy who suddenly declared his feelings for her? Feelings that he assured her were long gone? Did she now care about him because he was a challenge? Was she looking for something that maybe could be there again? After all, he had liked her at one time. Was she just looking for someone to ease the pain of her feelings for Thomas? Feelings that she realised were minimal now.

She went home that evening and took out the yearbook from the previous year. She stared at Danny's picture for a long time, so long that Alfie grabbed the book from her.

"Who is it?" he asked.

"Nothing, no one," she said, trying to grab it back. Alfie was her big brother, and she certainly didn't want to confide in him about boys. He would just tease her, which she could do without.

"This one?" he asked, pointing to a boy in the picture.

"No!"

"He'd better be a good one," he said and let go of the book and sauntered away, the topic not interesting enough for him to pursue.

Fiona was relieved, and after closing her bedroom door, she spread the open book on the floor and lay on her stomach with her chin in her hands, staring at the photo of Danny again, surprised at the burgeoning feelings she was having for him. It confused her. Boys had told her they liked her before, and if she didn't want them back, she wouldn't encourage it or think much further about it. So why was she suddenly so attracted to this guy, one that she had never taken a second look at before? It couldn't just be his eyes. Something clicked. She could feel something different from what she felt for Thomas, a liking for this guy that made her stomach churn. She remembered something she had seen or read. Chemistry. Maybe that was what it was—something indefinable that couldn't be grasped.

Chemistry.

* * * *

"So, do you still like him?" Danny walked over to Fiona's desk in history the next day and slid himself into the seat beside her. His heart was beating fast, but he was trying his best to be cool, to look like he wasn't hung up on her as badly as he was. He decided that it was time to find out whether there really was a chance with this girl. He had spent the previous evening mulling over his inability to speak to her properly. After he had the guts to mention Thomas and tell her how he felt about her, he felt stupid. He watched later as she moved on the stage with Thomas, and although it was Danny's eyes she kept seeming to find, seeing

Thomas's arms around her, his smile and confidence sent his heart into a frenzy. He fisted his palms, trying to control the jealousy he felt at that moment. He spent the night fighting himself. He had to be who he was. He had to be confident, especially when he spoke to her, and if it sounded silly, well, he wasn't going to be this strange timid creature with her anymore. He needed to know once and for all. "So do you?"

"Who? Thomas?" Fiona replied, surprise in her eyes.

"Yeah," he said.

"No, I don't think so." She bit at her lip unsurely.

"When will you be sure?"

"I'm sure."

"No, I don't think you are," he said and got up. "See you." He could see her eyebrows arch in confusion, and he smiled inside. He went to his seat behind her and watched throughout the class as she moved nervously, snatching glances behind her and walking to the rubbish bin with a blank piece of paper she'd just torn from her book. He was still not certain that she was over Thomas and was not going to settle to be her sloppy seconds. Now that he'd made a move, he would wait to see if he was more than just a rebound guy.

For the next week, Danny controlled his impulse to talk to her. He stayed away from rehearsals, and although he acknowledged her when they crossed paths, he didn't make a move to converse with her, even when her eyes lit up at the sight of him or her mouth turned down when he didn't stop to talk to her. He felt like he was becoming his confident self again, that if Fiona did like him, well, she could wait until he was ready this time. He sniffed at that. He had been ready for a long time. He saw her at the soccer field every lunchtime and tried his best to impress her with his moves, and although he acknowledged her presence with a nod, he never approached her. But his heart was happy. She had never been to any of the practice matches before this. It meant something. He decided it was time to test the waters again. After all, if he left it too long, she would probably get snapped up by someone else, and he would have lost his shot altogether.

* * * *

When Danny walked back to his seat that day, Fiona had bristled, angry and a little irritated that she had now invested in something that would never be. She certainly wasn't in love with him, but there was definitely something interesting there, a strange attraction, a quickened heartbeat when he sat beside her, a disappointment when he walked away.

And when Thomas flirted, said hi and chatted with her, she had no interest in him anymore. She wondered what the attraction was in the first place. His looks? Sure, he was handsome, but that was it? She considered that. Was she that fickle? Did she just happen to move on, forgetting that she thought she was in love with someone else? But was she in love with Thomas? He had made her heart beat faster, sure. His disinterest in her had made her want him more, of course, but how could she transfer her affection to Danny in the course of a conversation?

She went home that afternoon with a sense of disappointment. She thought that Danny still liked her. Why did he ask about Thomas out of the blue? Why would he have told her about how he felt if he didn't still feel that way? The point now was moot.

*

The day was dreary, the weather not yet warming up in readiness for spring, and Fiona stayed in the study hall by herself after the school day was over, waiting for rehearsals to begin. It had been a week, and Danny had not materialised at rehearsals after the day he talked so freely to her, and he seemed to be avoiding her during school. Even in the classes they shared, he didn't look her way, not once, and when she went to watch his games, dragging a reluctant Victoria along, he barely looked up at her.

Her homework for the day completed, she watched the hands on the clock move sluggishly and sighed. She may as well make her way to the gym. Maybe others had arrived — she could use the company. She strolled to the gym, her heart not in it today. Things were not good at home, her parents having had a massive argument the evening before, and there was more tension than usual. This morning, her mother had *forgotten* to put on the Moka pot, instead fixing herself an instant coffee, the type her father detested. A frosty silence had permeated the air, and Fiona didn't want to be around them when they were in this state. She was glad she had rehearsal that evening, reminding her mother of it on her way out of the house. Sometimes she wished they would just pack it in and go back. Where would that leave her and Alfie? She didn't know. She sighed and took a breath, determined to put it out of her mind for now.

There he was, Danny, leaning against the gym wall, his gaze on the soccer field, his hands in his pockets. Her heart jumped, and she told herself to get a grip. Why would she be so vain to think he was waiting for her? Hearing her footsteps on the gravel, he turned to her and smiled. Broadly.

"Hey," he called.

"Hey, back," she said, turning towards the gym door and away from him.

"Aren't you early?" he asked, his brow furrowed.

"Didn't have much homework to do," she said, still walking, unwilling to give in so easily. She was not going to fall at his feet because he deigned to greet her after ignoring her for the past week.

"Fiona, hold on," he said, walking towards her, and she stopped uncertainly. "Do you want to just talk for a bit?"

She wanted to, so very badly, but she stood her ground, her hands crossed against her chest, her lips pressed tightly together.

"I'm sorry," he said, leaning forward, almost whispering.

"What for?" She stared at her shoes, moving the dirt on the ground, creating angel wings.

"I needed to be away from you for a while."

She looked up at him in surprise. "But why?"

"Because I needed to know how I felt about you."

"And how do you feel?" Her eyes narrowed.

He took her hand and led her to the log bench. They sat close together, their thighs brushing, and Fiona felt a shock of electricity run down her leg. It was unexpected, thrilling, and painful. "I know I was sick, almost physically, from not seeing you. It happened even before last week, before I talked to you about… you know. My weekends, I spent thinking about you, and you didn't know I existed."

"I knew you existed," she replied feebly.

"But not in the way I wanted you to know."

"And now?"

"And now that you know, I can't go back." He paused, and she looked the other way, embarrassed for him. "I just feel like an idiot telling you when you are so clearly hot for Tom."

"I'm not hot for Tom!" She turned to him in indignance.

A smile spread over his face, and he nodded in satisfaction.

Chapter Seven

They were so different, Danny and Fiona. But when he first kissed her, her head between his hands that were propped up against the gym wall, they just melded as if they were born to kiss each other. She was scared to touch him, to put her hands anywhere on his body, just managing to link her wrists around his neck. She felt the warmth of his lips, the freshness of his breath, and the butterflies that danced in her tummy.

Two weeks of flirting and getting to know each other after his admission to still caring about her had led to nervousness for both. They didn't want to break the spell they were under, the contemplation of being together. But they sat beside each other in history, spent breaks in rehearsals seated on the log bench, looking up in irritation when other kids interrupted their time alone.

But that evening under the stars, when he walked her to rehearsal, she knew the time was right. It was an ordinary evening, the cool wind sweeping her hair against her face, her palms clammy as they usually were when she was with him now. He walked close beside her, his hands brushing hers, and it just seemed the right time, the perfect moment. He lingered when she leaned against the cool bricks and mumbled something.

She laughed, a nervous tension engulfing her. She knew what he was trying to say but wanted to hear it clearly. "What was that?" She turned her ear to him.

"Will you go out with me?" he mumbled again, his hand against his mouth.

"Sorry, what?" She leaned forward with more confidence, a teasing lilt in her voice.

"You know what I said. I want you to be my girlfriend." He enunciated every word.

Fiona nodded, her heart wanting to burst right out of her chest. "Uh-huh," she mumbled back.

"What was that?" He cocked his ear towards her, a sly smile on his face.

"Yes," she said clearly. "Yes, I want to be your girlfriend."

"Good. Can I kiss you now?"

*

They were inseparable after that evening. They spent every spare moment in each other's arms during the school day. From the moment Fiona woke up in the morning, Danny was in her head, and she'd hurriedly shower, get dressed, and rush to the bus stop. And he'd be waiting for her, sitting on the bench, eagerly looking out for the bus. When she hopped off, she'd throw herself into his arms, and he'd spin her around before placing her on the ground and kissing her. Then they would walk to school, fingers entwined, talking of nothing in particular, sometimes not talking at all, just happy to be together. They had their spot, their log, where they would meet at lunchtime, sit together, talk, hold hands, and cuddle, always jumping apart when a teacher walked by.

One afternoon after the bell rang to signal the end of lunch, they lingered too long at the soccer field, his lips on hers, her arms around his neck, and so lost were they in each other that they didn't hear a warning whistle from Jeff.

"Fiona! Danny!" They jumped apart to the sound of the principal, who was rounding up the latecomers. "Office. Now!"

Fiona wiped her lips, and they slunk to the principal's office. They waited outside, standing apart. She looked at him, and he was staring back with a mischievous smile. She tried to suppress a giggle and had to look away. They got a lecture, but Fiona thought she caught a brief grin on the principal's face as they both slunk back to class with a warning.

Those first few weeks were glorious. They skipped school, a first for Fiona, to hang out at the waterfall in a nearby park. He drove her around in his mother's car, not yet having his licence, and she sang loudly to the blaring music that emanated from the radio. She enjoyed being a rebel, not an open rebel, but a rebel, nonetheless. And when he gave her the first, and probably only, hickey that she ever got, she showed it around at school, making sure to wear a scarf when she got home. Her father would kill her if he ever caught something like that on her neck. According to him, she was a good girl who went to church on Sundays and studied to be a nurse, apart from participating in extracurricular activities such as the school play.

Fiona had considered nursing, but the time to decide her future was a distant thought, and she secretly harboured hopes of being an actress. She knew it was a pipe dream, but how she felt on stage was too glorious to ignore. She let her parents believe that she was headed down the path they wanted for her, her mind at this time not on anything else but Danny.

Fiona loved that Danny was so different from her. While he loved hard rock and heavy metal, she always had a yen for old music, that of the sixties and seventies, the music she had grown up with. While he was an athlete, she was not a sports fan, but she could watch him work up a sweat on the field all day. He lived a world apart from her own rigid life at home. He was free to go where he pleased, even having his very own bungalow in the backyard of his mother's house, where they canoodled when they escaped school between classes and sometimes during.

Fiona baked him a chocolate cake the night before for his eighteenth birthday, which she told her mother was for a teacher, and took it to his bungalow early the following morning. Danny was getting ready for school, and when he opened the door and saw her standing there, balancing the cake in one hand, the other on her hip, his face broke out in a massive smile.

"Get in here," he said, taking the cake from her and placing it on the table. He put his arms around her waist and drew her close. "Birthday kiss," he said, and Fiona let him kiss her deeply. She moved him to the bed and pushed him down on it. She sat atop him and felt him spread little kisses on her neck. She felt her loins twitch and pushed him down on the bed, leaning over him and kissing his lips again, letting her tongue slide over them. She felt his hand glide over her bottom, and her breath became heavy, her need for more overwhelming.

Danny sat up, taking her with him, and she looked at him in question. "Let's look at that cake," he said, and Fiona cleared her throat. She felt confused, rebuffed, but with it was a sliver of relief. She was close to being an adult herself, but only now she realised she wasn't ready to go all the way. It was too soon, but how her body reacted to him was unlike anything she could describe.

*

Fiona looked forward to school more than ever, and when she left Danny at the end of a Friday, knowing that a whole weekend would go by when she wouldn't see him, she was in despair and roamed the house aimlessly thinking about him.

"What are you moping about?" Alfie asked one Saturday evening as he was heading out to pick up his girlfriend, Maria. Fiona knew Alfie was getting suspicious by this time. He always narrowed his eyes at her when she sat by the window, staring out into the darkness, or when she completely ignored him, unaware that he was talking to her.

"Nothing," she said, knowing he would persist. Maybe she could talk to him. Perhaps he could help.

"Is it a boy?" he asked. Fiona shrugged. "Tell me," he said.

"His name is Danny. We've been going out for a few weeks." Talking about this to her brother felt awkward, but Fiona knew he would understand. He'd been living under the same roof as her for her whole life, after all, and even though he was allowed to have a girlfriend, the parents still warned him about *unwanted* things that could happen. Alfie would nod and pretend he was listening to them, taking their advice, and Fiona would try to hide the smirk, knowing well what her brother must be getting up to. She paused, nevertheless.

"And?"

"I just miss him, that's all. I can't see him on the weekends, and I miss him."

"I would like to meet him. If Mum and Dad are not going to, then I have to be the one to meet him," he said, his chin high, his chest broadening slightly, and Fiona wanted to chuckle at his big brother act. "Can he come out with us sometime?"

Her head snapped up. "What do you mean?"

"I mean, like we can all do something together?"

"Yeah? Can we?"

"I think we should, but not tonight. I have plans. Maybe next Saturday, okay? Ask him."

"Thanks, Alfie," Fiona said and couldn't help wrapping her arms around his neck.

"Yeah, yeah. Okay." He pulled away, and she couldn't wait to ask Danny. They could go on an actual date, sure, a date with her brother in tow, but a date, nevertheless.

The following weekend, Alfie pulled up to Danny's house, and when he hopped into the back seat of the car, Alfie put on a fatherly voice and turned around, giving Danny a stern handshake. But it was a wonderful evening. They all watched a movie together, Alfie glancing over often, ensuring that Fiona and Danny's hands held each other's and didn't stray elsewhere. They stopped at *McDonald's* on the way home, and there became an easiness between the two boys, Maria winking at Fiona across the table. Alfie approved.

Chapter Eight

Danny knew he was already in love with her long before she even knew he existed. But what he felt for Fiona wasn't just love. It was a fierce protectiveness, a need to have her around all the time, to look at the picture she gave him when she wasn't with him, and when he wasn't at training or out with his friends, he was moping around at home, thinking about her.

"So, when do I get to meet her?" his mother asked, deliberately casual, as they stood together at the kitchen sink, Danny drying the dishes Grace put into his hand. Danny had told Grace that he had finally got up the nerve to ask Fiona out, but he knew his mother, as much as she wanted to know more, didn't want to pry.

"I don't know..."

"You love her?" Danny nodded. "She loves you?"

"I think so."

Grace paused her washing and looked at him, raising her eyebrows. "You *think* so?"

"Well, she hasn't said it, but I feel like she does." Nobody could be the way she and Danny were if it wasn't love.

"And you don't want me to meet her yet?" Grace's eyes narrowed in question.

Danny wanted to bring Fiona over to meet Grace, but he was terrified his mother and Fiona wouldn't get along, or his mother would find fault with her. It wasn't in Grace's nature to do that, but he cared about what Grace thought, and he wanted the two women he loved to love each other. "She's, well, it's hard because her parents are protective, and she can't get out too much."

"Have you met them?"

"No! They would have a fit if they knew she was even talking to a boy, let alone seeing one." It was something that troubled Danny but he hoped with time, it was a hurdle they could climb together.

The crease between Grace's eyes wedged deeper. "Whenever you're ready, Danny, I'm here," said Grace, patting her hands on the dishcloth and kissing the top of his head.

She left the room and Danny stared out of the kitchen window at the moon so bright it lit up the side of his bungalow, and he felt a tug at his loins. He wanted Fiona so much, and yet…

When Danny asked Fiona to meet his mother on an afternoon before her rehearsals for the play began, her eyes grew wide in alarm. "What if she doesn't like me?"

He put his arms around her. "She will love you." He wanted to tell her that he loved her, but he needed the time to be right, to know that she loved him too.

"Okay, if you think it will be okay." She bit at her thumbnail, a fearful look on her face.

He could see her nervousness and tried to cover his own. "Come on, let's go."

They needn't have worried. Both Fiona and Grace talked tentatively at first, and soon they were chatting and laughing, and Danny sat back and watched with a mixture of pride and love for them both.

Danny recollected those few months as the most innocent, most fun time he'd had as a teenager. He had friends who Fiona got along well with, which made things easier. They went out together, skipped school together, and spent time on the phone, talking about what he didn't remember, but every moment she was with him was bliss, and every second she wasn't, he was in pain. He even wrote letters to her, inane words that tried to express how he felt. And she wrote in kind, words of love and passion, something they were both beginning to understand.

* * * *

"I love you," Danny whispered, and Fiona froze.

They were in the back of Alfie's car, Maria and Alfie chattering away in front, the music blaring out tunes of *Dire Straits*, and he had suddenly held her hand and leaned in close to her ear. They were dropping Danny home after they had all gone into the city. They had shopped, went on a tram ride, rode the Ferris wheel at the carnival, and when it was time to leave, they were exhilarated, their cheeks pink with an excitement that permeated the air in the car.

"Did you hear me?" he asked, moving closer to her ear.

Fiona's heart skipped a beat, and she nodded and looked the other way, out the window. It was the last thing she expected, and it hadn't even been two months since they'd been together. She really didn't know if she was in love with him. She had never been truly in love with someone, infatuation, sure, but love enough to tell someone? Besides, she didn't want him to declare his love for her in the back seat of her brother's car!

She watched the cars go by and felt his hand leave hers. He was rebuffed, disappointed she didn't return those words, but she couldn't tell him something she wasn't ready for. Fiona was as impulsive as any teenager could get, but she was not a liar. When they got to his house, he kissed her cheek quickly, said goodbye to Alfie and Maria and walked straight inside without looking back.

Fiona went to bed that night worried. Would he leave her because she didn't return his words? Wouldn't that mean he didn't really love her? But did she love him? Were they just words thrown around in a fit of passion? She'd heard her father say it to her mother as he held her face tightly in his hands, but that didn't stop their fights. And yet they were still together, crazy and happy. It was all so confusing.

When Fiona looked out anxiously from the bus window on Monday morning, there he was, waiting for her on the bench as he always did, his face lighting up when he saw her. She jumped off the steps and threw herself into his arms in relief and sheer joy.

During the next few days together, they resumed their infatuation with each other, not a word spoken about that moment in the car. She looked for some awkwardness from Danny, some resentment, but there wasn't any. The play was in its final stages, and it went for a three-night run, and Fiona, so caught up in the hustle and bustle of it all, tried to let that moment pass.

It was after the final show, at the after-party held in the school hall, when he held her close, his body moving in sync with hers, the sound of *Richard Marx* pervading the air, when she knew. She wanted to be close to him forever, to feel his hands on her. She wanted to be consumed by him, to be as close to him as she possibly could. The thought that they would not be together was not something that entered her brain, but when she squeezed up against him, her head resting on his chest, the thought suddenly struck her. What if they broke up? What if they were not going to be together forever? The sudden realisation hit her like a hammer, and she felt herself breaking into a sweat. She jerked back and looked up into his face. His smile turned to a frown, and she knew she had terror written on her face.

"I love you," she said with some urgency.

He broke away from her, and the crinkle between his eyes deepened. "You don't have to say it if you don't mean it."

"I don't think I've ever meant anything more in my life." She meant it. She knew right then that she had loved him already. He bent down and kissed her lips.

.

Chapter Nine

Where did it go wrong? Danny couldn't pinpoint it exactly, but a number of little things became big things. She envied his freedom, and it wasn't long before he resented her limitations. They argued fiercely and always ended up in each other's arms. Danny knew his jealousy played a big part in how they fell apart. He couldn't bear it when another guy looked at her, and he couldn't control his emotions when she talked to a guy, as platonic as it might have been. When she went to a party, which she was now sometimes allowed to go to with Victoria, and if it was a party he wasn't invited to, or he had somewhere else to be, he would seethe with jealousy, always wondering if someone else was making moves on his girl.

"Who was there? Did anyone hit on you? Did you see anyone you liked?" And as the words left his mouth, he felt sick with himself. She always kissed him passionately and told him it wasn't the same without him, and she missed him and wished he was there, and that sated him for a while, but his jealousy bordered on obsession. He wanted her all to himself and when they were alone, he just wanted to hold her, touch her, kiss her. It came to the point where they were neglecting everything else, and their friends were starting to fall by the wayside.

Danny had, for the most part, been a loner with a couple of good friends, but when he came to Freemont High, his social life had expanded. And with his training and games, sometimes interstate, every minute he had he wanted to spend with Fiona. It began to bother him when Jeff and the others went out without him because he felt he was missing out on time with them. He felt left out when they talked at school about what they did the evening before when he had been with Fiona. And after he spent his lunchtimes with her, he would hear them talk about what they did or continue a discussion they had begun when he wasn't there, and he would nod and smile, trying in vain to be part of their conversation.

"We probably need some time to spend with our friends, apart from each other," Fiona said to Danny one day as they walked to school one morning.

Danny nodded in agreeance. "Yep, Jeff is getting a bit annoyed that I don't hang with them like I used to."

"But I want to spend every minute with you," Fiona insisted, squeezing his hand.

"Me too, babe," he said. "But I get it. And Coach is getting shitty about me not practising like before."

"Okay, so how about we try to divide our time up."

Perhaps that was the turning point in their relationship. It was annoying to Danny that Fiona couldn't be open with her parents and that he couldn't be her boyfriend openly, and because of this, their time together depended on her. Lately, it always seemed to coincide with time with the boys, and Danny was feeling very left out.

"It's not her fault," Grace said when Danny voiced his frustration to her.

"She's not a kid," Danny said.

"Well..." Grace said, and Danny felt irritated. "She is a kid to her parents. She's seventeen."

"I've just turned eighteen myself. You don't stop me from seeing her."

"Sure, but people are different. She's also a girl. Parents worry about girls more."

"You don't worry about me?"

"Yes, of course, I do. But I know you're responsible. You've had to be."

"So is she." Danny could feel himself become more agitated.

"Yes, I get that, but..."

"No, this is so stupid!"

"What's really the problem?" Grace kept her voice even.

"I don't know, Mum. Everything."

"It's been, how long now?"

"Nearly five months."

"Do you think that you should really be in a long-term relationship at this age?" Danny looked at Grace in horror. Grace shook her head emphatically. "No, I mean there's so much on your plate. With your training, your matches, your school, your friends."

Danny nodded. He knew time was a big part of his resentment towards Fiona, but he couldn't think of spending less time with her. They barely had enough time together as it was. "What do I do?"

"See how it plays out."

Danny nodded. He knew he couldn't let Fiona go, but he needed to prioritise. They were getting irritable with each other, their constant bickering taking the fun out of their once playful relationship. The passion was still there. His need for her physically never waned, so much so that even when they argued, they ended up in each other's arms, their kisses becoming more urgent, their hands straying, their bodies yearning.

Fiona was waiting for Danny one evening when he returned from training, finding her on the steps of his bungalow, playing with Cruz.

"You could have let yourself in," he said, patting the dog's head and kissing her.

"I don't mind hanging with Cruz," she replied. "But Alfie is coming to get me soon."

"I need to have a shower," he said. "How long do you have?"

"He's coming in..." She looked at her watch. "At nine. So..."

"So we have nearly an hour," Danny said, a twinkle in his eye. "Hey, come shower with me?"

"Danny!"

"No, no! That's not what I mean," he said, reddening.

"Well, I just want to be close to you," Fiona replied.

"Come on." He pulled her to her feet.

"Hmmm, cutting it close," she said as she jumped off the stoop and headed to the bathroom. They stayed in that shower, the spray hitting their hair, their bodies close, arms wrapped around each other, barely moving, content to just be together as the water flowed over them until it grew cold. They had just gotten out when they heard the beep of Alfie's car. He was early.

"Shit," Fiona cried, and Danny could see her distress.

"It's okay. It's Alfie." He tried to calm her by taking her hand.

She pulled it away roughly. "For goodness sake, Danny. He will kill me just as much as my father."

"Why?"

"Stop talking. Help me find my socks." They scrambled around for their clothes, but Fiona could do nothing about her hair, and she tried to tie it back, disguising its dampness.

She rushed to the door and kissed him quickly, and Danny tightened his jaw in frustration. Alfie was supposed to be their ally. Why couldn't she just tell him the truth? He was a guy with a girlfriend. He should understand that they were together, even if it was his younger sister. They hadn't even had sex yet! He couldn't understand the whole thing. Maybe Fiona was being dramatic. Maybe Alfie wouldn't be angry with her.

He wanted to call her to see how she was and if Alfie had noticed anything or had told her off, and he became even more frustrated that he couldn't contact her. A simple phone call he couldn't make to his girlfriend. His resentment towards her, towards the whole situation, was starting to become a constant in his life.

* * * *

Alfie was no idiot.

"Why are you wet?" he casually asked as Fiona got into the car.

She shut the door slowly, searching her brain for an answer. "We were in the pool," she said, hoping he wouldn't notice the cool temperature outside.

"He has a pool?" Alfie looked impressed.

"Yeah, didn't I tell you?" Danny did not have a pool, and Fiona hoped it was something her brother would never find out.

Alfie was silent for a few minutes, and Fiona hoped that was the end of that, but then he came back with, "What did you wear?"

That was not what she was expecting, and she was flustered. "Um, my underwear." She wanted to change that immediately. What she should have said was she borrowed his mother's swimsuit, which would have been so much better, but she thought about that answer much later.

His face turned into a scowl, and his lips pursed. She didn't want to upset her brother, for him to think less of her, and she didn't know what to say, but she felt his disappointment. His mouth drooped, and his brows furrowed. Her big brother, who was so close to her, and yet, she couldn't confide in him about some things, had to lie about something so stupid. There was a stoic silence on the ten-minute ride home, and as they pulled into their driveway, he gazed at her with a look that made her feel so small, so stupid.

"Seriously, Fiona," he said, using her full name, making it clear he was angry with her. "Why would you do that?"

She wanted to protest, tell him she was a seventeen-year-old who had already been on the pill for the last two months in readiness for the expected, but she sat and looked at her hands.

"I'm not going to tell Dad, but I'm not going to cover for you forever."

*

"I'm over this," Danny said the next day when Fiona related what Alfie had said and how she felt about it. "You're not a child." They were children, that was just it, but he was angry, and she knew this was going to turn into another petty argument. "How can your family be so silly?"

"Don't talk about them like that."

"But you're seventeen. My mum knows about us — she can remember what it's like to be our age…"

"So terribly sorry that I don't have a family as cool as yours." Fiona felt the heat rise in her.

"I barely see you. I can't call you. I have to wait for you to call me. I think about you and want to hear your voice, but I have to wait until it's safe for you to call me."

"I know." She softened at his words.

"Are you ever going to tell your parents about me?"

"I can't right now. I can't even talk to a guy without them asking about it. Even my brother's friends…"

"You talk to your brother's friends?"

Fiona was taken aback by the venom in his voice. "I guess so."

"What do you talk to them about?"

A thrill of excitement rushed through her. He was jealous. He loved her. "Just stuff," she said.

"Do they come on to you?"

"No!" She didn't want him to think she was flirting with Alfie's friends! In fact, one of his friends had made advances towards her, and she had stayed away from him, but she knew how much to tell Danny. He already fumed when a boy looked her way or when he thought she was looking at another guy. But she knew this was because he loved her, and she felt the same when she was in the same position. She understood it.

But lately, this had been happening a lot. A possessiveness that she had for him, and she knew he had for her, was becoming the basis of all their arguments. Even when she talked to his friends and made an effort to be one of them, she could see the frown on his face, and she felt uncomfortable even though she knew they didn't see her as much more than Danny's girlfriend.

"Mamma," she said, stirring the pot while her mother chopped onions beside her.

"What is it, Fiona." Fiona loved the way her mother said her name. *Fee…ona.*

"How did you and Papa know you were ready to be together?"

Her mother looked sideways at the backdoor, ensuring her husband was not in earshot. He had been working on the car, which was broken down again, but he wasn't a man who gave up on something easily. "You're too young for this conversation, no?"

"I just meant, you know, how do you do it?"

"Do what?"

"You fight all the time."

Her mother let out a hearty laugh. "We fight?" She looked at her daughter with an incredulous look on her face. Fiona thought she was in a parallel universe. Of course, they fought — all the damn time. Her mother cocked her head in thought. "Ah. Maybe." She let out a little giggle.

"And?"

"And what?"

"How do you do it?"

"Do what?"

Fiona shook her head in exasperation. "You fight, you make up, you fight, you make up. What is that?"

"Sometimes I hate that man. But I will always love him."

"But why are you so mean to each other?" Fiona thought for a second about how to put it. "And the jealousy. Why is that?"

"It's the fire. The passion. It keeps love alive."

"But, Mamma, isn't it, I don't know, bad?"

"Sometimes bad, yes." Her mother grabbed the knife again and hacked the onion in front of her in half.

* * * *

"Do you want to stop?" Danny asked after they returned to his place after an evening spent at the beach together. He had just gotten his licence and wanted her to be the first he took for a drive. They had cruised along the coast. Fiona had her head sticking out the window, letting the wind blow against her hair. It was exhilarating, and afterwards, they had shuffled into his bungalow, the sweetness of the evening lingering. He backed her against the door and bent down to kiss her neck, feeling her hot breath on his face. His hands found their way under her shirt while hers roamed slowly below his stomach.

"No," she replied and leaned in closer. "We're adults now."

"It's my first time, though," he said, lifting his head, searching her eyes for any hesitation.

"Me too." She looked back with longing and pulled him closer.

"But are you sure?"

"Danny, I love you. I want my first time to be with someone I love. That is you."

"But you won't regret it?"

"No," she said, pulling at the zipper on his jeans.

*

It wasn't what he had expected, and by the look of Fiona, it wasn't for her either, and they both lay together afterwards, staring at the ceiling, awkwardness in the air. Fiona finally sat up and pulled her bra on. She seemed embarrassed, and Danny reached out and stroked her back.

"I'm sorry," he said.

"There's nothing to be sorry about," she replied. Then she turned to him and placed a kiss on his lips. "I'm glad it was you. I always will be glad it was you."

"Me too," he said and pulled her to him again, encircling her in his arms, and they lay on the bed wrapped in each other's nakedness. Even though it wasn't what they had thought it was supposed to be, the fumbling, the pain, the mess, right now with Fiona in his arms in his bed, so warm, so soft, the way her hair fell over his chest, he was in heaven.

* * * *

The summer holidays were nearly upon them when the unthinkable happened. Two things, really.

The first was a party, Victoria, her very best friend's party, to which Danny couldn't go as he had another party to attend. It was just as well because also invited was a boy who Danny had been terribly jealous of, and Fiona was relieved that Danny wasn't going to be anywhere near him.

His name was Justin, and he was handsome in a Tom Cruise sort of way. He had been a friend of Fiona's for a couple of years. They mixed in the same circles, studied together with their friends, and Fiona had known for a while that he was keen on her. Once Danny and Fiona had gotten together, Justin took it upon himself to have little digs at Danny, not by his words but by how he behaved when Fiona was around. He made his affection for Fiona evident by giving Danny dirty looks, and Justin sidled up to her whenever Danny was nearby. Although Fiona knew how he felt, she never had any interest in him other than being a friend who was in most of her classes and had the same interests as her, namely the school play and similar tastes in music and movies, which is what they mostly talked about. But apart from that, Justin never attempted to be more than a friend. Only Victoria, who was closer to Justin than Fiona, told her that he had been hankering for her attention for a long time.

Danny and Fiona decided to go to their own parties and forfeit one evening with each other. Fiona had fun, danced the night away and tried not to think of Danny and what he was up to with his own band of mates. At the night's end, she went home and thought that was that. It was an enjoyable evening, she had missed Danny, but she fulfilled her role as best friend.

*

"How was it?" Danny asked as soon as she hopped off the bus.

"Good, yours?" She kissed him lightly. "I missed you."

"Yeah, me too," he said brusquely. "Tell me about it." He held her hand as they walked towards school, a scowl on his face.

"We had fun," she replied. "I danced so much." Danny was not a dancer and didn't enjoy dancing, and their differences were becoming so much clearer lately. But she couldn't deny that she liked something just because he didn't. Besides, didn't opposites attract?

"Who did you dance with?" She could feel Danny's hand tighten on hers.

She ran off a list of people at the party, including Justin, and Danny's face turned to thunder. She continued, pleased that he was jealous, that he loved her. "And there was dirty dancing, too…"

"With him?"

"Justin? Yeah, we did." She quickly bit her lip, knowing she had perhaps taken it too far. There was dancing, and sure, she had danced with Justin, who'd wanted to grind on her, but she hadn't allowed that to happen—she would never have with anyone but Danny.

Danny's hand pulled away from hers, and he quickened his pace. Fiona clenched her teeth. Another fight. Why did she have to tell him that? It was all very innocent. She didn't think he would be that upset. It meant nothing. She stepped more quickly to catch up and tugged at his sleeve.

"I'm sorry," she said. "It was nothing."

"If I was doing that with Tanya, would you care?" Tanya was an ex-girlfriend of his that made Fiona's blood boil. She stopped and thought for a second. Perhaps she would have been. Not perhaps. She would have been furious. But it was too late.

"I'm sorry. I said I'm sorry."

"I can't deal with this shit anymore." Danny stopped and faced her, his lips pursed, his fists clenched.

"What do you mean?" Fiona's heart began to thump fast.

"I am so mad. I can't breathe." His face was on fire.

"But you have no reason to be. I love you, only you," she cried, trying to grab back his hand, which he kept firmly by his side.

"But you do this to me." He was softening, and Fiona knew she could convince him to forgive her. "And I love you so much. I can't take it anymore."

She reached up and, pulling his head to her, she kissed his forehead, his cheeks, his neck and his lips, and he put his arms around her, hesitantly at first, and she felt herself relax in his arms. She knew it was going to be okay. It was just another stupid fight.

But not long after, the second thing happened, the proverbial straw that broke everything. Alfie, still sore at Fiona for bathing in Danny's pool in her underwear, or so he thought, had been offish, and Fiona didn't mention Danny's name in any conversation with him. Their outings as a four-some stopped, and he didn't want to hear anything about them. It made things harder for Fiona and Danny to be together as much as they had been, but she knew better than to try to talk to Alfie about it. However, a week after they argued over Justin, Alfie caught Fiona sneaking in late at night after spending the evening with Danny, her hair a mess, a look of guilt written all over her face.

"With him again?"

Fiona squared her shoulders. "Yes," she said boldly.

"Just don't go getting pregnant."

"What's it to you?" she said. She had had enough of his treating her disdainfully, like a child. They had always been on the same page about everything, and she was sick of being treated like a pariah by her brother.

He turned to her, putting his hands on his hips. "Really? How about if Mum and Dad knew?"

"Who's going to tell them? You?" She said it with more bravery than she felt.

"Okay, yeah. Me," he said and marched into their mother's room.

Fiona stood frozen on the spot, unbelieving. He wouldn't. Her heart began racing, and just two minutes later, she heard her mother call her name.

* * * *

He knew it had to be done. He loved her, but he needed space from her. His time was not his own anymore. And he just couldn't deal with the drama anymore. Her family were crazy, strict, and mean, which made it so much more difficult. But ultimately, and he tried to dismiss it as a minor reason, he wanted to spend more time with his friends, to be part of the group again, and to have fun as an eighteen-year-old boy should. There was nothing wrong with wanting that. And he was sick of being in a relationship based on jealousy and possessiveness. A girlfriend should be making him happy, not worried or irritated. He knew he would break her heart, but something had to give.

He had just arrived home after training on Saturday when she called him in tears.

"He told Mum," Fiona sputtered into the phone.

"Who?" He sat on the kitchen chair and put his head in his hands. *Another drama.* He felt guilty for his thoughts and pressed his fingertips over his eyebrows.

"Alfie! He told Mum about the shower thing."

"Why?" Danny sat up, concerned for her now.

"Because I came in late, and he knew I was with you and…"

"Where are you?"

"At a phone booth. Everyone is home."

"Can you come over?"

"Yeah. Can I?"

"Sure. I have to shower first. Just let yourself in."

"Thanks Danny," she said in a small voice, and Danny hung up the phone.

"Trouble in paradise?" Danny raised his head to see Grace standing in the doorway.

"I'm just over it, Mum."

"You need to do what you need to do, Danny," Grace said, and she came to him and kissed him on the top of his head. "I'm going out for a bit." She walked back to the door and turned around. "Hey Danny?" He looked up at her. "Trust yourself."

*

He stood in the shower feeling the needles of cold water hit him. He knew he had to do it, to end it. Now. The thought of not being with her scared him too. What if he was making a mistake? What if what she'd said was true? He had no siblings. How would he know what it was like to have one, to be one? To be part of a family that was so different to his? But he also knew it was so much more than that. He wanted, no needed, his freedom.

He got out of the shower, his heart still beating fast, hating what he was about to do. He towelled himself dry slowly and threw on a t-shirt and track pants. He opened the bathroom door slowly and walked into the lounge room. He saw Fiona on the sofa, and she jumped up and ran into his arms. He kept his arms by his side as much as he wanted to hold her. She stepped back and searched his eyes. He knew it was now or never.

Chapter Ten

1992

Fiona came out of her class, exhilarated. It had been a gut-wrenching performance, and she knew it by the look on Mister Tarp's face. He sat on the edge of his chair, leaning forward, his eyes wide, his jaw slack. When she'd looked up after she ended on the stage scrunched up in a ball, he quickly cleared his throat and changed his expression to his usual one of casual indifference.

"Good. Okay, good, Fiona."

She wanted to smile, but she knew he wouldn't like that. She got up and moved offstage to pats on the back from her fellow students, and once she was behind the curtain, she breathed a sigh of relief. She knew she had to impress him for even the slightest consideration for a bit part in the production in a small theatre in Melbourne. To get a role, even a small one, would be a boon for her career. She walked to her flat, a tiny two-bedroom she shared with her friend Alice, hoping she wasn't home so she could call Danny over. Unfortunately, as she opened the door, she heard the kitchen tap running and Alice called out her name.

"Hi Alice. Did Danny call?"

"No," Alice called back. "Are you seeing him today?"

"I don't know." Fiona frowned. They hadn't seen each other in over a week, but it was not unusual. She picked up the phone and dialled, but his phone rang out. "Hey Alice, you wanna go out tonight?"

"Yeah sure," Alice said, bouncing out of the kitchen.

Fiona smiled. Of course Alice would want to. She was like Fiona's shadow. The same age, the same height, with much larger boobs and shorter curly hair, she seemed to dote on Fiona. Having had a tough life, Alice was grateful when Fiona offered to let her stay when her parents kicked her out of the home. For what, Fiona didn't inquire, but she knew Alice had always argued with her parents for as long as she knew her, towards the end of high school. Fiona always tried to talk to her at school, wanting to know what was wrong and if she could be of any help. Alice would gratefully sit by her side but was not keen to divulge her problems at home, so Fiona distracted her with funny anecdotes or gossip about teachers, which made her laugh.

Fiona kept in touch with Alice after they had completed high school, and often she found her on her front porch waiting for Fiona to return home from wherever she had been. When she appeared one night with red eyes and an overnight backpack, Fiona offered to let her stay for a little while, and there she remained for the last year, emulating everything Fiona did. But Fiona didn't mind. She loved the girl, who was no problem, except that she clung to Fiona's coattails a little too tightly, sometimes smothering her.

She had even immersed herself in Fiona's group of friends, and Victoria was not pleased one bit.

"Watch her. She's a little *Single White Female* if you ask me," Victoria warned.

"That movie scared the bejesus out of you, didn't it?" Fiona laughed. They had just watched the movie a couple of months earlier, and Victoria referred to Alice once they had come out of the theatre.

"Just saying," Victoria said.

"She's fine," Fiona replied. "She's just a bit lost."

"Watch her," Victoria repeated.

"Oh, Vic. You are suspicious of everyone."

"Maybe." Victoria had cocked her head in thought. "But someone's got to keep your head straight."

"She's okay," Fiona said, understanding that Alice had very few friends, barely saw her family and seemed lost, lonely. "She just needs a friend."

"Hmmm. Well, I don't like her," Victoria said.

"Yes, I got that." Fiona chuckled.

Fiona smiled at Alice now. "I'm trying to call Danny. See if he's free."

"Oh, I talked to Jeff. I think they were going out somewhere."

Fiona felt a little surge of irritation and scolded herself. It was okay that Alice was friends with her friends, but they were all getting a little too cosy, and because Fiona spent so many evenings rehearsing and practising her lines, she missed out on many of their outings. But she couldn't have it her way all the time. Her career was important, and if it meant foregoing some of her social life, that was what she had to deal with. Alice always happened to get wind of the outings with her friends, particularly her friend Daria, who was now attached to Danny's friend Jason. She seemed to have become quite friendly with Alice lately and invited her to wherever they went, and Alice happily went along with them. Fiona knew she shouldn't be so catty, so possessive, but she had just felt like they were leaving her out of everything more and more lately.

But what was Fiona to them anymore anyway? She still clung to the hope that Danny would love her, even two years after they had broken up. But he had been her first in everything, and she wanted him to be her last.

Now at twenty, Fiona was a woman who had her share of dating, and each time she thought she felt the remotest bit of attachment, there was Danny again, with his smile, his words, driving up to her apartment in his car, asking her if she wanted to go to the beach or a movie — or calling her late at night to chat about something or the other. And her hopes would rise again, and she would dump the poor sod who thought he stood a chance with her.

She still remembered well their break-up all those years before and shook her head at the ridiculousness of it. They cried, they kissed, they made love, and Fiona went home, sure that this was just another spat. But when she saw him the next day, he was determined it was over. Fiona held her head high and let the vultures swoop in.

And when Danny started seeing a girl seriously six months later and Fiona found out about it, she hurled insults at him, promptly called a guy she had been seeing casually, and let him make love to her in his car. A horrible sweaty affair, one she regretted terribly and tried to forget. And then she proceeded to tell Danny about it. She wanted to hurt him, to make him jealous, to make him want her again, and convinced herself that it would be the same as it had been with Thomas, that someone new would sweep her off her feet and she would forget him.

But once they had graduated and Fiona was allowed a certain amount of freedom with her parents, she took advantage of it, going out to clubs with Victoria, and sometimes by coincidence, Danny also ended up at the same clubs, and it made her heart beam with pleasure when he saw her dancing with another guy, a thunderous look on his face. Inevitably, she would leave the guy and go to him, and it became a routine for them to hook up and leave together, always going back to his place. Once she moved out into her own apartment, he often spent nights there.

"Where is this going, Danny?" she asked one night when they lay together, their arms wrapped around each other.

"I'm going to marry you, Fi," he replied. Her heart clanged, but she turned from him, trying not to show him her beaming face. "Not today," he continued, squeezing her shoulder. "But one day, I promise I will ask you to marry me."

"Sorry, I don't mean to sound needy," she said. "I know we're young. We have so much we want to do still."

"We do," he replied, turning her around and wrapping himself around the back of her body, leaving a light kiss on her neck.

To Fiona, it was magic. Being with Danny was the only thing she wanted. But three years of being his friend with benefits and nothing had changed. Danny didn't commit to her. He still professed his love for her but told her he needed time. Fiona was sick of waiting for him and resolved to get on with life without him. But each time she met someone she felt she could be interested in, he came waltzing back into her life, and she was his once more.

She tried. She went on a date with a boy from work, almost fell in love with him, and then realised she couldn't be in love with two people. No, she knew he would come around. He was still young, and so was she. There was much to do in life before that kind of commitment.

* * * *

Danny knew he was going to end up with Fiona. He loved her. That was certain. How much he loved her, he wasn't so sure. Could he commit to her at this point in his life? No. There were too many obstacles, distractions, and insufficient time to commit to the type of relationship she wanted, and he knew she wanted it all. He knew he was still bitter with his father. He knew marriage was not all it was cracked up to be. Jumping into it required thought. Danny was as impulsive as the next twenty-year-old, but his outlook on marriage was not promising. He still sometimes caught his mother gazing at the moon, a glaze in her eyes, and knew she was thinking about his father. What if their love faded? What if he wasn't enough for Fiona? What if he was just enamoured right now? What if he was like his father and fell for another pair of legs that walked through the door?

But Danny couldn't not have Fiona. He knew he was being selfish, not allowing her to be rid of him. It would be easy for her to move on, but he couldn't let her. He still needed her in his life.

He cringed when he thought about how she must have felt when she saw his arms around another girl. He had hurt her so many times. He still remembered her anger, the vicious words she flung at him.

"I hate you. I am done," she had said when he told her he was seeing Louisa.

He stood there looking down at his shoes, not wanting to hurt her, but he liked Louisa, who didn't come with all the drama Fiona did. Louisa was nice and pretty and came with a family that was not as erratic as Fiona's. It had been more than six months after their split, and he knew they had to move on. It would never work with them, they were too different, and their families lived in different universes. He still seethed with jealousy when he saw her talk to a guy at school. And Justin. Oh, he had pounced almost immediately. That slimy bastard! She had thrown his name into the mix when she tried to hurt Danny, but she had nothing to do with Justin, not in that way. She had told him later, and for some reason, it gave him a slight sense of satisfaction.

Yes, even though in those six months they had been apart before Louisa eyed him, they still ended up in each other's arms on occasion, especially when Fiona seemed to get close to anyone else, particularly Justin. But he knew he had to do something to end it. It was not healthy for either of them. And Louisa, who watched as he played soccer almost every day, seemed to be a good choice. He knew he had to tell Fiona about Louisa before she saw them together or heard about it from anyone else.

Fiona had not taken it well as he knew she wouldn't. She stormed out of his house, her face dry, thunderous, and he followed her, not saying anything to explain himself, not trying to stop her. He hurt for her, for himself, knowing that this had to happen for them both to move on.

Then Fiona stopped at the gate and turned around.

"I hate you," she yelled with venom. "You know how much I hate you? For your information, I haven't been sitting around waiting for you either. There's been guys," she said, rattling off the names of three boys she'd kissed at parties, and with each name, he could feel the dagger that pushed deeper into his heart. He still didn't say anything. She was allowed to be mad. It would make her feel better. "Oh, and Justin," she said. "Yes, Justin, too." He clenched his teeth as she strode away, allowing his chest to rise and fall.

Louisa was lovely — sweet, caring, and kind. Grace liked Louisa too, but although he felt he could see himself in a long-term relationship with her, the passion he shared with Louisa was lacking. Sure, they kissed, cuddled, and played, but the temptation to ravage her as he had felt with Fiona was missing. However, even with Louisa, he couldn't stop thinking about Fiona. Perhaps once school was done, he convinced himself. But before school was done, he was also done with Louisa, and their romance fizzled out within a couple of months.

Danny got a part-time job at his father's firm, and his secretary Rebecca was now a housewife with two children, his half-siblings. He was glad he didn't have to see her there. It was enough to have to be at their wedding. His father tried to make peace, to combine their families, but Danny was not having any of it. He had broken their family and trust, and he was not going to betray his mother by becoming part of something that broke them up. He knew he was being unreasonable, but it was how he felt. His relationship with his father deteriorated, and Danny was gobsmacked when he was offered a position at his firm.

"Take it, Danny," Grace urged.

"I don't know," Danny said. "It will be weird there."

"She doesn't work there anymore." Danny could see that Grace was trying to be strong, but he didn't want to betray her. "He's trying, Danny."

"He didn't try with you."

"That's different," Grace said. "You're his son. He wants to help you."

"I don't want his help," Danny said with warmth. "Where was he all this time? Holing up with that woman..."

"That was a long time ago. You have to move on from that."

Danny couldn't understand why his mother was sticking up for his father. "But seeing him every day."

"Whatever he is, he's a good businessman. You would learn a lot from him."

Danny shrugged, a little more casually than he felt. "Well, it is part-time, I guess. I could make a little bit of money. And he gets my soccer. So..."

Danny took the job, learning the ins and outs of advertising. He watched through the glass windows of the conference room as people came in and spread out their little boards on stands, their actions animated, their voices loud and passionate. He saw his father survey their selling prowess with a banal look, masking his thoughts. He saw the grand man that his father was, and a little stab of awe for him embedded itself into his psyche. He hated that he wanted to be him.

But soccer was still his passion. Danny continued to play, now travelling interstate almost every fortnight and coming home elated whether his team won or lost. His aim was to play for Australia, to be selected for the national team, to represent his country. But there were still stepping stones he knew had to be manoeuvred carefully.

Two weeks after he was selected to play for the Victorian team, he crashed his car after returning home from a match, toppling it on its head and breaking an ankle and wrist in the process.

"It will be okay," Grace said when he got home from his three-week stay at the hospital. "You will fully recover. You will get back on the team." She fluffed the pillows behind his back, trying to make him comfortable, knowing she wasn't succeeding.

"I think that's done," a sullen Danny replied.

"Stop it, Danny!"

"No Mum, I don't think I can even bend my wrist," he said.

"You're not meant to now. It will heal."

Danny was gutted. He was in a funk and couldn't get out of it. For months he sat around trying to forget everything, barely eating, watching soccer on television and replays of his taped matches. He refused to see anyone and neglected everything around him, including his friends, preferring to be alone. When his phone rang, he didn't answer it, and when there was a knock on the door of his bungalow, he ignored it. His dog, Cruz, was the only thing that comforted him, and Danny would cry into his fur, the animal licking away the teardrops that fell from his eyes.

One afternoon, he was sitting on his bed, flicking through a magazine, when he heard a soft knock on his door. He rolled his eyes. He was tired of Grace trying to bring someone over to see him. Couldn't she understand he wanted to be on his own? He would get out of it, whatever it was he was going through in his own time. He didn't answer.

"Danny?"

He sat up. Fiona. His heart began to thump. It had been so long since he had seen her. Not since school was done. They hadn't spoken since their break-up. He smiled wryly. His mother had brought in the big guns. "It's open," he said despite himself.

She came through the door tentatively and hovered near it, her hand still on the doorknob. "I just found out. I bumped into Jeff." He motioned for her to sit on the armchair that sat beside his bed, which she did, looking relieved. She glanced around the room, her gaze resting on the picture of them together pasted on the side of his desk. He could see her trying not to smile, and he felt flustered. He'd been meaning to take that down. After Louisa was out of his life, he pulled out the picture he had tucked into his drawer and placed it back on the table. His mother had rolled her eyes when she had come into his room one day and playfully slapped the back of his head. There it had stayed, and he looked at it every day.

"How are you feeling?" Fiona asked.

He shrugged. "Yeah, okay, I guess."

"I thought you'd be wrapped in plaster by the sound of things."

"What do you mean?"

"Well, Jeff and your mum, they said that you were pretty bad." She looked down at her fingers, which she twiddled together. "I'm sorry I didn't know about it until today."

"That's okay," he replied, slightly uncomfortable. He wondered why he hadn't heard from her and was a little irritated that she hadn't checked on him. But he knew he had hurt her. They hadn't had any contact, and there was no reason she should care about him or how he was. But seeing her here, right here in front of him, unnerved him. He still wanted her.

"Can you walk?"

"Yeah. It's better now."

"What about soccer?"

"Don't know," he said and looked away.

She left her chair and moved to sit beside him on the bed. "Is it okay that I'm here?"

Danny wanted to pull her to him, kiss her, hold her close, and smell her scent, which he missed so much. But he leaned back slightly and noticed her frown. She had mistaken his gesture for rejection. He grabbed her hand. "How are you?" he said quickly.

She looked down at their hands, leaving hers in his. "I'm good. I'm at Uni with a Bachelor of Arts, but I'm considering transferring to performing arts. I don't know if I can get in, but I'm in the next play as an extra, and I guess I just have to do the hard yards." She laughed lightly, and Danny felt his throat clog. He just realised how much he missed her, how much he missed her laugh, her voice. "I just wished I knew what I wanted six months ago. I guess I knew what I really wanted. But I wasted the last couple of years pining over you and didn't really think past high school."

"I'm sorry, you know." She nodded, and her eyes shimmered. "No, no," he said softly. He didn't want to make her cry and pulled her to him. He felt her sniff into his neck and softly shudder.

"Me, too," she mumbled. "I'm sorry, too." She removed her head from the crook of his neck and looked into his eyes.

Before he knew it, his lips were on hers, and she hungrily took them. He leaned forward and laid her back on his bed. He lifted his head to look at her, and she nodded, her arms already circling his neck. He leaned down and kissed her neck, the dip in her chest, feeling the same desire he always felt when he had her in his arms. He could feel her hands searching for him, touching him and sliding her hands into the back of his pants. He cupped her breasts and moved his mouth down her stomach.

Danny wondered if that should have happened. They had made love, a more urgent love than before, a more tender love than before, and when they were sated, they had lain together, her head on his chest, as they used to, comfortable, happy. Then she'd looked at her watch and sat up.

"Well, now that I know you're okay, I have to go." She laughed.

"Fiona," he said and hesitated.

"Don't flatter yourself, Danny. I don't think this is the start of something beautiful. For old times' sake, right?" She laughed again, a forced laugh. "Hey, let's catch up again sometime, okay?"

"Yeah."

And they had, not particularly on purpose, but when Danny began going out with his friends again, they seemed to bump into each other often. It had been nearly two years since they had been together, but he still seethed when he saw her with someone else. He remembered clearly the time he had bumped into her at the cinema and had gone over to say hello. He was with Jeff, waiting for a couple of other friends, and she was standing by herself, looking up at the session times.

"Oh, hey Danny, hey Jeff," she said, looking around her furtively.

"What are you doing here?" he asked, wondering if Jeff would be okay if he asked her to join them.

"About to watch a movie. I'm thinking *Point Break*. Maybe *My Girl*."

"Who are you with?"

"Um, just waiting for a friend."

Danny felt the heat rise in him. "A guy?" She nodded and looked at the floor. "Okay," he said. "Have a good time." He walked away with Jeff hot on his tail.

"Hey, man, are you okay?" Jeff called after him.

"Yeah, fine," he replied, but his jealousy blinded him at that moment. "I'm going to go home. I'm not feeling too well. Say hi to the guys for me."

He rushed away without waiting for a reply and drove home, his heart thumping, his head almost exploding. He burst into the house and went to the kitchen, pouring a large glass of water and drinking it all at once until he spluttered. His breathing was heavy, and he felt himself fall to the floor. He was losing her. He crumbled into a ball and wept.

Chapter Eleven

"So Daria wants to know if you want to come on the camping trip," Alice said. She and Fiona were in the middle of watching a movie, and this came out of nowhere. "Spring Leaves. Do you know it?"

"Yeah. We went up there last year." Fiona remembered how beautiful it had been. A little rained out, the raindrops pattering on the tarpaulin, but being holed up in the tent with Danny was the most romantic thing. She sighed, wishing she could go back to that place. "You're going?" Fiona paused the video and looked at Alice in surprise.

"Yeah. If that's okay. They asked me if I wanted to."

"When?"

"We met for coffee yesterday," Alice said with some hesitation.

That was news to Fiona. That Alice had now very firmly embedded herself into Fiona's group, even more than Fiona had been lately. She felt a stab of jealousy, but what could she do? And why should she do anything if she could? Alice was entitled to be friends with whomever she wanted. She didn't need Fiona's permission, even if they were Fiona's friends. "I meant when is the trip?" Fiona snapped and swallowed down her irritation.

"This weekend, Friday." Alice didn't seem to notice Fiona's ire.

"I don't think I can. I have rehearsals. The show begins in three weeks."

"That sucks," Alice said, and Fiona thought she caught a wisp of a smile on her face.

"Is Danny going?"

"I think they all are," she said. "Jeff, Daria, Jason and Sandy. Maybe Paula and Dina, too."

Fiona nodded. Her friends, no, Danny's friends. She didn't see much of them anymore, only when they went clubbing. Daria popped over to spend the night occasionally, but even that was petering out. But Danny. She hadn't seen him in a while and these days it wasn't uncommon. Even though they were only two people who hooked up because they couldn't stand to be apart for too long, she was less and less sure that he would commit to her. She was losing faith in him.

She thought of Kevin and a smile involuntarily crept onto her lips. Kevin had been flirting with her for a few weeks, they had gone for drinks on more than a couple of occasions, albeit with friends on the play, actors, backstage people and even the director. But Kevin had asked her out to dinner on Friday and she had declined, citing an early morning, but she felt a little poke in her belly; she was more than interested in him. The only thing holding her back was Danny. She was not yet ready to give up on them. She still believed they would end up together. But Kevin.

Kevin was smart, a little too reserved, tall, and dark, with wavy locks of hair. He reminded her of her favourite movie star, Pierce Brosnan, and although they had only been out a handful of times, she could see that he was the serious type, not one who could have his heart broken easily. But what did she know about men?

She went into her room and picked up the phone, dialled. "Hey Kevin? Is that offer for dinner on Friday still on the table?"

Dinner with Kevin was unexpectedly fun. It wasn't that Fiona didn't think Kevin was a fun guy, it was that Danny had hardly entered her head, and she knew she could fall for him. They talked about the play, they talked about their families, they talked about everything, and when they walked back to his car, she slipped her hand in his. And when they arrived at her apartment, he walked her to the door, taking her hand again.

She turned to him when they reached her door and Fiona was suddenly shy. "I had a great evening," she said.

"Me too," he replied and leaned forward.

Fiona wanted to kiss him, and she moved towards him, putting her arms around his neck. She gazed into his eyes as he felt his arms encircle her, and saw his dark eyes crease in pleasure. Then she felt his lips on hers and a rush of warmth invaded her belly. And then Danny popped into her head and Fiona let go of Kevin. "See you on Monday?"

"Yes," he replied. "Monday."

She reached out, pecked his cheek and went into her apartment. She closed the door and leaned against it, her knees weak — the first time she felt more than an inkling for another man who was not Danny. She wished she could have invited him in. Alice had left that morning for the weekend with Fiona's friends, and she had the apartment to herself. She wanted to talk to someone about Kevin, about Danny, but it was too late to call Victoria, and she wished Alice were home so she could discuss her burgeoning feelings for Kevin. No, she couldn't let it happen. She couldn't let Danny down. She needed to know now if what they had was going to go anywhere.

She had an idea and looked at her watch. It was too late to go now, and besides, she had rehearsals early in the morning. But she packed a bag. She would go straight from the theatre. Spring Leaves was only a three-hour drive, and she would get there in enough time to spend at least the evening and a night there. She could tent it with Danny. He would be more than happy for her to, as he had been the previous year. She was excited to see him, nervous about giving him an ultimatum, and barely slept that night. Her nerves were ragged.

The next day, the phone rang as she was rushing out the door, having slept in.

"Hi Fiona," Kevin said cheerily.

Fiona bit her lip, wishing she had left the phone ringing. "Hey Kevin. I'm on my way out. Rehearsals."

"No problem. Just wondering if you want to do it again tonight."

"I...I have to, um, I have rehearsals now..."

"It's okay. Too soon?" He chuckled a nervous giggle.

"Yes, maybe," Fiona said honestly. She needed time. She liked Kevin a little too much and knew he was a serious man, fun, sweet, but not someone who just had casual flings. "I'm going away for the night with some friends. I should be back tomorrow. Rain check?"

"Sure," he replied, and Fiona sensed the disappointment in his voice. After she hung up the phone, she contemplated not going to Spring Leaves. Maybe this was the sign, the thing that was to break whatever spell she and Danny were under. But no, she had to talk to Danny about it all, make a clean break or commit. She couldn't just wait around for him to be ready anymore.

She went to the theatre, hurried through her scenes and asked to leave when they were done. Anne, the director, frowned but let her go. Fiona was excited. She was finally taking control of the situation, not waiting for Danny anymore. She felt elated and empowered. Even the long drive didn't make her determination wane. This was it, the beginning or the end. Either way, it was a new chapter for her.

When she finally got to the campsite at seven pm, she parked in a spot next to Danny's car, and hearing a rumbling noise in the distance, turned her head to see the flames flying into the air. She smiled. They were already at it — the bonfire. She could imagine Jeff wailing at the moon, Danny slightly embarrassed but also letting his hair down, and Daria cleaning up the moment someone dropped something on the grass. She missed this — time with her friends. She was glad she had come.

She grabbed her backpack, wandered toward the fire, and grinned at the sounds emanating from there. The first person she saw was Daria, and Fiona waved her hand. Daria began a smile that quickly froze on her suddenly stricken face.

"Hey," Fiona called, looking around for the others. Jeff, Jason and Sandy sat around the fire, lost in a song, their faces raised to the sky. Paula and Dina were not there, and neither were Danny nor Alice. "Where is everyone?"

"What are you doing here?" Daria moved towards her a little too quickly.

"You invited me." Fiona frowned. Something wasn't right. "Where's Danny?"

Daria's gaze shifted to the tents about twenty metres away from the fire and returned quickly to Fiona's face. A fear settled into her eyes. "Out," she said. "Maybe at the rock. I thought I saw him go there."

Fiona turned to the rock in the other direction and stepped that way. But suddenly, she turned around and found herself dropping her backpack and heading towards Danny's tent, her stride widening as she drew near. She heard a laugh — not Danny's.

Before her mind could protest, she drew back the flap and stared. Danny was lying on his back, shirtless. Alice was leaning into the crook of his neck, kissing him. Fiona's insides felt like they were falling out of her, and her face became hot. She could never remember that feeling completely when she tried to later. Something always blocked it out. She recalled returning to her car, fumbling for her keys, and Danny calling her name. She was already in her seat, the door closed, and he was at the window, banging on it. Fiona looked behind her as she reversed, not allowing herself to face him.

She drove home numb, not quite sure how she got there, and when she looked for her backpack, she realised it was still back at the camp, sitting on the grass.

Here's a letter. I wanted answers. I got them. Stay the fuck away from me. And thank that little wench for me. She managed to get rid of the shit that was stuck under my feet for so long.

Chapter Twelve

1996

Fiona sat at the kitchen table, knowing it was over. Her marriage was doomed from the beginning, and all she could think about now was Danny. Her anger for him bubbled into something that scared her. He had set the bar for the way all her relationships after him would go, and nothing stood up to it—not even the man who had loved her deeply, who understood her, who wanted the same things as her. She went to the bedroom, now devoid of Kevin's things, and flopped herself on the bed. She let herself think of Danny now, cursing and still loving him simultaneously. She hadn't spoken to him since she walked out of his life, and she hadn't looked back, refused to think about him whenever the image of his face, his blue eyes gazing at her with that fierce tenderness, tried to invade her brain. But she knew she hadn't let him go completely.

When she had seen him three months ago while shopping in the city with Kevin, she had frozen, her heart had thumped at her chest and her ears buzzed. He was standing on the other side of the crossing, waiting for the lights to change. He was by himself and hadn't spotted her yet.

"Fiona, honey," Kevin said, nudging her, and she realised that people had already begun to move across the street. But not Danny. He remained immobile now, a mirror of her shell-shocked self, his eyes directly on her, his face unmoving. She stepped onto the street and averted her gaze as she moved past him, turning her head the other way. She had gone home dizzy and had a glass of wine and a long hot bath, letting herself come to terms with the fact that he still lived in the same universe as her. There would be a time when they bumped into each other, and she had to accept that. But she wasn't prepared for what she felt when she saw him. Nothing had changed, at least not for her. And she was married to the nicest, most wonderful man in the world.

The situation with Kevin was complicated now. Things had been going downhill for a while. She didn't know what it was, really. Perhaps it was because they spent so little time together, his job as a photographer flying him away at the whim of his boss at the agency. And when she was in the throes of a new play, she was barely home. It was time to finally acknowledge that as much as they wanted to be together, it was over. The final nail in the coffin was when Kevin had to move to Queensland, a major promotion, and Fiona wouldn't leave. Not from Melbourne, the heart and soul of Australian theatre, of which *her* heart and soul were firmly entrenched.

The doorbell clanged her out of her snooze, and for a moment, she hoped Kevin had returned, had changed his mind, but it had been weeks, and he had called to let her know he was in Brisbane, safe and sound. At least it was amicable. She sighed and pulled herself out of bed, wondering who on earth had decided to visit so late on a Saturday night.

Victoria stood at the door, and when she saw Fiona in her track suit pants, she lowered her gaze and raised it again, a frown of disapproval on her face. "Looks like I've come at the right time," she said, pushing Fiona back into the house. "Come on. We're going out."

"Out where?"

"You can't sit around having a cry. You made a decision…"

"I didn't," Fiona started.

"You did, and he did too." She ushered Fiona into her room, and Fiona sat on the bed. Victoria opened the wardrobe and ruffled through Fiona's clothes, pulling out a pair of jeans and a black lacy top. "Here, this is good."

"Where are we going?"

"To the bar."

"No!"

"Yes!" Victoria put her hands on her hips. "You can't just sit around and mope," she said.

"The ink is not even dry on the papers," Fiona replied and pouted, crossing her arms like a stubborn child.

"Well, you've been sitting around in your pyjamas for days now, so it's time to get up and get going." She came closer, sniffed Fiona and wrinkled her nose. "Go have a quick shower, too."

Fiona sniffed at herself, not finding anything wrong with how she smelled. Maybe a bit of pasta that she had made yesterday. She reluctantly went to the shower, let the water hit her back, and tried not to cry. It seemed that was what she did whenever things went wrong. And things were very wrong now. No, not wrong, just over. She was divorced at twenty-three. Everyone had told her not to do it, not to marry so young, and she thought she had it all worked out. Now they were going to laugh at her. Her parents did the *I told you so* thing and then promptly returned to Italy.

She thought of Danny again. If he hadn't—

She turned off the tap and shook herself out of frustration. There was nothing to be done about it now. Music was wafting through the house, Madonna. She couldn't help but chuckle. Victoria always knew what she needed—a good dance. She stepped out into the bedroom and watched as Victoria held the hairbrush to her mouth, mouthing the words to *Holiday*, their favourite song to karaoke to. She couldn't help moving her hips to the rhythm, and grabbing a comb, still wrapped in her towel, she sang along, both squealing in the most inharmonious tones.

"This is what I need," Fiona said. "Hell yeah! Fuck men!"

*

Maybe she willed him there.

Fiona was coming out of the ladies' room, having wiped the sweat off her neck and thrown water over her face to freshen up and cool down after an energetic bout of dancing. She stopped dead in her tracks. There he was, Danny, just leaning against the wall, a look of anticipation on his face. She stared for a moment, and without thinking, she ran to him and threw herself into his arms. She felt him grip her tightly, and she let go and looked at his face, which was filled with surprise.

"What are you doing here?" she asked, wondering if the right thing to do when she first saw him was hug him. She blamed the tequila that she'd been throwing back all night.

"Same as you," he said, his eyes searching hers.

"Did Victoria tell you we were going to be..."

"No."

They walked to the dance floor, and Fiona leaned against a table, watching Victoria shaking her bottom about. She smiled, but she was acutely aware of Danny's proximity, so close she could smell him despite the various scents of alcohol and sweat that permeated the air. It was so silent above the music, and she swallowed. How could he still make her feel this way? Did she do the same for him?

"Did I ever tell you how sorry I was? How sorry I am?" he shouted, trying to be heard above the din.

Fiona swallowed again and shook her head. She didn't want to hear this, not here. "Nothing to be sorry about."

"Fi," he said and gently touched her arm.

She could feel a tear begin to well and was determined not to give him the satisfaction. He had seen her cry too many times already. "Vic is calling for me," she said, bouncing a little too enthusiastically on the dance floor. She didn't look back at him and, after a few songs, lost the mood, and they left soon after. Every bit of her wanted to return to where he was, where she knew he stood and watched as she flirted with other men on the dance floor, knowing how much it would make him fume. She knew she would forever have that effect on him and was taking full advantage of it. Sure, she was being immature, but she didn't care. What was that saying—revenge is a dish best served cold? Well, this was as cold as she could get right now.

* * * *

Danny walked out after he saw her chatting with some guy, and he clenched his teeth, angry, irritated. She still had that effect on him, and she knew it. She was doing it for him. It should have made him happy that she still cared enough to try to make him jealous, but it was the actual jealousy that he couldn't deal with.

He had seen Victoria on the dance floor before he knew Fiona was at the club and had bumped his way through the crowd, trying to get to her.

"Danny!"

"Hi Vic. Haven't seen you in ages." He had to yell to be heard.

"No, it's been a while," she called back.

"How's…how is she?"

Victoria bobbed her head towards the ladies' room. "Find out for yourself," she said with a grin.

"She's here?" His heart was already beginning to crash against his chest. Victoria nodded, and Danny went to the bathroom and waited, leaning against the wall outside, wondering what he would say to her. He had rehearsed it often — how he would apologise for his actions. What a terrible mistake he had made.

He could never fathom what possessed him to kiss Alice. Well, she had kissed him, and he had kissed her back. What an absolute dick he had been. It had come entirely out of the blue, and his mind had been on Fiona that night. It was a warm night, a night of romance, one that he should have been spending with Fiona, not out here in the wilderness with his friends, who had too much to drink and were singing at the top of their lungs. He had left the bonfire and had moved to the edge of a fence on which he leaned.

"You know she's seeing someone." Alice was behind him, and he turned to her. She seemed to be everywhere, Alice, but she was nice and fun and had bonded with the group. He wondered why she had come along when Fiona hadn't.

"Who? Fiona?"

"Yeah. He's nice. Good looking. She seems happy."

Danny felt his blood curdle as usual when he thought of Fiona with another guy. "That's good," he said. "She deserves to be happy."

"So do you," Alice said and leaned close to him.

He turned to her, and before he knew it, her lips were on his, and his arms were around her.

When he thought about it later, he knew it would mark the end of his and Fiona's constant cycle of fighting, loving, and doing whatever they had done with each other for the last three years. And he liked Alice. Of course, he knew he had just ruined their friendship, but something had to be done. He and Fiona were toxic together, and it had to end.

When she drove out of his life, a determination on her face that he'd never seen before, he didn't really believe she would remain gone, but when he heard that she was to be married, not even six months later, he knew he had made the worst mistake of his life.

Alice was long gone too. Their relationship had fizzled out two months after they had begun, and he suspected they were never really all that into each other. And when he reflected on it, the only thing he felt about his time with Alice was the hurt he must have caused Fiona. But it was too late. He had fucked up, big, this time. And he had lost the thing he loved the most in the world.

"She's getting married," Jeff said one day when they had gone out to play pool.

"Who?"

"Fiona." Danny felt the familiar stir in his belly when he heard her name. He nodded slowly. Jeff put down his cue and scrutinised Danny's face. "You guys are done, right?"

Danny nodded, a little more surely this time. "Yeah. Haven't seen her in a while." He nodded at the table. "Take your shot," he said and blinked back the tears that were about to escape his eyes.

He got drunk, caught a taxi home, and when he reached home, he drank some more. Then he let his tears fall. She was happy now, about to be married, and he would not cause her any more heartache. She had been through enough with him.

When he stood outside the bathroom waiting for her to come out, his heart beating so hard and so fast, he prepared again what he needed to tell her, how he was going to explain it all. And when he saw her come out, looking as beautiful as she always did, her face in that constant smile, her eyes lighting up the moment she saw him and hurled herself at him, all those words he had so carefully prepared flew right out of his head.

Chapter Thirteen

"If it were meant to be, it would have been," Fiona said to nobody in particular.

Right now, she had to deal with a failed marriage. What a shambles. She looked at Kevin's side of the bed, which she had yet to stretch over to. It was too soon — if three months were too soon. She didn't want to leave the bed but knew she had to. She whined as she scrambled to the shower and got ready for work. Another day at the zoo — rehearsals were like that, people rushing around everywhere, bumping into each other, screeching at each other from the back row of the theatre to the stage, behind the stage, in the hallways, but Fiona thrived on it. She loved the hustle and bustle of the place. The energy fused into her body, and she soaked it all in. She was lucky she had secured a job at the theatre company, and being part of the chorus was a stepping stone into the big leagues. She was still idealistic enough to believe she would make it even though her feet literally bled sometimes when she got home after a long night. But she loved her job, trudging to the theatre, mixing with like-minded, if sometimes self-involved people.

She sat on her stool now and stared into the mirror. Today she didn't like what she saw. The bags under her eyes were packed to the hilt, and her eyes were still red. She wondered if it would be a good idea to take another day off, but she knew she couldn't, she had already taken three days off in the last three months and even though she wasn't the star of the show, it would reflect on her ability to show up when needed. Sure, they would understand, but for how long? And this was different, even though she balked at the thought of allowing Danny to mess up her life again.

She faced Danny a night ago. Danny, whom she hadn't seen since before her wedding. Actually, a long time before that, too. Why couldn't she stop thinking about him? Why was he permeating her brain again? She thought that after Alice, she could never forgive him. One little *I'm sorry* would not cut it. And what was he sorry about anyway? They weren't together when Alice happened. But he should have known it would be a mistake to go there. She still didn't know why he did it. Maybe he wanted to hurt her. Perhaps it gave him power over her, a control, or maybe that was their unfinished business. Perhaps that was what was needed to close the chapter on their romance that would never go anywhere. It worked. She moved on.

She shook her head. Why was she thinking about Danny again? Maybe because she didn't have to feel guilty about Kevin if she did. Kevin and Fiona had been happy. Having really put her mind to not thinking about Danny had worked, and she loved Kevin, forgetting Danny existed for a while, and she was genuinely happy. But then it fell apart, and a little piece of her knew it was supposed to, that as much as she loved Kevin, he would never be Danny.

And Danny, well, he was still Danny. He still managed to make her swoon by just being there, being in her presence. She frowned. Why did he have that effect on her? She wanted to hit herself for letting him off the hook so easily, for dismissing his apology instead of making him crawl and beg for forgiveness. But she had never been one to do that, to let herself be pitied, to let someone feel sorry for her. She had been fine, it had been the best thing, and he had done her a favour by letting her go, even in the manner he did.

She fluffed the powder on her face and let out a breath, feeling a little better and more justified about her dour mood. She would forget him again.

The only problem was that now she didn't have to feel guilty about thinking about him, and all she wanted to do was think about him. She went to the theatre more dejected than ever.

Chapter Fourteen

Fiona toyed with the phone after Victoria left the following Saturday evening. It had been a week since she'd seen Danny, but he'd been floating around in her brain since then. The work week had been a letdown, with not much for Fiona to do but watch the rehearsals of the mains, keeping her mind more distracted with Danny than ever. She thought about Kevin and missed him. Perhaps it would distract her from thoughts of Danny, but every time she let her mind stray to her ex-husband, they automatically reverted to Danny in comparison. And she knew she shouldn't think about Kevin anymore. It was over, and she had few lingering feelings for him. She refused to have regrets about that.

She sighed. She also intended never to have lingering feelings for Danny, but here she was, not a few months after her separation, thinking about him.

She dialled his number. She knew it by heart and hoped his mother hadn't changed it. She knew he still lived with her, even though his father had passed a year earlier. They still had friends in common, so it was natural that she heard about him. But when she did, her stomach scrunched up tightly, and she usually stayed out of the conversation. She didn't see many of those friends anymore. It was clear they had sided with him after the whole Alice thing, and to be fair, they had been more his friends than hers, so that was natural too.

She heard the phone connect and ring, and her throat caught. She hung up and looked at the phone. "Don't be a wuss," she said to herself and dialled again.

"Hello?" His voice was tentative.

"How sorry are you?" she blurted.

"Fiona." His voice was sad but didn't register surprise at her being on the other end of the line.

"I mean it. I want to know."

"Are you busy?"

"I'm on the phone with you."

"Can I see you?" he asked.

She felt a tear plop on her wrist. She didn't know until this moment how badly she wanted to see him. "Yes. Where?"

"Come to mine?" he said, an urgency in his voice.

"Is anyone home?" She couldn't stand the thought of seeing his mother. She just couldn't face her after all they had been through.

"No. No one's home."

"I don't know." She didn't want to return to his place after all this time. It just seemed weird—soiled. *She* had probably been there.

"I can meet you. Anywhere." His voice was more urgent now.

"Come here." It was an impulsive decision, but this new apartment didn't hold anything of Kevin, so she didn't feel like she was disrespecting him.

"Are you sure?"

"Yes." She gave him the address, and he said he would be over in half an hour.

She paced the floor, angry with herself for going back in time. If they were meant to be, they would have been, she told herself again. But why now was she so terrified and so exhilarated to be seeing him again? She jumped into the shower to freshen up and threw a quick splash of makeup on her face. Her eyes had already reddened from the tear spillage, and she didn't want him to see her cry. She had wasted enough tears on him and certainly didn't want him to know it. He was the one who stuffed up. She didn't do anything wrong. She still had her pride.

She rehearsed how it would go. He would come in, and she would get him a drink. She didn't know what he drank. They weren't together long enough to know his adult life. But she had wine and beer, staples for when Victoria came by, and they spent a late night chatting. She drank the odd wine now and then but never on her own. She poured herself one.

He would come in, and she would offer him a seat, and maybe he would explain why he did what he did. But she already knew why he did it. Her best friend — it wouldn't have been something he did lightly. "Maybe he did," she said to herself. "Maybe I was really nothing to him." And she would listen to whatever explanation he gave, as lousy as it was, and she would forgive him, and when he was leaving, she would hug him. Then there would be closure, and she could get on with her life.

By the time he arrived, Fiona had already finished the full glass she had poured out of pure nervousness.

It hadn't helped, and she was a mess again. She wished he would take longer, giving her more time to prepare her mind. She didn't expect to see him—maybe she did.

But she didn't expect her heart to drop right through her insides at the sight of him standing on her doorstep, and for a long moment, they just stared into each other's eyes. It seemed like yesterday since she had seen him, since they first kissed, and it seemed like a lifetime had passed since then.

She found her bearings, ignoring her hammering heart, and stepped aside. "Come in."

He reached forward and kissed her cheek, and she moved back. "Sorry," he said, and she pointed the way to the living room.

"This is a nice place," he said, looking around. "Did you…"

"I moved out of our house," she said quickly. "I've been here for a month." She moved to the kitchen. "Beer? Wine? Coffee?"

"Whatever you're having," he said, eyeing her now empty glass.

When she returned to the living room after pouring their drinks and trying to calm herself, he sat on the sofa, his head bent, staring at the floor. He took the glass from her and placed it on the table. She sat opposite him and sipped at her wine, not knowing how to start, where, and what to say. He seemed in a similar state, so she reached for the remote. Maybe some distraction would help the awkwardness.

"No, don't," he said. "I just wanted to tell you how sorry I am."

"For what? The breakdown of my marriage?" She didn't know where that came from, and she pursed her lips.

"No, I mean, yes…I mean…"

In spite of herself, she tried not to smile. "Okay."

"For Alice. It was the worst mistake of my life."

"Why? Did her boobs not do it for you?" She couldn't help herself, the bitterness she'd locked away for so long seeping through her seemingly calm veneer.

He frowned. "It was the worst thing because I lost you forever."

"Oh." She was quiet for a moment. "Did you think I'd come back to you again after that?"

"No…" Danny looked at the floor.

"I came back to you again and again…"

"We came back to each other." He raised his head now, looking steadily into her eyes.

"But how could I have forgiven that? My best friend." Everything she had felt, she was going to make him understand.

"I don't know why. Maybe it was the boys…"

"You can't blame them," she said, feeling her temper rise. He could always do that to her too.

"No. No, I'm not blaming them. It was me, all me."

"But why her? I got over Louisa."

"We were not together. With Louisa or Alice. I never cheated."

"I know it wasn't cheating, but surely you knew how that would affect me. I lost my best friend and the man I had been in love with for three years!" She balled her fists, her body tense.

"I think it was because of that. We just went back and forth for too long." He leaned forward.

"Why was that?" She gritted her teeth and leaned back on the sofa, crossing her arms.

"I don't know, Fi, but I think I was just so tired of doing it. The other guys you went out with…"

"The other guys," she cried, raising herself out of the sofa, standing over him. "All the other guys were because of you!"

"I loved you."

She turned her back to him, couldn't look at him anymore. It was too difficult. Every fibre of her being wanted to rush to him, to throw herself in his arms, to feel those lips she loved so much, but she swallowed and sat down again, gazing away from him, out the long glass window. Rain was pattering on the pane, and it took her back again. It made her think about Kevin. Three years with Kevin, a rushed into wedding a couple of months later, but they stayed together for three years. Did she love him? Shouldn't she be thinking about him right now? She had thought about him for the last three months and almost changed her mind about how things went, but she remained steadfast in her decision, unwavering no matter how lonely she became.

Now here she was, Danny, sitting less than a couple of metres away from her, so close if she reached out she could touch him, and she was on fire.

"Maybe I should go," Danny said, rising from his seat, and she turned back to him.

"Yeah, maybe."

"I guess I just wanted to say I'm sorry. It haunts me what I did to you."

"Thanks," she mumbled and led him to the front door. He walked out of it and turned around as if he was contemplating saying something else. Fiona held the knob of the door tightly, fearing that if she left it, there would be no going back. Then he turned around and walked back to his car.

"Don't go," she called out, astonished the words had left her mouth, but before she could say anything else, he was back at the door, his lips hard on hers, and before she knew it, he had kicked the front door closed and was carrying her to the living room. He placed her on the floor and stared deeply into her eyes. She knew right then that she had never stopped loving him and that he had never stopped loving her. Her arms went around his neck, and he squeezed her so hard it hurt, but it was a beautiful pain, and for a moment, she was back on that dance floor, feeling that she could never be separate from him, that she would die if she were.

But she hadn't died. She'd survived the breakup and everything that came after that. And as she watched his face, eyes closed in sleep, a peaceful look of satisfaction the next morning as dawn broke through the window, she wondered if she had the nerve to go through all that again.

It had been six years, and sure they were just teenagers, but had things really changed that much?

* * * *

Danny slept a peaceful, beautiful sleep. His arm around Fiona, her head stuck in the crook of his neck, as she used to do, and when he woke in the middle of the night, thirsty, he couldn't bear to move her as she lay there, little noises escaping her mouth. He loved that. Those same little noises she made when she kissed him.

He let his mind go back to last night when she had made those sounds, a little cry of want. It was new to him. She had never done that before, and he wanted to crush her with love as she moaned in his kiss. They had remained encased in each other's arms, her back against the wall, his body pushing against hers. She moved her face away from him.

He let her go. "I'm sorry," he said.

"No, don't be sorry. Not for this."

He pulled back, but she reached for his waist and pulled him to her again. "We can stop," he said, hoping she wouldn't agree.

"I don't want to."

"But..."

"I should want to. I should want to slap you. I should want to hate you, but right now, I just want you to kiss me again."

"I'm sorry, Fi."

She reached up and kissed him, feeling his lips hard on hers, his mouth sucking her lips into his. She lifted her head, and he ran his lips across her neck, and before he knew it, she dragged him to the sofa, allowing herself to drop into it, taking him with her. She grappled with his shirt buttons and pulled his hands under her blouse. He felt her need, her want, and it made him crave her. He hadn't had this feeling with anyone else but her, and he paused for a moment, looking into her eyes, which gazed back with need.

"Are you sure?"

"Fuck me, Danny. I want you to fuck me."

"I don't want to fuck you, Fi. I want to make love to you."

"Then make love to me," she said, pulling him back.

They had made love on the sofa, and it was nothing like he had felt before. Three years since she had been in his arms and things had changed, but nothing had changed either. That passion he thought might have dulled with time was still there, burning more fiercely than ever. She lay atop him, her legs sprawled over his, her hair splayed over his chest, and he was content, a strange satisfaction he hadn't felt in his life. He stroked her hair.

"What was that?" she asked softly.

"I don't know," he said truthfully.

"Let's call it closure," she said.

"Call it what you want, but I don't think that's it."

"Thirsty? Need a drink?"

"Yeah," he said, not wanting her to leave his side but understanding that she may want to get her bearings after this. "I'll get it." He began to rise. "But you need to tell me where the kitchen is."

She rose, wrapping a throw rug around her while he put on his jeans. He followed her to the kitchen and watched as she removed a glass from the cabinet. "Tap?" she turned around with a smile, and he nodded.

Gosh, she's beautiful, even with her hair all mussed, her eyeliner smudged, just her shoulders peeping out of the blanket. He leaned on the table, and she poured the water and offered it to him. He set down the glass and pulled her to him.

"Don't say you're sorry again. I will kick you out." She laughed. Danny chuckled. He was, in fact, going to, but he bent down and kissed the bare shoulder instead, and she let the blanket drop from her.

"Stay with me tonight?" Her voice was urgent, demanding. He nodded, and she kissed him with her little moans as she led him to the bedroom.

Chapter Fifteen

Fiona watched as he stirred, and as his eyes opened and saw her gazing at him, he grinned.

"Coffee?" Fiona asked.

"What time is it?"

"Barely seven."

"I'm going to be late for work," he said but pulled her to him again, and as they made love, not the love of teenagers, but the love of love, she knew it would take much more than a quickie marriage to get over him.

They lay in bed until her alarm clanged, and he groaned. "Do we have to go to work today?"

"Yeah, I will have some very annoyed actors and some very irritated directors if I don't show up for work again."

"Did I ever tell you how proud I am of you? Of what you've become?"

"What have I become? A divorcee?"

"I'll take that," he said, pulling her down on his chest. "But really. You're doing what you want to do, what you've always wanted, pretty much since I met you. You're living your dream."

"Hah! I'm still a bit player in a small theatre company. It's going slow, but at least it's going, right?" She ran her fingers along his chest, and he put his hand on hers.

"I'm still climbing the corporate ladder. And it's going to take a long time to get where I want."

"And where is that?"

"New York."

"Oh, okay. That sounds ritzy. What about soccer?"

"I think I had to move on. After the accident, I played for a while, but life expects more."

"That sounds dire. You're still so young to think that way."

"I'm twenty-four. And I got over it. I found something that I love too. Advertising!" He snickered dolefully.

"Like your dad?" He nodded. "Do you think you gave up too easily?" She knew it was the wrong question when his eyes turned dark.

"I couldn't," he said, and Fiona bit her lip.

"Sorry. I just knew how much you loved it. I thought you would be playing forever."

"It was a pipe dream. A short-term thing. It was time to grow up." His eyes were still creased.

"Well, I guess your dad would have been happy — you following in his footsteps."

"Yeah, I guess I had more in common with the old man than I thought. I found something I like and that I'm good at. Anyway, I need to leave this place and get away from here."

And me, but what is this anyway? One night of passion, some type of conclusion to our teenage romance. "I'll make that coffee," she said. "How do you like it?"

"I'll make it with you."

She smiled inwardly, and throwing the blanket over her shoulders, she went to the kitchen. He followed a minute later, still tugging on his jeans. She put the kettle on. "I'm going to have a quick shower while it heats," she said.

"Can I join you?" he asked, raising his eyebrows. "You know, for old times' sake."

She laughed and ran to the bathroom, Danny hot on her heels, pulling his jeans back down again.

*

They made it to two months exactly before it started again. Two months of bliss, two months of loving each other, two months of secrecy — they didn't want to share what they had with anyone for fear of it erupting again with other people in their proximity.

"You still wear your wedding ring," Danny said one evening, a week after seeing each other for the first time in years. The lounge room was warm and lit with candles, soft music playing in the background. Danny leaned against the sofa, and Fiona lay with her back against his chest, her fingers entwined in his. He had raised her finger and ran his thumb around the ring.

"Yeah," Fiona said, not knowing why she didn't take it off. It wasn't like Kevin was returning, nor was she still in love with him. But she had loved him, and it was hard to remove the symbol of that love. After all, he was the man that had set her free, even if only for a few years.

"And..." Danny pressed.

"Sorry, I didn't know there was a question in that," Fiona said, stalling for time.

"Why do you still wear it?"

"Does it bother you?"

"I don't know."

Fiona felt a sliver of irritation. He had been back for less than a minute and was trying to control her again. "It shouldn't," she said and made no move to take it off. She would be ready in her own time.

"I love you, you know," Danny whispered in her ear.

"How can you love me, Danny?" Fiona shot back, not letting the words sink in.

"I never stopped, Fi."

"You stopped long enough to move in on my best friend."

She felt his fingers tighten around hers. "You know, I don't know if you know, but I never slept with her."

Fiona sat up and turned to him. Then she put her hands together in a loud clap. "Well done, Danny. You must be so proud of yourself." Sarcasm was etched all over her voice.

"Sorry, I know that's not important."

Fiona sank back and bristled. "No, it's not. Besides, from where I was standing, it looked like you two were quite comfortable..."

"We were not..."

"I don't care about what you did with her," Fiona said, even knowing it did matter to her.

"Will I spend the rest of my life explaining to you what I did? How I fucked up?"

"No, you don't have to do any explaining at all. At least, so far, you haven't."

"I'm sorry. I don't know how many times I need to say it. I don't want to keep reliving what I've done."

"Yet, you should," she replied, still feeling the raw spot in her heart that had not fully healed since he punched a hole in it. "No, I didn't mean that," she said quickly, although she did. She wanted an explanation, something better than *I don't know why I did it.* It wasn't good enough.

"I don't know how many times it will take for me saying I'm sorry, but I will do it, and I will mean it. I don't think I ever..."

"Stop, please stop," Fiona said, and she turned to face him, wriggling her body around so her chin sat on his chest. "I want to tell you I love you because I do," she said and then chuckled. "I just did, didn't I?" She stared into his eyes, and he tucked away a lock of hair behind her ear.

"Can this work?" he asked.

"I don't know. We haven't tried as adults, you know, real grown-ups." She felt a stirring, but she wasn't sure if it was too soon to make any sort of commitment to him. "We are still so different, want different things."

"If you need excuses not to be with me..." he said, raising one eyebrow.

"What exactly are we?" she asked.

"We're with each other. Do we have to put a label on it?"

"Yeah, maybe," she said, tapping her fingers on his chest.

"Okay, what do you want to be?"

Not forcing you to be with me, she wanted to say. "We're okay the way we are." Fiona wasn't so sure. When they had been together, all of those five months as teenagers, they were exclusive, wrapped in each other without exception. When they had been seeing each other for the next three years, there were so many ifs and buts and maybes, and Fiona had spent all that time in a state of confusion, of insecurity. She didn't want that, but she didn't want Danny to think that she forced him to be with her when he really didn't want to be.

* * * *

Danny wanted to give himself to Fiona completely. He had never felt this way about anyone, a woman who could make his heart palpate out of control, and when he was not with her, she was in his brain, an obsession that could only be sated when he saw her again. He was fixated with her, and it scared him. He hoped that maybe in time, when they were more settled, more comfortable in their position with each other, when his heart didn't beat out of control for her, and when she had fully forgiven him for what he'd done, he could make a commitment—a full commitment to her.

He thought about it—a commitment. A shiver rushed through his body, and he sat up in realisation. That was what he should do. That was the way he could fix everything. He would prove how much he loved her, that the terrible thing he had done meant nothing, that he'd overcome his insecurities about her and wanted her and her alone.

"Mum," he called, running into the main house.

Grace was preparing dinner, chopping onions, and looked up at Danny with a smile. "Hi honey."

Danny stopped for a moment. Should he be asking his mother about something like this? Then again, he sought her advice on a lot of things, and she never pushed him to do anything, just gave him options. What if she didn't think it was a good idea? When he mentioned Fiona in passing the other day to gauge her reaction, she'd frowned at him, and he quickly changed the subject. But he needed to talk to someone about it. Jeff or any of his other friends were not ones to give advice on women, spending most of their time picking up and dropping women as often as they changed their clothes.

"What is it? Going out?"

"No." Danny sat on the stool and swept the potatoes and the peeler from the countertop towards him. Grace raised her eyebrows, encouraging him to go on. He began peeling, and his mother continued chopping, glancing up at him now and then.

"Okay, what is it?" Grace asked and pulled the peeler from his hand.

"I want to ask Fiona to marry me." Grace didn't flinch. She just placed the peeler on the countertop and stood back, waiting for more. "I know I didn't tell you but we've been seeing each other again."

"Okay. For how long?"

"A couple of weeks."

"And you're ready to be her husband."

Danny choked on the word. *Husband.* That sounded weird. But that was what it was. "I just think, why wait, right?"

"I'm not saying aye or nay, but two weeks?"

"I've loved her for six years."

"And she feels the same way?"

"Well, I haven't asked her yet. I wanted to talk to you about it first."

"What about New York?"

"Well, she's an actress," he said, almost bursting with pride. "Did I tell you that?"

"You haven't told me anything," Grace said.

"Well, she is. A stage actor. And where do all actors want to end up?" He didn't wait for Grace's response. "Broadway. We are both headed down the same path anyway."

"Wasn't she already married?"

"Yeah, but that didn't work."

"How long ago did they break up?"

"About three, four months ago." As the words came out of his mouth, he realised how stupid it sounded. Him wanting to marry a recently divorced woman after being with her for only two weeks. But the reality was that they had never stopped loving each other, but to say that again sounded cheesy. "But I think she married him because I hurt her."

"So, have you figured it out?"

"What?"

"Why you hurt her?"

"I still don't fully know, Mum. It just happened, you know." He saw his mother blanch. She couldn't stand Alice, and he had rarely brought her to his home. "I think sometimes maybe it's because I wanted to see other people because I knew she was seeing other people. I mean, don't get me wrong, she never cheated on me. She couldn't be cheating because I never committed to her."

"And that's what you think this will be?"

"I guess so."

"A bit full on, don't you think? What makes you think it will work out this time?"

"It has to. I can't not be with her."

"Then do it," Grace said, and Danny pulled a face.

"Devil's advocate, hey?"

"No, Danny, I mean it. If you want to spend the rest of your life with her, you should. Grab love with everything you've got. You just don't know when that person won't be around anymore."

"Oh Mum, I'm sorry," Danny said. After his father passed away, his mother lamented never having tried harder to keep him, even though Danny realised it would not have made any difference to his philandering father.

"Just wait a month, Danny, maybe two. That's the only advice I will give you, which you don't have to take."

Danny nodded. He was already thinking about his bank balance and what type of diamond Fiona would like.

* * * *

Fiona boiled with jealousy, her temples throbbing with anger, as she watched a bunch of girls run up to Danny, pushing her out of the way. They were at a soccer match at his old club, and even though he hadn't played for years, he was still somewhat a legend there. They threw their hair back, their mouths wide open in come-hither smiles and take-me looks. Danny beamed with pride and nodded and chatted with them. He happily posed for photographs with them, and her blood was boiling by the time they left. She hated how she was feeling, so childish, so stupid, but those feelings always managed to come to the surface when Danny talked to another woman.

"What's the matter," Danny asked when Fiona pushed his hand away as he tried to grab onto hers.

"Why don't you go hold *their* hands?" she retorted.

"Oh, for goodness sake Fi."

"Don't, *for goodness sake Fi*, me," she said.

"They were just chatting."

"Well, go back and chat with them again then," she said.

"What do you want from me?"

"To ignore them and be with me, tell them I'm your girl," she said. She didn't see the harm in that at all.

"You are my girl, my gorgeous girl." He put his arm around her shoulder and wedged her closer to him.

Fiona rested her head in the crook of his neck as they walked to the car parked at the far end of the lot. "I'm sorry," she said.

"Fi, do you know how much I want you, just you?" he said when they had gotten into the car. She looked into his eyes, so sincere, his want for her apparent, and she leaned over and let her lips graze his lightly. "I want you," he said, and she let her tongue roll over his lips, knowing how much that turned him on. "I don't know if I can wait," he said, pulling her to him.

She turned and looked out of the window. "Then it's lucky that the car park is deserted," she said as she watched a car beside theirs drive away. She leaned over and put her hand on his chest, letting it slowly roll downward.

*

Fiona lay in bed that night alone. Danny had gone home, and it felt strange now, being alone in the bed again. She tossed and turned, punching the pillow in frustration, but sleep evaded her. Eventually, she got up and made herself a cup of chamomile tea, which she didn't enjoy but helped calm her nerves. She sat on the sofa and turned on the radio, letting it softly hum while sipping her tea. She looked at the clock — one am. Danny would be asleep now, so there was no point in calling him, and if she did, they would probably find something to argue about anyway. She sighed. The cycle had not changed in six years, as much as they thought they had grown up. Fighting, making love, the jealous tantrums. Nothing had changed, and Fiona wondered if it ever would.

They had spent every waking moment together after that first night, making love, watching movies and going out to watch soccer matches, where Danny still had a good following, but his little groupies were starting to irritate her, and she could feel the old jealousy creeping up whenever they went. Fiona had wanted to let him go by himself, but she also wanted not to let him go by himself. It wasn't that she didn't trust him. He wouldn't be with her if he didn't love her, but the same insecurity kept popping back in her head and going with him was a sort of self-mutilation. She didn't want to live in a fantasy world, a denial that had brought her to her knees before.

She saw it in Danny too—the jealousy, the angry looks at anyone of the opposite sex that walked by. She knew how much it irritated Danny when another man talked to her, and he began to question her incessantly about her co-stars at the theatre.

"Do you have to kiss anyone today?"

"I didn't. And if I did, it's called *acting*, Danny."

"Do you *act* when you kiss me?"

"Stop it, Danny," she would reply.

It became tiresome, but Fiona understood it and in a perverse way, enjoyed it. Being jealous meant he loved her. That was what she grew up believing, and even being in a secure relationship with Kevin that didn't involve those tactics, she still bound together jealousy with love. However, she didn't want to walk down the street with him and look straight ahead of her just in case she was accused of looking at another man. It was exasperating, Danny preparing to begin a fight with someone who just happened to glance her way from the other side of the room. But for the sake of peace, to take a break from their arguments, Fiona kept her eyes ahead of her and refused to go out with her co-stars, as she used to, and she made excuses.

"I know you guys are glued to the hip now, but I want to go out with you. Just you," Victoria said one evening. "Not as a group. I know Jeff is funny and nice, but I want to just have a girls' night, you know."

"Yeah, maybe," Fiona said thoughtfully. She missed hanging out with Victoria as they used to.

"Don't maybe, me," Victoria said. "Why can't we go out together, you know, not clubbing or anything, but just out for dinner, or even spend a night at my place, or I could come to yours."

"Danny's pretty much moved in," Fiona said with a laugh.

"Does he pay you rent?"

"No, of course not! He doesn't actually live here, but his things are here, and he spends almost every night here."

"Tell him to stay at his own house for one night. We can stay up late, eat pizza, sing loudly, watch a movie maybe." Victoria pouted.

"Yeah, okay. I'll try."

"You'll try?" Victoria's expression changed to one of scorn. "Who *are* you?"

"Stop it, Vic," Fiona said, feeling irritation, which she knew was partly built on the truth of what her friend had said.

"Things haven't changed, have they?"

"What do you mean?"

"He still is the possessive jerk he always was. And you..."

"Don't say that about him," Fiona said, her hackles rising.

"Are you the same?" Victoria asked carefully.

"How do you mean?"

"You know, the stupid jealousy thing?"

"I don't know, I guess."

"What is it, Fiona?"

"I still think about it, you know. Her."

"Yeah, well, that was a blow. I'm glad I got to punch her in the face."

"Thanks," Fiona said, recalling when Victoria told her of how she had gone to Alice's place of work after Fiona had told her what had happened and punched a gobsmacked Alice smack bang in the face. She had stood there and watched as Alice put her hands to her nose, and Victoria had challenged her to hit her back. All Alice said was, *tell her I'm sorry.* Victoria had thrown a barrage of insults at her and left. Fiona appreciated the gesture but wished she hadn't done that. She didn't want Alice to think it mattered to her as much as it did.

"Well, you shouldn't think about that nobody. Good riddance."

"Yeah, but he's back in my life."

"And why I'll never know." She looked at Fiona, and her expression softened. "I don't mean that. I know you never got over him. I just thought he was smart enough to stay away after what he did."

"You've never liked him anyway," Fiona sulked.

"No," Victoria said thoughtfully. "I like Danny. I don't like what he did to you, and I don't like who you were when you were with him."

"Who was I?"

"Who you seem to be turning into now," Victoria said with a sigh.

* * * *

Danny turned the red velvet box around in his hands. He knew she would love it. It was simple, a square cut, not massive, expensive as hell, but nothing less would do. He thought about the ring she wore for so long on her finger, which she thought she had discreetly removed, but he always saw it twinkle, and it did something to him, consumed him with a fury. So when he came over to take her out one evening, and it was gone, and without a word from her about it, he was overjoyed.

He did wonder about her marriage, three years of her life that she never talked about, and he never asked. He wanted to know, of course, who was this man who she had loved enough to marry? What were they like together? Were they playful like he and Fiona? Did they make love with a passion like he and Fiona? Did they go out often? Did they cook together? Did she love him more than Danny? But Fiona never mentioned Kevin, and not long after Danny and Fiona resumed their love, he noticed the two pictures of the handsome man, one of Fiona in his arms in a casual unposed shot, the other their wedding photograph, had disappeared. He never asked about the pictures or her ex-husband.

It had only been three months, and sure, they had their share of arguments and jealous bouts, him as well as her, but something stirred in him whenever he saw her glance in the direction of another man. He knew he was being unreasonable, and it bothered him that after all this time when he thought he was mature and over petty jealousies, things had not changed when it came to Fiona. The girl he dated, Tanya, whom he spent four months with and thought he came close to loving, never did that to him. She talked to other guys, had guy friends and talked about her male co-workers, and he never reacted like he did with Fiona. He knew he would always react that way, and he had to become immune to it and grow up. And maybe if she was his, truly his for life, perhaps his nerves would wane, and he wouldn't react as he did.

He had their evening planned. He was going to take her to a bar on the beach, one they went to from time to time, which served her favourite dish, seafood risotto, almost as well as her mother made it, she'd said. It was to be a regular evening. They would have dinner, a couple of drinks, take a walk on the beach and then, under the stars, he would get down on one knee. It wasn't extravagant. It was simple, something he knew she'd prefer and would never see coming.

"Such a nice night," Fiona said as she gazed at Danny, sitting on the barstool beside her. Danny was impatient. He wanted them to be put at their table so that they could get their dinner over and done with, and he had reserved a table so he didn't expect a delay. "What's wrong?" Fiona asked, and Danny realised he had been frowning.

"Nothing, my love. Just hungry, I guess."

"Shouldn't be too long now. Here, have some peanuts."

Danny shrugged and picked from the bowl of nuts that Fiona had slid in front of him. "At least they should have…"

"Fi!" a voice called behind Danny, and he turned to see Justin, Fiona's friend from high school, hurrying over.

"Justin!" Fiona was on her feet and had thrown her arms around the neck of Danny's nemesis. He felt the hairs on his neck rise. "How are you?"

"Great, so great! Just meeting my fiancée, Jess. She's not here yet."

"Oh wow! Congratulations," Fiona said, and Danny pursed his lips, trying not to allow his nostrils to flare. "Danny, Danny. Do you remember Justin?" As she turned to him, he saw a small crease appear between her eyes. She had remembered the past, and it gave him a little satisfaction.

"Hi Justin," Danny said, putting out his hand, which Justin took, but he didn't miss the mischievous smile on Justin's face. "Been a while."

"Yeah, a long while." Justin looked at Fiona. "Didn't know you two were still going strong." Fiona cleared her throat and looked uncomfortable. Justin looked back at Danny, a confused look on his face.

"We're...um..." Fiona looked flustered.

"We're together," Danny said, and Fiona's forehead creased again.

"Well, about time," Justin said and grabbed a barstool, sitting it near Fiona. "You look fantastic," he said. "What are you doing with yourself?"

"I have to use the men's room," Danny said. He didn't. He needed a moment away. His nerves were raw. What if she said no? He hadn't considered that and his stomach twisted when he realised this was quite a possibility. She didn't even know what to reply to Justin when he asked about the state of their relationship. And Justin. Of all people to bump into on the night that he was going to ask Fiona to be his bride. He was still creepy, the way he just threw himself at her, even in front of him.

He took a deep breath and walked back out to find Justin leaning in close to Fiona, who was giggling, animated. He could feel his blood boil again, and he clenched his teeth, walking slowly back to them. As he got there, a waiter appeared and told them their table was ready, and Danny felt relief. Fiona kissed Justin goodbye, and Danny just nodded at him as they followed the waiter to a spot near the window.

"Are you okay?" Fiona reached out and put her hand on his.

He felt irritated, but he left his hand under hers. "I'm fine."

"Fine? You're not okay," she said, peering into his eyes, willing him to say more, but he couldn't, and through the corner of his eyes, he could see Justin, still sitting at the bar, looking their way. He was sick of it. He had to shoulder people, no, men, away from Fiona everywhere they went. She thought she was being ignorant of it all, but he could see she revelled in the attention. It wasn't her fault that she got looks from people. In fact, it made him proud that she was with him, on his arm, but it still didn't stop him from wanting to break their necks. And now, on the evening he was about to propose, they bump into Justin, the guy he truly despised.

They ate their dinner in relative silence, and when he had paid, he considered whether to continue his plan. He took a deep breath and decided that it was now or never. But as he led her towards the door, Justin rushed up to them.

"Hey, you didn't say goodbye," he said and pulled Fiona to him, hugging her for a moment too long. She opened her mouth in a laugh, and he realised that no matter where they went, people would always still want her. Her beauty, her effervescence just drew people to her. He knew he couldn't cope with it all his life.

He headed straight for the car.

* * * *

"I don't think I can do this again," Danny said, standing at her door, his head drooping forward.

"Do what?" Fiona asked, her heart already starting to thump. She knew it was coming. She could see his irritation begin when Justin appeared and ruined a perfectly good evening.

"What we do to each other. What we did to each other all that time ago."

"What did I do now?" She rolled her eyes.

"Forget it," he said and began to walk away.

"Really? You're going to do this?"

"I don't think we can do this. I have spent the last couple of months so happy, but my heart is always in my mouth, waiting for something to happen, to go wrong."

She stood there trying to comprehend what he was saying. "Why?"

"Because I have the urge to hit something, hit someone, when that someone looks at you."

"How the hell is that my fault?" she shouted, angry that he made it seem like her fault.

"You know what you're doing."

"No, I don't. Tell me."

"You look the way you do — you smile at everyone. People want to talk to you. Men, oh my gosh, men have their tongues hanging out…"

"I'm sorry I'm nice." She was still trying to fathom how this was her fault.

"You know what you're doing."

"Oh, I've had enough. You're right. Nothing's changed."

She watched as he let his head slouch again, his gaze falling to the floor. "Do you know what I was going to do tonight?" She didn't answer, but her eyes widened as she watched him remove a little box from his jacket pocket. "I was going to give you this."

Fiona drew a quick breath and stared at the red velvet case he held in his hand. "Why didn't you?"

"Because I realise you will never be mine."

"But I am yours," she said, her voice croaking.

"I can't do this, Fi."

She felt her blood heat. "Well, don't then. You didn't anyway. Why are you telling me what you were *going* to do?" He shook his head sadly, and as much as she wanted to reach out to him and draw him to her, she didn't. "You're right, Danny. Nothing's different."

"So it was a mistake to go back." It wasn't a question.

"Damn right," she said and, walking into her house, slammed the door in his face.

She slumped to the floor and put her head in her hands. He was right. Nothing had changed. They still loved each other, but it was a selfish love, one born of jealousy and possession. They both felt it. She hated him for it, and he hated her for it, but there it was, and nothing would change that. She spent the next two hours gathering and putting his things in garbage bags. Then she called him. "Your things are outside my house. Please pick them up before I get sick of seeing them there." She hung up. She went to bed in tears and woke up the following morning with an anger that she hadn't felt since she left him those years ago. She wanted to hurt him like she was hurting.

And she tried to forget again, just as she had before, by clubbing with Victoria and going out with her friends from work again, and soon she began to feel normal, as normal as it felt when Danny wasn't around. She survived before, and she knew she would again.

A few months later, Fiona began seeing a young man, Tony, tall, good-looking, with a hint of playboy in him. They had met at a club and hit it off, but as much as she was attracted to him, she knew he was a rebound and warned him as much. But he was quite okay with that and replied that he was having fun, and as she was having fun, too they should just go on seeing each other. He took her mind off Danny, but never for long. She hadn't seen Danny since that awful night, and as much as she longed to call him, she stood her ground. They were just not meant to be together, and they should have realised that from the beginning.

Tony loved to dance, something Danny was not fond of, and Fiona took advantage of the fact that she had a partner who could match her moves on the dance floor, and they spent many evenings at her apartment, the music playing, jiving, shaking their hips and her arms around him as they swayed to their favourite tunes. Tony and Fiona spent many a Saturday evening when Fiona wasn't on stage, burning up the dance floor at a local club, so much so that they were recognised as regulars. *I didn't have this with Danny,* Fiona thought triumphantly, but then she remembered the first time she told Danny she loved him on that dance floor so many years ago. "Don't go back," she told herself repeatedly. "Don't think of him."

"This is nice," Fiona said, her hand on Tony's as they sat at their table waiting for dinner. It was a rainy evening, and the drops pattered on the window by which they sat. The bar was getting more crowded, so they were lucky to have secured a table, especially at peak hour on a Friday.

"Better in here than out there," Tony said.

"Did I tell you I used to run around in the rain as a kid?"

"No, but why did you?" He screwed up his nose.

He didn't get it. "It was just a feeling of freedom. I loved the rain. It used to rain a lot where I grew up, and we'd all go out, my brother and I and our friends. My dad sometimes pulled us out of bed so we could dance..." The sudden nostalgia surprised her, and her mind went to her parents. She missed them more than she thought she would.

"I'm not fond of the rain," Tony said. "I'm happy to return to Perth, where it's nice…"

Fiona nodded. She was not going anywhere. She loved Melbourne, where it rained, brightened, and froze, all in the same day. She glanced out the window, wishing she could go out and turn around in circles with her lips facing the sky, tasting the drops of rain that entered her mouth. Her gaze stopped short, and her eyes widened. Danny was walking into the bar with Jeff. He was laughing at something and had not noticed Fiona's face, stricken, staring through the window at him.

It had been over three months, and she had not seen or heard from him, and she never expected to see him at a bar on the other side of the city. Tony was saying something, but she didn't hear him. She watched carefully as Danny and Jeff entered the bar. She swallowed the bile that rose into her throat, feelings of anger, love, things she couldn't describe, heating her cheeks.

"Fiona," Tony said, tapping on her hand.

"Sorry Tony," she said, clearing her clogged throat.

"Are you okay?"

"Yep. Geez, food is taking ages tonight."

Tony glanced around them. "Getting busy, I guess."

Fiona nodded and looked back to the bar where Jeff and Danny had squeezed through a gap in the crowd. She saw Jeff looking around, and when he spotted Fiona, he smiled broadly at her, a smile that quickly straightened on his face. Fiona wondered how much he knew about them, a random thought but one that she used as a distraction, something to take away from the fact that Danny was little more than a few metres away from her. Jeff looked back at Danny and said something to him. Danny looked over Jeff's shoulder, and his eyes widened. He dropped his head, and Fiona felt her skin bristle. Then they were moving towards her table.

"Hey Jeff," she said when they reached her, and she introduced Tony, who was taking a long swig of beer.

"Fiona," Jeff said. "It's been ages. How are you? Danny's with me," he said, lightly kissing her cheek.

"Hi Danny," she said, and when he leaned forward, she offered her cheek to his lips. But the electricity that she felt when they touched her was still there. She felt an anger surge through her. All these months, he hadn't called. He hadn't tried. He had just forgotten her again. "This is Tony," she said, clutching Tony's hand tight.

"Hi," Danny said, and Tony returned the greeting.

"What are you guys doing here?" Fiona asked.

"Party up at Jason's. He just moved in, so it should be a banger. We're pre-drinking," Jeff said with a laugh.

"Oh, nice," Fiona said. "Give him my best."

"Okay, well, you two have a good night," Jeff said, and Danny nodded, and they moved back to the bar.

The waiter brought their food to the table, and as they ate, Tony chattering about his work, Fiona's gaze kept returning to the bar, where she saw Danny repeatedly glance in her direction. Something about the whole exchange, the cool interchange between them, made her blood boil, and she hated that he had gotten over her so quickly. She had the urge to make him jealous as she used to do. She laughed idiotically at things Tony was saying, things that weren't funny. She was incensed with her behaviour but was powerless to stop it. She wanted Danny to want her again.

Tony glanced at the bar, and his gaze fell back knowingly on Fiona. "Someone interested?" he asked.

"What?"

"Nothing," he said, but the smirk didn't leave his face.

"He's just an old...friend."

Tony was silent for a few moments. "So I'm your showpiece tonight?"

"What are you talking about?"

"I'm not an idiot," he said.

Fiona put her hand on his, not on account of Danny this time. She knew what she was doing was terrible, not just for her and Danny but for the man who was sitting in front of her. "I'm sorry," she said and lowered her eyes. This was ridiculous, the way she was behaving, the whole thing. She knew it was the idea that Danny was watching, and the thought of him being jealous ignited her. She wanted him to seethe, to hate that she was with someone else. Maybe they were never meant to be but it was still nice to see him squirm.

"It's okay. I get it," he said. "I know what it's like." Fiona looked away through the dripping window and felt the urge to cry. And when she felt Tony's hand turn around and his fingers entwine through hers, she did. She didn't see Danny leave and was glad she hadn't looked back his way.

*

She lay in bed that night wondering what to do, how to get him off her mind. He had managed to ruin another potential relationship for her, this time without intention. Maybe it was time to get away from him completely, to move away, and she contemplated her next move. She didn't want to leave a job she loved, her brother, and her best friend who lived so near.

Fortunately, she didn't have to do anything. A week later, she got a call from Victoria. Danny had gone to New York. *So he decided to follow his dream after all.*

Good for him.

Fuck him!

Chapter Sixteen

1999

The seat was uncomfortable, too soft, and Fiona shook her bottom around, trying to get into a comfortable position. Henry was taking too long, and sitting in this fancy restaurant, waiting for her manager to arrive, was beginning to annoy her. She had been here for nearly half an hour, and the aromas of the food wafted past her nostrils, making her stomach churn. Henry was never late, but at least he had called the restaurant, leaving a message for her. He was stuck in traffic and trying to get there as soon as possible.

Fiona rolled her eyes. In this city, was he nuts to take a cab? He could have just walked here or taken the subway. New York was not the best place for driving — especially if you wanted to get somewhere on time.

New York. Where Danny was, or at least from what she heard. But she was never going to look for him, to begin where they left off and end up where they ended up. No. And she certainly had no intention of letting him think she had followed him there. She hadn't on purpose! It was the best place to be for her career, and Danny was not a part of that decision. This was about who she was and who she wanted to be.

When Henry had brought her out here nearly three years ago, she was doubtful. There was no way she was going to make it on Broadway. But she had. She never believed she had what it took to be a serious actress, as much as she loved being on the stage and felt like she belonged there. The head coach of La Flora, the theatre where Fiona performed in various productions, Teddy, had told her that she would never make it to Broadway. "A pretty face does not always a good actress make," he had said on several occasions. Fiona smiled in satisfaction now. She had shown him, the lousy bastard, who once she refused his advances, had it out for her. He had given her bit parts in productions for two years until Anne, his partner, had seen her potential and refused to budge until Teddy had accepted that Fiona was to understudy the star of *Anne of Green Gables*. She never got to play the part, but it was the learning experience she needed, and learn she did—enough to audition for *Phantom*, where she was heralded as the next big thing in the theatre scene.

All of this, in the wake of Danny, but at least it was the distraction she needed, and she threw herself into her work, rehearsing, perfecting her art, reading lines late into the night with Victoria, sometimes even Alfie, who patiently listened on the phone while his wife, Petra, put a pillow over her head, trying to sleep.

She thought about her first lead performance and chuckled. She had thrown up all day, and Victoria had run about trying to find energy drinks and glucose to keep her electrolytes up, and to keep her from doing it on the stage.

But once she was out there, in the glare of the lights, sure only a crowd of two hundred or so, every bit of nervousness left her, and she shone. Even her voice, which had to be further trained, didn't sound so bad, and she left the stage at the show's end in satisfaction. The reviews didn't rave, but they weren't bad either, and Anne read them with a satisfied smile on her face in front of the cast, including a very surly Teddy.

That had been the beginning of the ride. Fiona was exhausted most of the time but couldn't stop working or even take a break. The entertainment world was fickle, and if she paused, she would be completely thrown off the ride. Comebacks were uncommon, and she was quite aware that she had plateaued at the age of twenty-six. If she let herself go, it was all downhill from here.

"Sorry I'm late," Henry puffed out, and the frown beginning to form on her face at the sound of his voice softened when she saw that he had been running. Poor man. But he did need to lose some weight. He was only thirty-four, and he coughed like a ninety-year-old.

"All good," she said. "I'm starving though. I ordered. I hope you don't mind scallops."

"Sure," he said, and Fiona could see that wouldn't have been his first choice. She hoped he wasn't allergic. "I can order something else," she said quickly. "I can wait."

Henry shook his head. "No no. Scallops are fine."

"So, what did they say?" Fiona had waited in anticipation, and he was enjoying holding out on her.

"Straight to business," Henry said with a little smile.

"That's what I pay you for," Fiona said, and even as she said it, she knew it wasn't a nice thing to say. Lately, she couldn't help herself. Even Victoria had been put off by her snarky comments. She remembered that she had to call Victoria. She hadn't spoken to her for a couple of months. "Sorry," she said and looked down at her glass. "Wine?"

"Yes, thank you," he said, motioning for the waiter. He ordered a glass and put his hands on the table, folding them into a steeple. She wanted to smile. "Morgan's called. They want to do a screen test."

"A screen test?" She almost balked. "Why?"

"Because if you want to be in a movie, that's what you do…"

"Don't be snide with me Henry," she said. "I just meant that I don't know if I can…" She felt a rush of fear. She wasn't sure she was good enough for the movies. Even though most stage actors scoffed at film roles, she secretly thought it was perhaps because they weren't successful in getting them.

"It's easier than the theatre," Henry said. "Auditions in theatre are—"

"Yes, yes, I know." She waved her hand about impatiently. "But I've never done a screen test before."

"When you began in theatre, did you do an audition the first time?"

"Of course! I had to. When I came here, I had to all over again, and with my Australian accent, half of those people were snickering at me."

"But you got the jobs."

"I guess, eventually," she said, a little less unsure now. But she was still terrified. How would she go with a film? She knew how different it was between cinema and the theatre, and even though she still got nervous before a performance, it was part of her routine. Her stomach churned for about an hour before, and she would have to puke just before the curtain rose. It was a running joke, which she thought funny at the beginning, but now it was annoying when her co-star, especially the giggling Melville, stood beyond the stage with a bucket in hand. Of course, she never used the actual bucket, but the other players were ready and moved apart to let her through when she ran for the toilet, where she let out whatever was in her stomach. Oddly, it wouldn't happen before she got beside the stage curtains. She had tried plenty of times to let it out before she moved into position, but that didn't work. And when she didn't start on stage and had to walk on, she made use of the mop bucket that the stage director had placed beside the curtain, ignoring the one offered to her by her snickering co-stars.

She felt the churn in her belly now as she thought about cameras surrounding her. "When?"

"Next Wednesday."

"What? That soon?"

Henry was already waving his arms about in front of her, trying to calm her down. "I know, but there needs to be a change in—"

"Henry! I haven't even finished reading the script!"

"You'd better get a move on then," he said, and she wanted to reach out and knock the smug look from his face.

"Time Henry. This is my only evening off. I am run ragged..."

"This is the career you chose, Fiona. This comes with the territory. In film, it will be..."

She grimaced. Henry had been trying to woo her into the movies since he had found her on the stage in Melbourne, taken her on as a client, and brought her here. She wasn't even sure she wanted to be in film, but he pushed, and she eventually thought it might be the right path to go down. She couldn't count how often she had been propositioned to come into film, but she had always thought she had enough time to make the move. But at her age, she knew if she didn't try it now, her time would have passed. Yes, she knew of all the actresses who had remained in the film industry decade after decade, but she knew after her looks had faded, there were limited opportunities in the fickle world of film.

She returned to her apartment, her mind whirling, confusion and fear taking hold. She shed her clothes and ran a bath. She stepped into it and let the water burn her skin, trying to regain her sense of calm. She picked up the script and read. It was a love story, a dramatic forever-love story, and she put it down after ten minutes. Forever love story. That should have been her and Danny. The butterflies danced in her belly as usual when she thought of him.

He was here, in New York, and had been for the last four years. She had been here for almost three, and she was yet to bump into him. She was glad she hadn't, and yet...

She angrily picked up the script again and read it all. Henry asked her to audition using the breakup scene. She smirked. She knew that scene all too well. She had played it with Danny twice, actually, more than that. She had done it with Michael and Tony, but it had not been in any way dramatic. In fact, she could barely remember what had happened with them. Even Kevin, she wracked her brain to figure out what went wrong. No, they were utterly insignificant compared to how it went with Danny and how it felt with Danny, like somebody had ripped her insides out.

She let herself out of the bath that was now freezing and tossed the script on her dressing table. She got into bed and stared up at the ceiling, the lights from the street creating a kaleidoscope of shapes on the white paint. It should have been irritating, but it was somewhat comforting.

Film! She had never been attracted to that medium. She loved the stage, and she had since she was a girl. She loved how it felt when she acted, when she was becoming what people wanted her to be — even on that stage in high school. She remembered how Danny used to wait for her, his eyes shining and how she finished her performance and threw herself into his open arms, sharing her elation with him.

His face crept into her head and she smiled momentarily. Then she let out a little sigh.

Chapter Seventeen

Fiona walked out the door, exhilarated. Henry was there beside her, pumping at her arm, and when they got to his car, she threw herself into his arms.

"I think you have it," he said. "I could tell they were loving you."

"I don't know, but it felt good," she replied, biting her fingernail. "Let's go to the hotel and celebrate!"

"Of course, I'll take you to the hotel, but I have to go home to New York."

She cocked her head. "If I have to move here Henry, who will manage me?"

His face fell. "I couldn't do it from New York. I will find you someone —"

"No! You can't leave me." Fiona knew she had taken advantage of Henry. He was always on call, day or night, but who would she rely on if she was left alone in LA? She really liked the man, got to know his young family, bought birthday gifts for his kids and went to their parties. She'd even organised his last one, a surprise party held at the *Ritz*.

"It's okay, Fiona. We'll work something out."

"Like what?"

"Like nothing now. We have to get this job first. Let's not get ahead of ourselves."

Fiona frowned. Yes, there certainly was a possibility that it could go the other way. Nothing was guaranteed. "Okay, whichever way it goes, it's fine." She knew she would be more than relieved if she didn't get the part. At least she had tried. She could believe she had given it a shot and could return to the stage, where she preferred to be anyway.

"Come on then," Henry said, a resigned look on his face. "My flight is not for a few hours. Let's go at least have a drink."

Fiona beamed. "Thanks Henry."

*

The bar was packed, and Fiona was in a good mood. She wished she was going home tonight, back to New York, but she was also glad she was staying overnight. She needed to calm down, relax for a few hours, have a drink with Henry, return to the hotel, and soak in the tub with a good book.

"Maybe I should stay a little longer," she told Henry. "In LA. What's there to do? Where do people go?"

"What about Nina and Jared? They're here. Maybe they can show you around, introduce you to people."

"They're great," Fiona said thoughtfully. "I like them, but I always feel like I'm a third wheel."

"Well, you do have a break now. Nothing's on the cards for the moment. The show doesn't start until June. That's a few weeks away."

"But rehearsals," Fiona said, her stomach already tingling at the thought of opening a new show. *Pacific Heights* was a musical with dancing, singing and minimal acting.

"Stay here for a while," Henry was saying. "Enjoy the sights, enjoy…"

Fiona wasn't listening to what Henry was saying anymore. She was staring at the man in the suit that just walked through the door with a woman on his arm. Her body tensed, and her throat went dry. Danny was smiling and holding the hand of the woman, his eyes creased in laughter as he ambled over to the bar. He seemed to know the bartender, and Fiona watched from her table as he grinned and chatted with the man. Fiona turned her attention to his companion, a blonde buxom Hollywood knock-off. Fiona wanted to tear those blue eyes right out of her face, and she was unnerved by the degree of venom she could feel coursing through her veins.

"Fiona, what's the matter?" Henry had placed his hand on her arm, at the end of which her fists were clenched.

She tore her gaze away from the couple and looked back at Henry with a start. "Sorry, what?"

"Are you okay?"

She cleared her throat and nodded. "I need another drink."

"You've had quite a bit already…"

"You're not my father, Henry." Again she was unhappy with how she snapped at him but was too distracted to correct herself. Henry went over to the bar, and Fiona returned her attention to Danny, who had his gaze on his friend.

Fiona didn't know what to do. Should she go to him and say hello? It would be rude not to. She always imagined a moment like this in New York, but she at least expected it there. He was not meant to be here! She should go and greet him, but her heart was beating too hard and too fast to move. She hated herself for the way she felt so many years later, but perhaps it was just the shock. No, it was more than shock, and her face began to flush. Feelings of resentment coursed through her, and she looked toward Henry. He was at the bar trying to get the bartender's attention, and she rolled her eyes. She grabbed her purse and headed to Henry, who smiled apologetically when she approached.

"The bar is full…"

"I got this," she said, noticing she already had the attention of one of the barmen. "What will you have, Henry?"

"Nothing more for me," Henry said.

"Water then?" Henry nodded. "Scotch and soda and a water, please," she said to the man, who was giving her one of those grins she knew well while he made her order. She smiled sweetly and took out her card when he returned with her drinks.

"On the house," he said. He leaned over and whispered, "I'm Matt." Fiona curled her lips in thanks, but when they looked back to their table, it was taken.

"That was embarrassing," Henry said, his eyes narrowed at Matt. "I could have been your boyfriend for all he knew."

Fiona laughed and suddenly realised that Danny was here, buying drinks from this same bar. She leaned over the bar in search of him, and her gaze fell on his, which was on her. His forehead was crinkled, and his mouth was open in disbelief. Fiona felt her heart thud again, and she smiled shakily at him, lifting her hand slowly in a wave. She saw him disappear out of sight, and in a second, he was behind her, taking her in his arms. She felt her own go around him, and an immediate sense of belonging hit her, that familiar scent, that familiar feel.

"Fi," he breathed when he let her go. "What are you doing here?"

"Hey Danny," she said, not wanting to let him go. "An audition. For a movie. Just in town for the night."

"Wow." He stood back to look at her. "You have not..."

"Daniel?" Fiona could feel her heart sink when the blonde entwined her arm in Danny's. Danny turned around and looked somewhat surprised that his companion was there.

"Mel, this is Fiona," Danny said. "Fi and I, er, grew up, no, went to high school together."

Fiona could already feel her blood begin to boil. Went to high school together? *No, I was the goddamn love of your life!* She wanted to scream. She gritted her teeth, irritated that he could still get her so mad. She cleared her throat. "This is Henry. He's my manager." Henry shook Danny's hand, and they all exchanged pleasantries while Fiona stared into Danny's eyes, which avoided hers now.

"Join us for a drink," Danny said, but all Fiona wanted to do was get away from him and his girlfriend. She swallowed the scotch in one gulp. "I have to get back to the hotel. Henry has to leave tonight."

She saw Danny's eyebrows knit. "Already? Can't you stay for a while? We have so much to catch up on."

"Have to go," she said, knowing she couldn't stay and converse with the man she evidently still loved while he was almost physically attached to another woman. "Bye Danny, bye Mel."

She grabbed Henry's hand and pushed past the two of them, and when they were in the car park, she leaned against the car, her knees weak, her heart still hammering.

"What is it?" Henry asked. "Who was that?"

"No one," she replied. "Just give me a minute." She wished she had listened to Henry and hadn't had so much to drink. She felt weak, faint, and her stomach was starting to complain. Henry opened the door, and she fell into the car seat, her head spinning. She closed the door and waited as Henry got in. She heard an urgent knocking on her window as he began to back out. She jumped in surprise and saw Danny's face on the other side of the glass. She rolled it down.

"Where are you staying?" he panted out.

"*Hotel Normandie,*" she blurted.

"I'll be there in an hour." He turned on his heel and strode back into the bar.

She stared after him, annoyed that he expected her to agree, that there was no question about it, but also elated that he wanted to see her.

Chapter Eighteen

Fiona paced up and down the hallway, a strong feeling of déjà vu taking over. She had been in this position many years ago, but then he had been coming over to try to make up for his hurting her. Now he was coming over for? He was with another woman who was obviously more than a friend. But the way he breathed out his words at her through the window, she thought she saw what she used to, a longing in his voice, a desperation, that he would die if he let her leave. But he had also mentioned catching up when they were at the bar. Maybe he just wanted to reminisce about old times.

Old times! Were there any times they weren't fighting or making love? Was there even an in-between for them?

The phone on the wall buzzed, and she picked it up and told the concierge to allow Danny into her room. Her head was still spinning, and she wasn't sure if it was from the scotch or the thought of seeing him again. Her stomach was in knots, and she tried to figure out how she would greet him. Surely she had enough restraint not to throw herself at him. She rushed into the bathroom and gargled with mouthwash, taking a quick look in the mirror. Yes, her hair was still in place, her face fresh. She'd had a quick shower the moment she got back to the hotel room to try to quell the fluttering of her belly.

A soft knock on the door, and she took a deep breath. When she opened the door, her knees almost collapsed beneath her. He was the same Danny, albeit with a three-day growth, but the same look of love and want emblazoned on his face.

"Hi," she said and moved to let him through. He didn't. He took her in his arms and put his mouth on hers, hard and determined. She should have protested. She should have pushed him away. She should have slapped him for his assumption, but she didn't. She let him feel her lips on his, and he kicked the door closed, and she dragged him into the bedroom, his arms still holding her tightly.

It was the same, and if possible, there was more. The way he knew her—how to make her moan, how to kiss her on just the right spot on her neck that almost brought her to tears. And she let herself cry while she held onto his hair, allowing her body to succumb to the pleasure she had felt with only him.

His head was rested on the pillow, his eyes locked on hers, and she lay beside him on her stomach, her chin resting in her hands, and gazed back at him. They were talking about everything, about their friends, their jobs, their lives. He had achieved everything he wanted to, a successful businessman, about to open his own advertising firm. She told him about her new venture into film.

"Poor Henry." She laughed. "He looked scared!"

"Poor Henry," he said. "Poor..."

"You know it was never going to work with us." Fiona kissed his forearm and rested her head in the crook of his arm. She didn't want to know about the other woman. Tomorrow Danny would be gone, and so would she. And he would go back to Mel, whoever she was. Well, he was hers first, she justified. She would always have that.

"Why?" He turned her face back to his. "Why wouldn't it work?"

"Because we tried so many times."

"We were young then, dumb, hot-headed."

"We weren't that young the last time," she said, running her fingers along his chest.

"We were twenty-three," he said with a laugh.

Fiona wanted Danny to be with her forever but knew it was another road to heartache that she couldn't deal with, not right now, maybe never. "Can we just enjoy tonight and not think about more?"

Danny's eyes grew sad, and he turned his head from her. "Sure," he said.

"Danny." Fiona touched his face, turning it towards hers again. "I love you. I will always love you, but I can't do this again."

"I can," he said.

"You went and started a new life in another country."

"You weren't sitting and moping over me," he said, and she could feel his resentment. "You moved on."

"You moved across the planet to be away from me," she said, her temper rising. "And what about that girl on your arm."

Danny frowned. "She's..."

"You can't even say it, Danny. What are you even doing here?" She rose from the bed and wrapped the sheet around her naked body.

"I don't know," he admitted. "When I saw you, I went out of my mind."

Fiona lowered her head. "Me too. But this is a road we've been down, and it never ends well." She bit her lip, knowing she was trying to convince herself of it too.

* * * *

Danny leaned against her closed door and put his head in his hands. Always the same. Everything had changed, and nothing had changed. He knew he still loved her. He never doubted it, no matter how much he tried to move on. He sighed. Mel would be waiting for him, wondering why he had decided to drop her home early and take off again. She was nice, Mel. They had been seeing each other for a few months, and she was fun, but they knew it was not going anywhere — they certainly weren't exclusive. She had just decided to accompany him on this trip because she had a few days off from work, and he was happy to have her company. He didn't even have to lie to her about where he was, but this was Fiona, the love of his life. And he didn't even want to admit to himself that he would throw everything away for her again.

He still fumed when he thought about her at that restaurant, doing everything she could to make him jealous. After that, he kept pushing for the New York position he knew would eventually be his. It was ironic, as he thought that was where they would go together. He couldn't believe it when Fiona told him she'd been living there for the last three years. He wished he knew. He would have found her. But maybe it was better he didn't. He needed to focus on work, and he had been too upset after their split to let himself be distracted by her.

But he did let himself find distractions in the arms of women that he met at work, clubs, and the café. None of them were Fiona. None ever came close.

Now that he knew she had been there all that time, it was too late, and she likely would move to LA. He walked back to his car and drove to his hotel slowly. How would he ever forget her if she was going to be a movie star? Her picture would be plastered everywhere, and of course, he would watch her on screen the moment her first film came out. A surge of pride flowed through him. He just wished he could be by her side as she went through it all. He kicked himself that he hadn't looked out more carefully at the stage shows in New York. Had he known she was there, he would have searched for her. The theatre was not his scene, and he was too busy building his portfolio to think about entertainment of any kind. But he knew as much as they wanted each other, they were too different, that they would always clash. They still hadn't grown up as much as they thought.

He shook his head in frustration. This time she didn't even want to try. She just wanted to make love for old times' sake, already knowing that was all it was. He wanted to. The moment he saw her at the bar, he wanted to be with her, and when he had driven to her place, all he had thought about was the ring that he still kept in the drawer of his side table in his New York apartment. He wished now that he had just proposed that night. Maybe they would still be together.

"A lot of maybes," he snarled to himself.

He reached the hotel and sat in his car for an hour, willing himself to forget she existed again. It was not going to work. It never did.

Chapter Nineteen

2004

Fiona looked around and lowered her sunglasses, hoping to see him soon. She scanned the cafe and found a somewhat secluded booth, a little table wedged behind a bigger one and the fronds of a fake plant covering the front. It would not end well for either of them if she were recognised. She wished she didn't have her face splashed on posters across the mall. She pulled down her navy scarf at the sides, hoped he would hurry, and sidled into the booth.

"Can I get you anything?" A bored, middle-aged waitress stood before her, and Fiona tried not to look up at her.

"Waiting for someone," she muttered, her hands shaking so much she had to clutch the salt shaker to stop them. The woman shrugged and walked away.

Where was he? She looked at her watch — it was still early. She wished she had more self-control, but she didn't, never with him. But it had been what? Five years since they'd seen each other? That was five years of a lot of self-control. Sure, she had been busy, and things had moved so quickly in her professional life, but he never left her mind through the crazy years that went by so fast. Even through the other flings she had over the years, none came close to what she felt when she was with Danny.

She had contemplated contacting him, especially when she was back in New York, but stopped herself. What was the point? A night of passion, months of back and forth, fighting again, and then the most challenging part, trying to move on, trying to forget. It just played with her head, and as much as she wanted to ask him to stay with her that night in LA and never to leave her again, she had used all her self-control to stop from clinging to him when he walked out of that hotel and out of her life again. She had spent the next few days wondering if she should have, knowing that she was doing them both a favour by letting him leave.

But now she had contacted him just two months ago, and what possessed her to search for him, she didn't know. Maybe she was lonely and had too much to drink as she sat by the window in her apartment, listening to sad soppy songs, most of which brought Danny to mind.

Mason had been away doing his movie, and she had the sudden urge to speak to Danny, to know where he was, what he was doing and whether he ever thought about her too. She searched the internet for a phone number, some way to get in touch and found his email address on his company's website. She shuffled through the website to see what he was up to and raised her eyebrows in admiration. He was vice president of an advertising company based in New York—he'd become the businessman he always wanted to be. She wondered why she never thought to actively search for him before, just to see what he was doing. Sure, it took time to find him, but there he was, so accessible.

She typed in his email address, and her fingers hovered over the keyboard. She didn't know what to write, her heart beat fast, and she bit on her lower lip, wondering if it was the right thing to do. What if he was with someone? What if he felt pressured to answer her back even if he didn't want to?

Hi Danny, Fi here. Make it sound casual, she told herself. *You just came to mind, and I was just wondering how things were with you.* She let her finger hover over the send button, and she hit it before she could change her mind.

With her heart still beating a hundred miles an hour, she leaned back in the chair and willed his response. Her mind was spinning. She wasn't doing anything wrong, she reasoned, and the way things ended the last time, she knew it wouldn't lead to anything. She just wanted to know how he was doing, she justified.

She beamed as she opened her email account the following morning, and his name popped up.

Fi! So good to hear from you. I thought with all that's going on with you, you had forgotten me! How are you?

She couldn't keep the stupid grin from her face, and all the guilt she felt last night flew away. This was Danny! She noticed he had finished the email with a question, which meant he wanted her to reply. Wasn't that what that meant?

I'm doing okay. I don't know if you know, but I've made six films since I last saw you. Two bombed, but I think the others did quite well. She didn't want to sound like she was bragging and wanted to know how he was doing. *What about you? I see that you've become vice president of Viesta Media Group. That's massive. I'm so proud of you.* She lifted her fingers from the keyboard. Did that sound condescending? No, this was Danny. He knew her better than anyone. He wouldn't take it like that. *How about everything else? How is your mum? Are you with anyone?* Again, she cocked her head and thought about that question. Was it too forthright? Was it suggestive? She wasn't sure she wanted to know the answer to that question. She deleted the last sentence. *Are you married, kids?* Yep, that sounded more casual. She clicked send and went to take a bath, her skin tingling with expectation, with the fact that she had just been in contact with the man who had always put her off-kilter, as he was doing right now, without even knowing.

He had already emailed back by the time she came out of the shower, and she realised he might be online now. She sat expectantly at her computer to read his response.

Thanks for the kudos, but I'm about to go out on my own, so this will be a huge step. Yes, I'm married – two years now. Her name is Leah. You will like her. I hope you get to meet her one day. When will you be in NY next?

Fiona's heart went crashing through the floor. Of course, he would be married. What did she think was going to happen? That he was going to wait around for her? For someone who was not coming back to him, who had literally pushed him out the door? But she only just realised that he would move on, for real, and she sat back in her chair and stared at the computer screen, a sudden urge to cry. She got off the chair and went to the kitchen. She needed to busy herself with something, so she poured some cereal but hurried back to the computer, and she ate her breakfast while she read his message repeatedly.

Who was she to feel bad about the state of his love life? She was with Mason and had been for the last year, no, nearly two, she suddenly realised. She knew it was a farce. She had met him at the request of her manager David, a man who was so far removed from Henry that Fiona almost fired him, but Henry had coaxed her into staying with David because he was good. He was the best. When he asked her to meet with Mason, the biggest thing in film since Al Pacino, she thought it might be worth it.

In the beginning, she quite liked Mason. He was handsome, funny, and reminded her of Danny in some ways. The way his hair fell over his eyebrow, the sea blue of his eyes. But that was as close to Danny as he came, and Fiona went through the motions of their relationship, well knowing she was only with him for the sake of publicity and that he had other girls, starlets that dropped to their knees when he clicked his fingers together. And since all she thought about was Danny anyway, Fiona didn't see anything wrong in what he was doing. She had been unfaithful in her heart from day one.

However, the moment Danny's message pinged her inbox, and her heart almost sprang out of her chest, she knew it would never be over for them. The impulse to see him lately had been immense. She didn't know why. It came out of the blue. There were days, weeks that she didn't think of him any more than a passing thought, but there were times when she was alone, when her thoughts of him pervaded her brain, took hold of her so acutely that she had to hold her breath to stop her tears from falling.

She bit on her fingernail, wondering how to reply to that message. *Congratulations! I'm so happy for you. She must be special, and I can't wait to meet her. I may take a trip to NY soon. I haven't been back since I left nearly five years ago.* Fiona had no intention of going back, especially now. She didn't want to meet the woman who had taken the heart of the man she loved.

She's great, Fi. Have you been back to Melbourne?

I went last year. I went to see Mum and Dad, too, in Italy. They are loving it there, but things are the same with them. I speak to them often. How's your mum?

Mum's good. Happy. Found herself a husband. Not sure if I told you the last time I saw you.

The last time he saw her. Fiona sighed. The time when she could have asked him to stay, to be with her, and she let him go, and now...

Every morning Fiona jumped up at the break of dawn to check her email, and her heart skipped a beat when she saw one from Danny. At first, their messages were casual. *How are you? How is it all going?* They discussed their careers—his plans to build his own firm, and hers, on the screen, now in full swing. Her move into film had not had its downs, but Fiona had fit in, and although she missed the theatre, she adjusted to a film set just as easily. Two months later, they were still messaging each other, talking of old times, reliving their crazy moods and the way they loved each other.

*

"Fiona," Victoria said sternly. "I don't think it's a good idea at all."

"But Vic," Fiona said, wanting her friend to support her, to tell her it was okay to see Danny. "He's married now. I'm with Mason…"

"And you're putting a spanner in the works." Fiona could hear the disapproval in her friend's voice over the phone. "Don't do it, Fiona."

"Mason's a farce anyway. We both know it."

"Sure, but what about him, Danny? Are you willing to be the other woman?"

"Who says we are going to be anything more than friends?" Indignance filled Fiona's voice, but she was more indignant with herself. What did she want from Danny? Why did she need to see him? Their email conversations were becoming more flirtatious, and she loved the feeling of him needing her. She needed him too. She just didn't know why.

"Okay Fiona. I'm all the way back home. I can't stop you. But be careful. If you two were supposed to be together…"

"We aren't going to be *together*," Fiona said. "I just miss him."

"Keep to emails. Don't let things get out of hand."

Fiona hung up the phone and wondered if she should keep her date with Danny. He was going to be in town for a few days, and she wondered if he had created a situation at work where he had to be there just so he could see her. No, she thought, that was vanity. He had a busy life, and he wouldn't just up and leave across the country to see her. Well, she had considered doing the same, so...

She always wondered if Danny thought about her when he saw her posters slung up on walls and her movies on television. She hoped that maybe he stopped and smiled or thought about her somehow. Now, as she sat with her hands still on the saltshaker, waiting for him, she looked at the billboard on the far side of the centre and cringed. She didn't like herself in print—in big print. It was one of the things she missed about the theatre—that her picture wasn't splashed everywhere. Sure, there were advertisements and some publicity shots, but they were limited, and the public mostly didn't care. A film actor was different. Her face was plastered on posters, on the pages of magazines, on tabloid newspapers...

Her gaze was drawn to the man who stood in front of the poster, his gaze not on it but on her, and her legs turned to jelly, and as he strode towards her, his eyes glowing, she could tell that this was not over, not nearly over.

"Hey," she said, motioning for him to sit opposite her. He didn't. He sidled in beside her and put out his arms, and she fell into them, unable to let go. Her nerves got the better of her, and she jerked away from him. "Coffee?"

"Yeah," he said, looking slightly jilted. He moved to the other side of the table and looked like he couldn't keep the smile from his face, yet his forehead was crumpled.

"Sorry, I'm a little nervous."

"Me, too," he said, tapping his fingers on the table. "After all this time. How long has it been?"

"Five years," she replied. "And a half." She grinned, feeling the tension in her fingers loosen.

His lips curled even more, and his brows relaxed. "Just like you," he said. "Remembering details."

"I remember everything," she replied and chewed the end of her lip.

"I do too," he said. "Your hands are shaking," he said, reaching towards them but stopping halfway.

"I'm just nervous," she said.

"About being seen here with me?"

"No," she said, waving her hands about. "It's being here with you."

He grinned. "How long has it been since we first started dating?"

"Fifteen years. When we were just children." She gave a short laugh. "I feel like a schoolgirl right now."

"You are not that girl anymore," he said, putting his chin onto his hand, and looked at her like he was inspecting her.

Fiona looked away, embarrassed. "So what now?"

"Now?" He chuckled. "Do you know how much I want to..." He left the sentence hanging.

"Can we go somewhere..."

"Tempting fate, aren't we?"

"I guess," she said, feeling her heart drop in disappointment.

He leaned forward. "But I desperately want to."

"How long are you in town?"

"Four days."

"Busy days?"

"Yes, and no."

She nodded, hoping he would ask to see her, but he didn't. "How's Leah?"

"Fine," he replied and pursed his lips. Clearly, his wife was not a topic he wanted to get into, and as much as Fiona wanted to jump across the table and put her lips on his, she knew it was one thing to make love to a man who was attached but to tempt him from his wife of two years was not something she could take lightly.

"Good," she replied.

They talked like they had never been apart, discussed old times, their high school teachers and friends, and Fiona was despondent when it was time to leave. She raised herself from her seat and went over to where he stood. She let her arms wrap around his neck and held him tight, feeling him squeeze her, and she resisted the urge to kiss him.

"Can I see you tomorrow," he said. "Just as friends?"

Fiona smiled wryly. "Were we ever friends, Danny?"

"No Fi. But I want you to be. My life without you in it sucks, and I want you however I can have you."

"But we fight, Danny."

"We fight because we always want something else from each other, something more. But if we can be friends, then maybe that part of us will go."

"It makes sense, at least in theory," she said thoughtfully. "I guess that's something we haven't tried."

"Then dinner tomorrow evening?"

"I still can't be seen with another man, Danny, especially an ex-boyfriend."

"Your image, yeah, I get it. How about you bring your boyfriend, and I can bring Leah."

"She's in town with you?" Fiona felt a stab of jealousy.

"She's arriving today."

"Mason may not be back by tomorrow. But if he is…"

He pulled her to him again. "Let me know. I want to see you, and I don't care how."

"Okay." She took a deep breath of his scent to hold onto after he was gone.

Chapter Twenty

Fiona could see Mason was not in a good mood and was certainly in no mood to go dining with anyone, let alone someone who would not help his career rise even further.

"Do we have to go?"

"Yes," Fiona replied. She was determined to make a friendship with Danny. Then perhaps the insistent tug in her heart would not pull so hard each time she thought of him. *Friends*. That was one thing they never were. It was clear they would never forget each other, so maybe a friendship would work.

"How do you know this guy?"

"A friend from high school," Fiona said. "I bumped into him at the plaza. We haven't seen each other in years."

"And were you involved with him?"

"We had a little fling back then, but we were friends. He will be bringing his wife, so I thought a sort of double date would be nice."

"Yeah," Mason said, scratching the stubble on his chin thoughtfully. "I guess so." He rolled his eyes. "Can it be an early one?"

"Sure, yes, just a catch-up dinner."

"Where?"

"I booked *Valentino's*."

Mason raised his eyebrows. "On the assumption that I would be home on time?"

"Well, you were due to get back this morning…"

"And what if I didn't? Would you have gone anyway?"

"I don't know," she replied, slightly taken aback by his question. "Why?"

"Oh I don't know. I don't like the idea of you going out to dinner with an ex-boyfriend, even if it was a little fling like you said."

"That's rich," she replied. "Didn't I see you with Trudy in *The Tribune* three days ago?"

"Trudy's an old friend. You've met her. We were just catching up."

"An old girlfriend, you mean? And you will meet Danny today too. It's the same thing."

"Look, I'll go, but don't expect me to be best buddies with the guy."

"Sure, whatever you want. But I want to see him…and his wife."

*

When Fiona walked through the door, her gaze fell on Danny immediately as he stood up and waved at her from the other side of the restaurant. Her skin tingled as usual when she saw him, and she smiled widely at him, forgetting for a moment that Mason was just behind her.

"She's a looker," Mason said a little too loudly, and Fiona's gaze moved to the brunette, who had turned her head to greet them, her big blue eyes tentative, her mouth in a half smile. Fiona's breath caught in her throat at the gentle beauty of this creature, who rose to greet them.

Mason jutted out his hand, and when Leah offered hers, he put it to his lips. Fiona looked at Danny, who wasn't looking at the scene Mason was making but was staring directly at her. She felt her face heat and turned away, moving to the seat beside Leah. Leah retrieved her hand and faced Fiona.

"Hi, I'm Leah. Danny's told me so much about you." Nervous, yet warm.

"Fiona," Fiona replied and put her arm around Leah in a quick hug.

Mason realised the only seat left was between Fiona and Danny, and he reluctantly took it.

After the introductions, a bit of nervous chatter and a couple of drinks later, an easy conversation followed until Mason began to slur his words.

This brought the attention of other diners, who suddenly realised who was eating beside them.

"Can I have an autograph," a young lady who seemed to be in her early twenties asked Fiona.

"Sure," Fiona replied, taking the offered pen and scratching her name on a book. Mason looked slightly miffed that he wasn't asked for one when the girl beamed and took her book away.

Another young girl and a boy, who looked bored, came up behind her and offered a napkin. Fiona smiled and did the same, and when people began to turn around to them, noticing the commotion, Fiona realised it was time to leave. She didn't want to. She wanted to sit opposite Danny all evening and gaze at his face as she found him sometimes staring at hers.

"Drinks?" Mason asked as they passed the bar, and Fiona looked to Danny and Leah, who both shrugged and nodded to each other. Fiona felt a stab of jealousy at the ease with which they talked. She had been with Mason for nearly two years, and there was no sense of closeness or togetherness. It was him, and it was her, and even though they lived together, they barely saw each other. She knew she would have to end things with him, no matter what their publicists said.

At the end of the night, Fiona said goodbye to Danny and Leah, and she was happy with how the evening eventuated—she was hopeful they could be friends and have him in her life. Mason was in no mood to return to their apartment, having tried to sidle up to a not so forthcoming Leah.

"Yeah, I don't think I like the idea of you two being friends," Mason said when they got into the apartment. He had thrown his jacket on the bed and flopped himself onto it, looking up at the ceiling.

"What do you mean?"

"I just don't like him," Mason replied.

"Well, that's not my problem," Fiona replied, a little grizzled. They had all had a good time, and by the end of the evening, she thought that perhaps there was hope of her and Danny becoming friends and that they could still be in each other's lives without fighting or being jealous as they had no further claim on each other.

"You're with me, so yeah, it becomes my problem, too," Mason said without emotion.

Fiona sighed and pulled off her shoes, rubbing at her stockinged feet. "No, Mason, I don't think it should be your problem." She had no feelings left for him. In fact, she realised she never did, and they were two years with him that she had to forego. Sure, he had helped her career, but she had helped his too. He didn't need her anymore, and this charade was more of an embarrassment for her, with the tabloids loudly yelling whenever he was seen with someone else in a café or bar or wherever. He was tired of hiding it too, she supposed. Mason just shrugged.

But what about Danny? Establishing a friendship with him as a single woman would be hard. As lovely as she was, Leah would probably not go for it either. Still, she had to end this pretence. She just didn't know how to broach it. It was always an uncomfortable topic.

"So, what do you think we just go our own ways?" She just blurted it out. That was the only way.

"What do you mean?" She felt him sit up on the bed behind her and resisted the urge to turn to him, to face him. Her resolve may crumble.

"I don't know. I think we've run our course, don't you?"

He was still for a moment, and Fiona massaged her foot, her mind focussed on what he was doing behind her, how he would respond. "No."

"No?" She didn't expect that, so abrupt, so sure. She turned to him now and saw his brow knitted in confusion.

"No. Why do you want out?"

"Mason." She snickered, more to loosen the tension than anything else. "You don't want to be with me anymore. You want to be free to run around and do your thing, sow your wild oats and all of that." He looked at her cautiously, and she chuckled again. Then she sobered her face. "I don't want to know anything about what you do, or did. I just think it's time you did what you wanted to."

He lowered his head. He didn't deny it. At least he had the decency not to insult her. "What about the publicity?"

"I don't think anyone will care much anymore. They've made their money on our time, and they can't force us to stay together."

"It's not like we signed anything that says..." A hopeful note crept into his voice.

"No, I guess not," she replied.

"But the movie. It comes out in two months."

"Well, I guess I can put up with you for two months then," she said, leaning over, kissing him on his forehead.

He pulled her to him. "One last time, for old times' sake?"

She laughed and pulled back. "Not on your life," she said.

* * * *

"She's lovely," said Leah.

Danny nodded. Leah was not the jealous type, which perhaps had been the attraction. Sure, she was pretty, with long straight hair and large blue eyes that pierced through him when he met her at his boss's dinner party at the *Hilton*.

She had been there alone at the bar, sipping delicately at her glass of wine, gazing absently at the people that moved past her, oblivious to the looks of passers-by, and Danny had come through the doors and headed straight for the bar. It was going to be a long night, and he needed to survive it, so he ordered a scotch, set himself down on a stool, and scanned the place, looking for no-one in particular. Mr Jives always arrived late at these shindigs, and Danny wasn't sure why he got there early, but there were always people to meet and things to discuss. Many a deal was made on a handshake at these things. He was already close to the top and just needed to seal the deal. He knew he was a shoo-in when the promotions came up in the next year, and he was already handling his own accounts.

He looked around the room, and his gaze fell on Leah, who quickly looked away from him, a shy smile forming on her lips. He tried not to grin but was flattered, and his gaze kept returning to her, but she never returned his glances. His mind went to Fiona, and he frowned. He still wanted to call her to see how she was, but he knew she didn't want him to. She had made her choice that night in LA, and he would not try to convince her otherwise. He had hurt her enough, and she didn't need such disruption. Her star was climbing, and he admired and loved her for it. Who was he to impinge on her life? Their time had passed, and although he wished they could have tried again and worked harder to settle their differences, particularly working out their petty jealousies, he knew he wasn't good for her. She had made a life for herself, and he didn't belong in it.

He still sometimes shook his head in amazement when he saw a picture of her face pass by on a bus or a poster displayed on a wall in a mall. He had been to see her first movie, *Rebel Love,* and he couldn't tell what the movie was about because he fell in love with her on-screen all over again, but yet when she kissed her co-star, he still felt an unbridled jealousy pierce through his pores. But he went back and watched it four more times, finally buying a copy when it came out on DVD, and whenever he had a hard day at work or needed to relax, he played it, pausing the film on her face, gazing into the eyes he still loved.

But he moved on, not with Mel. She was a distraction, and both had no illusion that it was more than that. It ran its course, and Danny dated other women, none of with whom he found any lasting bond.

But Leah. Oh, he wished he had known that she was the niece of Harry Jives, his boss. But thinking back on it, it probably wouldn't have made a difference. When he finally decided she was playing too coy, he approached her. She turned to him, and a giggle erupted from her mouth.

"About time, you're thinking?" he said boldly.

"Something like that," she replied. She held out her hand. "Leah. Leah Jives."

"Oh."

"Yes, not the daughter, the niece. Daughter of Nathan."

"Yes, Nathan." Danny had met Nathan several times. He worked in a top position within the company and Danny wasn't fond of the man who threw around his brother's name to get work done. His wife was Australian, and she left him to return home to be with her sons.

"And you are?"

"Danny. Danny Devoy."

"French? You don't sound it. What's the accent? Don't tell me, Australian," she said, screwing up her face, which formed a cleft in the middle of her eyes.

"Guilty," he said. "No French blood. Not sure where the name stems from."

"Well, that's something we have in common. My mother's from Sydney." She leaned her face on the palm of her hand and studied him. "So, Danny, how do you belong here? Another suit in the company?"

"Guilty again," he said, sitting beside her without waiting to be invited.

He fell in love with Leah quite quickly. She was easy to fall in love with. She was easy-going, reserved, and pretty, and they enjoyed being together, going to dinners, spending evenings at his apartment or hers, and cooking for each other. He thought about Fiona less often, and within six months of meeting Leah, he asked her to marry him. She was everything Fiona was not, and it was the peace and the quiet acceptance of his life, and his of hers, that appealed to him.

"Hi honey!" His mother's voice always calmed him and gave him a sense of belonging. "Why are you calling? Are you okay?" Danny laughed. Ever since he had left Melbourne, she always answered the phone like that. A note of worry etched into her voice until he told her all was well. He did, and he could hear a little sigh of relief through the receiver. "What's news?"

"All good here. How's Peter?"

"Peter's well. The move went well. He had all his burly friends help, so that was easier than we thought."

"And you're enjoying living life in the Stix?" Danny had been surprised when Grace had told him of the new man in her life, a man so different from his father, a construction worker, tall, sturdy, gruff. Danny had flown back to Melbourne to meet him when he realised this was a serious relationship, that Grace had found love again. He was wary, but as he watched them together, his mother, a twinkle in her eye, the constant smile on her lips, he knew this man would make her happy.

"The Stix is great." She giggled. "A long drive from work, but I've applied at the local, and I think I may get it."

"I'm kidding, Mum. It's only a couple of hours from Melbourne."

"Enough of me. I spoke to you last week. What's going on? Why are you calling again so soon?"

"Well…"

"A girl?"

Danny chuckled. His mother always asked about his love life, and somebody inevitably dropped Fiona's name into the conversation. Not this time, he would make sure of that. "I've told you about her. Leah."

"Oh yes, of course. All going well?"

Danny couldn't keep the smile from his face. He could just imagine his mother clicking her little heels in delight. "Yes." He remembered the time he asked his mother's advice on marrying Fiona. He didn't like how that conversation went. But he wasn't asking now. He was telling. He knew his mother would like Leah, especially since she was the one to take his mind away from Fiona.

"And?"

"And I've asked her to marry me."

His mother was silent for a few moments. Then a shriek of glee. "Oh, Danny! Danny. Danny! When do I get to meet her? When is the wedding? Tell me more."

"Okay, Mum, okay," Danny replied. She was so predictable, so comfortably predictable. "All in good time. We're coming to Melbourne next month. Her mother lives in Sydney, so everyone will meet everyone."

"Is she good to you, Danny? Are you good to her?"

"Of course, Mum," he said, a little miffed. What did that mean?

"Sorry Danny." Grace clearly realised her gaffe.

"I know, I know," he replied. His mother was just looking out for him, trying to prevent him from making the same mistakes as she had, as his father had. And as Danny and Fiona had. Again, everything had to go back to Fiona. He shook his head, irritated that this hold on him would not be released as easily as it should be. "Gotta go, Mum. I'll call with the details. Say hi to Peter." He hung up the phone and stared at it. He was happy for his mother and that she had found love again. He clenched his teeth in determination. He had too. He was determined to make it work.

He smiled when he thought of Leah, gentle, calm Leah. Something was missing, not really something missing, just... He loved her, but he didn't want to ravage her the way he wanted to Fiona. "Grow up," he said to himself. "That's not what love is based on." He went through the motions of being in love without the terrifying jealousy, the frantic possessiveness he felt when someone looked Leah's way. He wondered at that. This was only the second time he had been in love, and he thought he would feel the obsession he felt with Fiona, the fear that she would be stolen away, that she wanted more than he could be.

He never felt that with Leah, and when men glanced at her, he pulled her arm into his in casual indifference, knowing he didn't want to rip out their eyes. Maybe it was the same thing as had happened with his mother. Maybe Danny needed someone so far removed from Fiona that there would be no comparison, no connection. Or perhaps he had finally grown up. He sincerely hoped it was the latter. He put her out of his mind...or tried to, difficult when she suddenly seemed to be everywhere.

"Hey, I want to see that one," Leah said one afternoon as they walked downtown past a cinema. She was pointing to a film advertisement on the glass front.

Danny turned around and looked straight into Fiona's face. *One Two Three*...the poster said. *Coming Soon*. He cleared his throat. "I know her," he said.

"What? You know Fiona McAllen? How?"

"Went to school with her," he said, thinking fast. He tried not to smile at her stage name. Macrone to McAllen was close enough. He would have to tell Leah the truth, of course, and honestly, there was no reason not to. Fiona may still pop into his head occasionally, but he hadn't heard from her since that night two years ago, and Leah didn't need to know all the details. He was sure there were some things about her past that she kept mum on, too.

"Oh yes, that's right. She's Australian too. Why didn't you tell me that?"

"What's to tell? I had a thing with her back then, and we have been friends since then, but we lost touch."

"She's getting big. I hear she's dating that guy from *Railway Blues*."

Danny felt his back stiffen. "I wouldn't know." He tried to sound nonchalant but could still feel his skin bristle.

*

The email came out of the blue, and Danny sat and stared at it for half an hour, his throat dry, his eyes unblinking. He looked at the time stamp. She had sent it last night. He threw down a glass of water and stared at the screen again, wondering how to reply to it and if he even should. He was never very good at the letter thing, the thing she always wanted him to do. A casual email she had written, nothing untoward, but his heart still beat at an abnormal pace. Casual. Okay. He needed to be the same. And he needed to tell her he was a married man—a *happily* married man. Was he, he wondered.

He hadn't been happy—content, maybe, not happy. Leah was still everything he wanted, but she was spoiled, and he tried to make her happy. Lately, all she talked about was getting pregnant. It was taking every inch of passion from their lovemaking. He wondered if there was all that much of it, to begin with, but he knew she thought her biological clock was ticking, and he had to admit that he wanted children too. Leah was a good choice, a safe choice.

But nothing on earth made his heart thump the way Fiona did, and she still had that power even through benign words on a computer screen. So he replied. The guilt he felt as he typed his response beat at his chest, and he tried to convince himself that they were not more than friends anymore. He hit send and waited in anticipation with more excitement than he should have felt.

When Fiona replied, he was excited to hear from her, but he had to put it out there that he was a married man, lest she get her hopes up. When she told him of her romance with the actor Mason Bent, his heart contorted as usual, but he had no right to feel any of that. Their banter was friendly, and perhaps that was what they needed to be, something that they never really were—friends. He hoped they could be. Surely now that they were in serious relationships, there was a possibility they could be in each other's lives. When he found a deal to be made in LA a few months later, he jumped at the chance.

"What do you think about going to LA for a few days," he called out to Leah.

"Why?"

"Business deal," he said.

"You can't do it here?"

Danny half hoped she would decline, but he also needed her to come along. It was safer that way. "No," he lied. Of course, he could, but he wanted to see Fiona, see if they could be in the same room and not want to tear each other's clothes off.

"Yeah, okay. Would be good to get some sun. I may catch up with Aunt Louise when we're there." She skipped out of the bedroom, looking excited.

"Good. I'll book two tickets. We have to be there by next Wednesday."

"Can't do — appointment with the doc. I can come up the next day. Maybe we can catch some sun while we're there."

Danny smiled at her enthusiasm, but a stab of guilt pierced through his belly. "Sure, that would work."

He wondered if Fiona would have time to catch up. He emailed her the next day.

Danny was pleased when Leah nodded her approval at Fiona after their evening out. He was excited at the new turn of events, that he and Fiona would now carve out a different path for their relationship — friends.

Chapter Twenty-one

The phone was ringing when Fiona pushed open the door of her apartment. She rushed to it and breathed a *hello* into it, flicking off her heels as she reached across the bed. Her feet were killing her even though she had taken them off in the limo. The premiere had been a lot of standing around, being photographed, smiling…the usual.

"How was it?" Danny asked, and Fiona smiled at the sound of his voice.

"Tiring, but I still quite enjoy it. I wish you could have come." She turned over onto her back and twirled the phone cord through her fingers.

"I did try," he replied. "But Leah's cramps are getting worse. This first trimester was not supposed to be the hard part."

Fiona swallowed. When Danny had told her Leah was pregnant a month earlier, she was glad it hadn't been in person. Her throat had caught, and her chest hurt, and it was all she could do to keep from bursting into tears. But she was his friend — she had to support him in whatever he did, but she didn't know how to empathise. She had never been pregnant. "I'm sorry. I hope she's okay." It sounded inane.

"I'm checking the television for clips." He chuckled.

Fiona squeezed her eyes shut, trying to picture him wherever he was, laughing as he flicked the channels in search of her. How she loved the sound of his voice. "Don't watch anything," she said. "I looked terrible. My hair was all over the place…"

"I fucking love your hair," he whispered, and a thrill ran through her spine. "Sorry, I shouldn't have said that."

"It's okay. We are going to stuff up a bit sometimes." This friendship thing was difficult when they, at times, said something inappropriate to each other out of sheer habit or a sudden compulsion of passion. "This takes practice, and we are doing well, I think."

"Yeah," he said, his voice brightening. "At least I don't miss you as much."

"That's probably not the best thing to say either," she replied, keeping her lips tight lest her following words be as suggestive. All she wanted to do was tell him she missed him, still loved him, and leave everything and get on a plane to see him, even for a night. But she couldn't. He had other responsibilities now, he had chosen to marry another woman, and now he would be a father.

"Sorry again…"

"Stop saying sorry." She laughed brightly, trying to lighten the mood.

"I have to go," he said. "Are you coming to New York anytime soon?"

"I wasn't planning to. I haven't been back for ages. Maybe," she said, thinking. "Next week, I have a couple of weeks on my hands, so I may think about making a trip."

"Good! We'll lunch, you and Leah can go shopping…"

"Okay, okay," she said, hearing the eagerness in his voice. If they truly were to be friends, it would be a good idea to spend some time with him…and Leah.

"Talk soon," she said, and before she could help herself, she blurted, "I miss you."

"Me, too," he replied, and she quickly hung up.

She felt a tear roll down her cheek and onto the pillowcase, and she closed her eyes, remembering the last time they were together alone, when he had his arms wrapped around her, when she knew it was the last time they would be together like that, and how broken she felt. She felt the same now and sat up in frustration, shaking her head wildly, trying to free her mind of the past.

She looked around in the dark. Before taking her home, the chauffeur had dropped Mason off at his own apartment, which they had set up some weeks earlier. He had continued to reside with her until opening night, and now the place felt cold and lonely without him. She would miss him. She knew that. After they realised they were not compatible as lovers, they turned out to be great friends, even though he did try to hint at more at times, in the couple of months they still lived together.

Well, now he was free to bed anyone he wished, at least after next week. They still had to keep up appearances for a little while. She wondered what he was doing and reached for the phone again.

"Miss me already?" Mason answered, and she laughed. He was so predictable.

"Actually, I do," she replied. "Are you with anyone?"

"No, not feeling up to it tonight."

"Want to come over? Celebrate?"

"Really?"

"Not like that," she said, laughing. "I just miss you, especially tonight."

"Okay," he said a little too quickly. "I'll be half an hour."

"I'm going to take a bath, so let yourself in. I haven't gotten the key back yet, so you should be able to."

It's Just Chemistry

Chapter Twenty-two

When Fiona saw Danny and Leah at the café, all her senses were awakened, and Fiona wondered again if this friend thing would work. But when Leah gave her a quick hug, and Danny gave her a quick kiss, she had hope. She didn't have the urge to fling herself at him, not with his wife standing right there, her arm entwined in his.

They talked about the pregnancy. Danny had been back to Melbourne to visit, and Fiona was becoming homesick. She had been feeling it more acutely in the last couple of years but could not give up what she had been striving towards. She thought there was plenty of time to go back to live there when her star had waned and when the call in her bones became more urgent.

"I think it's time I visited home," she said.

"You've been back a couple of times, haven't you?" Leah asked.

"I have, but when I return here, I miss it terribly and want to go home, so I just try to stay away. Even when I talk to my friend, Victoria, or my brother and his family, I feel so lost, alone, you know?"

"Yeah. I get it. We may be going back," Danny said.

"To live?"

"We've been thinking about it," Danny replied, looking at Leah, who smiled back. "I'm setting up a company. About time I moved out on my own, try it, and see how it goes. Maybe even before the baby is born."

"Oh wow," Fiona said, not knowing how to feel about it. Sure, she and Danny didn't see each other all that much, communicated via email or phone, but he was going to go back to live in another country, so far away from her. It felt weird, even though he had done it before. It was different now though. Fiona felt like he was going away from her to start a life without her that she couldn't follow. She swallowed and tried to grin. "That's really great, you guys," she said, looking at Leah. "How do you feel about that?"

"I miss my mother," Leah said. "And I guess having family around when the little fella is born would be nice."

"It's a boy?" Fiona jumped from her seat and hugged Leah. "That's so great! Well, it would have been great either way…"

"Gotta pee," Leah said and left the table.

"That's so great, Danny. I'm so happy for you." Fiona stopped her hands from reaching across the table and taking his in them. "You going to Sydney, then?"

"No, Melbourne."

"But Leah's mum is in Sydney, isn't she?"

"I think she wants to come live with us, so…"

Fiona tried not to smile. "Well, I guess that will be some help with the new baby and all."

"Yeah, it will help…with things, I guess." Fiona tried to read the look on his face, thoughtful, and he rubbed at his chin.

"You're not happy about it?"

"She's okay." He grinned a little too forcefully. "And Leah wants her to be with us."

Fiona nodded. She could see something was troubling him, but it wasn't up to her to help with his family problems. She certainly wasn't the right one to intrude on or give advice on anything, especially to Danny. "I really am happy for you Danny. You've done well. In everything."

"Thanks, Fi." He looked down at the table. "I will miss you."

She attempted a laugh. "We barely see each other anyway. We don't even live in the same city. But the travel time from LA to New York is a few hours. From LA to Melbourne…"

"You are not going to hop on a fifteen-hour flight just to see me."

Fiona nodded, considering. She would have in a heartbeat if she had any claim to him, but it would be odd… "Well, we still have phones, email, I guess."

"We can stay in contact. No, we *will* stay in contact." He looked towards the ladies' room. "It may be different, but I meant it. I will always love you and always want you in my life. However, that may be."

Fiona smiled at him shakily. "Yes, I want that, too."

"Friends?" He held out his hand, which she shook heartily.

"Friends."

Chapter Twenty-three

2006

Danny sat at his computer at work and smiled when he saw her name ping on his inbox.

How are things at home?

Good so far. Still settling in. Business is good, hard. Start-up was always going to be difficult. How about you?

I'm getting over the whole film thing. I really am thinking about going back to the stage. What do you think?

Does it matter what I think?

Of course!

I think you should do what makes you happy. If you want to leave LA, go back to New York. Maybe come back to Melbourne. Haha. He took a deep breath, hoping she didn't read too much into what he had written. She had been sick of film for so long now, had been complaining about it, the recognition, the false atmosphere, the takes and retakes. He always remembered the joy on her face when she was in front of an audience. She came alive, and he remembered how he couldn't take his eyes off her. Of course, that was back in high school when he was infatuated with her.

He thought about that. Was he still? Would he forever be? Or was she just something out of reach, something he knew he couldn't have, so he wanted it more? He shook his head. He was married and had no right to think about any of that. They were their past. Leah and baby Kane were his life.

He frowned. Things were not great. Leah had become different when they returned to Melbourne, more erratic, if that was the right word, since her mother moved in. Perhaps it was because she was stressed out with a new baby, and Danny spent so much time building his business. Either way, they were growing apart. She had always been a little removed from him, somewhat distant, reserved, but it seemed that they just didn't talk anymore, not about anything important, not about anything much at all.

I've thought about that. Melbourne is home. New York, I don't know.

Well, I'm in Melbourne. That should be some incentive. He narrowed his eyes at his words and then deleted them. It was too suggestive. But he missed her. How he couldn't fathom. It wasn't like they had spent any substantial amount of time together. But the idea of her being so far away unnerved him. *You've been unhappy for a while. Maybe change your crowd. By the way, how's Barry?*

Barry is good.

Danny couldn't resist a smile. She never wanted to discuss Barry, her new boyfriend, who she'd met at a baseball game. He knew she wasn't keen to discuss her love life with him, and even though he tried to encourage her to do so, telling her that was what friends did, he was glad she didn't. It still bothered him even though he had no right to be bothered with anything of the sort.

I have to go, Fi. I miss you.
Sure. Miss you too, Danny.

Chapter Twenty-four

"Cute baby." Fiona raised Laudie into the air and dodged a swirl of dribble aimed at her chin. She returned Laudie to her brother, who laughed and cradled his daughter.

"More coffee?" Petra stood up to go to the kitchen.

"Yes thanks, Petra." Fiona loved Petra. She was the perfect woman for her once introverted brother. She had brought him out of his shell and made him laugh again. She loved the ease with which they interacted, their open affection with each other and with their children without the volatility that her parents had. She wondered if she was the one who had taken after them, remembering the heated words and the savage love they shared, which she only now realised was reflected in her relationship with Danny when Danny was her lover.

"I envy you," she said to Alfie.

"Why?" he asked. "Because I have the perfect marriage? The perfect little children?" As if on cue, Bernadette, Alfie's five-year-old, ran into the room and plonked herself on Alfie's lap. "It's great. It's hard work at times, but the reward is...I can't describe it."

Fiona pushed her shoulder into her brother's and pulled Bernadette over, wrapping her arms around the little girl, wishing she could spend more time with them. As it was, she saw them just about once a year.

"Maybe I should move back," she said, almost to herself.

"Why don't you?"

Fiona didn't know why. It wasn't as if she was loving life on the big screen. "Maybe," she said thoughtfully.

"How's Danny? Have you seen him?" Alfie asked when Bernadette bounced off Fiona's lap and toddled in the direction of her mother.

The bolt that always pierced her belly at the thought or mention of Danny hit now. "Do you see him? Bump into him?"

"Not really. I saw him and his wife once at a restaurant in the city. He seemed happy enough." Alfie was looking at her closely. "Are you two in touch?"

"Yeah," she said, trying to remain even sounding. "We've been friends for a little while."

Alfie laughed. "You're not over him, are you?"

"Stop it," she said, waving her hand at him. "I'm great. I've had relationships…"

"But you will always hold a flame for him, right?"

Fiona shrugged. "First love, you know, that usually stays, right?" She wanted her brother to tell her, yeah, this was normal. No one really forgets their first love, and those feelings stay forever.

"I guess…" he began.

"What about Maria?" Fiona leaned forward and whispered.

"What about Maria?" he said, unblinking.

"Do you ever think about her?"

Alfie looked at her and frowned. "Not really."

"But she was your first love, right?"

"Yeah, I guess."

"And?" Fiona licked her lips, hoping for some words of wisdom, some hope that this feeling for Danny was normal, something that everyone went through. "Do you see her? Think about her sometimes? Does she hold a little place in your heart?"

Alfie laughed. "*Little* sis," he said. "You want absolution. You won't find it here. Yeah, Maria was my first love, but my true love? No. Will I think about her as someone special? Sure. She taught me a lot, and I did love her. But do I feel anything when I think about her?" He chuckled again. "I don't think about her, to be honest. I did see her a couple of times," he said, and seeing the earnestness on Fiona's face, he slapped his thigh in amusement. "No! If you're thinking there was a spark there, no."

Fiona tried to hide her disappointment. Then she had no hope of being happy. She would forever be in love with someone who would never be hers. She didn't like the look on Alfie's face, one that showed his disappointment for her. She changed the subject. "Do you miss them? The oldies?"

"Yeah. But they wanted to go back. They never really left."

"I should go to see them," Fiona said. "But it's been so busy."

"Life will always get in the way, Fiona."

"Thanks for the life lessons, big brother," she said and leaned over to swat Alfie on the chin. "They were loving it there when I went last year. But it was the same with them. Crazy as bat-shit."

"Haha, maybe that's why I've been avoiding it. Maybe at the end of the year."

Petra came in with the coffee, and Fiona left their house happy for her brother but with a sad heart for herself. She'd never given herself a chance — a real shot with anyone else. Even Barry, who she felt a little spark for, petered out after a few months. Would she ever be happy? Would she ever be satisfied with someone who was not Danny?

Chapter Twenty-five

"Cheers," Danny said, clinking his glass of whiskey on her glass filled with wine. They had met at a bar after Danny had finished work for the day. She had to see him at least once before she returned to LA, and Leah was too busy to make time to come into the city.

"So, tell me, how's Kane?"

"He's so beautiful, Fi." Danny's eyes glowed, and Fiona wished she could have met his son, who was over a year old now. She suddenly felt so alone. Everyone around her was moving on with their lives, and she was still pining for a man with a family, something she was not remotely part of. Her mind returned to the ring he almost gave her, and she shook her mind from it—no going back.

"Have you seen Victoria?" he asked.

"Yes I did when I got in, and we are going to catch up again before I go back."

"I see her from time to time."

"Yeah, she told me," Fiona said and chuckled. "She's got this beautiful kid, four now, and she's so happy. I've never seen her so fulfilled, a clucking mummy." Fiona grinned at the thought of Victoria, so independent, so spontaneous, hugging her daughter the whole time Fiona had been at her place. "She's a bank manager, you know."

"Yes, I do know. She works a block from my office in the city."

"How's that going?" Fiona leaned her head in her hands, gazing at him, genuinely interested in his life, not just how it affected her.

"Good, real good."

"Are you happy you moved back?" she asked him.

"Yeah, I think so. Business is doing well. I've even thought about setting up a branch in Sydney. I think that could happen. Can you picture it? *Devoy Advertising*—National or maybe even International." He laughed. "Maybe eventually."

"More like your dad than you thought, right?"

Danny frowned. "I didn't take a thing from him," he said. "Even his company, nothing."

"I didn't mean that, Danny," Fiona said, reaching out to pat his hand. He nodded. "How's Leah?"

"She's good," he replied quickly, sipping his drink. "What about you? Any new man on the horizon?"

"Not really. Barry lasted six months. That's five and a half more than the others." She snickered.

"You will find the right one," he said without catching her eye.

He's right in front of me. "Another?" She held out her glass.

"Not a cheap drunk, are you?" He downed his whiskey and ordered more drinks.

"Wanna dance?" He held out his hand.

"You dance now?"

"No," he said with a grin. "It's a slow song, and I can just stand there and move around a bit."

"Why not? For old times' sake."

She knew it was dangerous to be in his arms in the state they were in. Not drunk, but light, free. She knew it was dangerous to be in his arms full stop. But she threw caution to the wind and let him lead her to the floor, where other patrons moved slowly to Bon Jovi's *Always*, a song that always brought him to mind. Putting her arms around his neck and resting her cheek on his chest seemed so natural.

She could hear the beat of his heart, a soft thud, and she closed her eyes, a memory flashing back to her. She looked up at him. "Do you remember when we did this last?"

"I remember everything," he said.

"Including what I said to you?" He nodded. "I don't think anything's changed, Danny."

"I know, Fi," he said sadly.

She looked into his eyes, the world closing in, leaving only his eyes, his lips, and she reached up to put hers to them. He leaned forward, and as she felt his graze hers, a drop fell from her eye. She felt herself tug at him, pulling him outside, into the brightness of the lights of the sidewalk and then into the dark of the side-street, into the black of the back of the bar.

She let him place his lips on hers and let herself trail her hands under his shirt and up his chest. She pressed into him hard, feeling his fingers move her hair from her face, caress her neck. She wrapped her leg around his and felt his need.

She suddenly realised what was happening, what was going to happen, and she jumped back, and when she saw the look on his face, she realised that it was the right thing to do, to resist—his face registered horror, shame, and disbelief.

She let her arms flail about her and spun from him. "What the...what the..." she kept saying.

"Fi," he pleaded, but she didn't turn around, wiping savagely at the tears running down her face. There was silence behind her, and she turned to face him.

"What on this earth could possibly make us think we could be friends?" She didn't raise her voice. She wasn't angry with him. She was angry that they had both let it come to this.

"We can't," he said, lowering his eyes. "We clearly cannot be."

"We can't do this anymore, Danny," Fiona said. Her head hurt, her body ached, but what killed her was her heart. Two years of so-called friendship and she still wanted to be with him more than ever. It hampered every relationship she had, comparing every man to Danny. It was his emails she ached for, his voice on the other end of the phone that set her heart alight. And with each message, each call, they couldn't help but hint about how they felt. It wasn't fair to Leah, and it wasn't fair to her or Danny.

"I know, Fi."

"It's taking a toll on you, on me, not even to mention your wife and child. I have to leave you alone."

"What do I tell Leah?"

That question, for some reason, irritated her. "You're her husband, Danny. You will figure it out.

I'm sick of being the third wheel in this relationship, and I think we were mistaken. We cannot be friends."

"I know. I know," he said, fingering his brow. "But where does this leave us?"

"Nowhere, Danny. This is it. I love you. I always will, I've said it before, but this is it. We can't do this like we did before. You have more at stake now, and honestly, so do I."

He moved towards her, and she let him take her in her arms. She kissed his lips lightly and held him tight, feeling his arms around her, squeezing just as tightly. Then she let go.

"Bye, Danny," she said and walked away from him. Again.

Chapter Twenty-six

2007

Fiona met Terry on a yacht. It was a perfect summer day, not too warm, but the sun beaming down its rays in just the right quantity. It had been four months since she left Danny standing against the bar wall, and when she walked out of his life, she set about getting rid of everything that reminded her of him. She returned to LA and deleted her email account, erasing his number from her phone, not that she hadn't memorised it, but the gesture was symbolic enough.

She resolved not to even think about him anymore. She had to move on. She'd done it before. She kept busy. Two movies were wrapping up, and one was about to begin. She went to Italy to see her parents and returned happy that she didn't live in the same country as them. Alfie was right. They were still barking mad. She was determined to learn from them and become everything they were not. It would take work to rid herself of her foolish impulses and crazy jealousy. But when she thought about it, only Danny ever made her feel that way.

Fiona also resolved not to date. She was thirty-four years old, and dating for the sake of it was getting tiresome. No one did it for her, and she wasn't willing to sacrifice her ideals for a quick fix to ease her loneliness. She went out with friends and spent nights at home alone, reading, watching television, listening to music, and trying to become herself without Danny. When she spoke to Victoria, she never talked about him, and even though she knew that they bumped into each other on the odd occasion, Victoria never brought him up in conversation either. It was better that way. She had no news of him, and her determination not to think about him was working. She was happy. Maybe not so much professionally, she was well over the film industry, but in her personal life, she was content.

She thought it funny that what people said was true. Love would happen when she wasn't looking for it. For her, it was at a party for Henry's birthday — she still kept in touch with Henry, and he visited whenever he was in LA. Henry detested parties but acquiesced because Fiona and his wife had conspired to convince him it was what he needed. His teenage children helped to persuade him, excited to take advantage of a party on a yacht. It wasn't a big party. A modest fifty to sixty guests roamed the upper level of the yacht, women in string bikinis and men in very tight shorts. Music blasted from the speakers, and guests danced, drank, and talked about nothing in particular.

Fiona was in a good mood. Henry was happy, the guests seemed to be having fun, and she felt light-hearted, free. She did the rounds, conversed, danced and swam in the pool for a little while, and when she needed a break from the noise and the sun, she wandered down to the lower deck. She leaned her elbows on the railing, raising her face to the sky, her eyes closed, and filled her lungs with the fresh sea air.

"That's a pose," a voice said, followed by a little chuckle.

She felt her skin bristle. "That's audacious," she replied without turning to the voice.

"I wasn't being offensive," the voice replied, a hint of apology in it now.

Fiona opened her eyes and looked at the man standing a few metres from her, swarthy, wisps of his wavy hair flicking in the soft sea breeze. She hadn't met him before but had seen him perhaps at some shindig, but they were never introduced. "Okay. Thank you." She leaned towards him and held out her hand. "I'm Fiona."

"Hi Fiona," he said, shaking her hand. "Terry."

"How do I know you, Terry?" She cocked her head, trying to place the face.

"You don't, not really. I've seen you a couple of times. Once at Jasmine's opening night. Another at Peter Daly's annual house party. And…"

"Oh yes, I remember you at Jasmine's, but Peter's, not so much." She laughed. "But then again, that was a wild one, too many people, too much happening. It got out of hand this year."

"Yeah. I think you left early. I stayed around to help keep things in order."

"Are you a bodyguard or security guard or something?"

Terry smiled, and Fiona found herself drawn to his warmth. "Security, yes." He rolled his eyes skyward. "To the stars."

"Who are you with today?"

"Imelda Ramos."

Fiona had invited Imelda, who she had worked with on *Jackhammer*, her last film, who was also a family friend of Henry's. "Nice kid," Fiona said.

"Yeah, she's young but sweet, not full of herself."

"Like other movie stars?" Fiona raised her eyebrows.

"Well, I guess it can go either way."

"I went the wrong way for a little while," Fiona said, wondering why she was opening up to a man she'd just met. "It happens so smoothly that you don't even realise it's happening. One minute you're the new kid on the block trying to get noticed, and before you realise it, you're throwing temper tantrums and making stupid demands."

"Yeah, I know that about you." She could see he was trying not to laugh.

"How would you know?"

"It was only for two days, but I stepped in for Ronald."

"Ronald? My security? All that time ago? What was it, maybe ten years?"

He let out his laugh now. "Yep. That was me."

Fiona was trying to place him. Ten years wasn't that long. Surely, she would remember the man, especially if he was this nice, attractive, and sweet. She looked back into the crystal water, embarrassed at her thoughts. "Well, I'm sorry if I behaved like a brat," she said.

"No, you weren't that bad. Didn't give me a second look but you weren't rude or anything."

"Thanks," Fiona said, still trying to place him. "How long have you been doing this?" Fiona was more curious to know how old Terry was. His age was very well disguised by the looks of his smooth face, just a tiny tuft of hair beneath his full mouth.

"For about ten years," Terry said. "You were only my third fill-in. I was just starting out, so I was given fill-ins. You were just the beginning."

"Do you enjoy what you do? Like, I mean, are you a wannabe actor?" She wanted to kick herself at the insensitivity of her question. "No, no, what I mean is, was this just a pathway…"

Terry laughed. "No. And no offence, I would rather eat raw fish than do what you do."

"Well, people do eat raw fish." Then she put her hands on her hips in indignance. "And why not?"

"Well, for one, I'm no actor. I couldn't act to save my life. And secondly, seeing the amount of attention you guys get, I don't think I could deal with that, everyone wanting a piece of you, prying into your lives…"

"Have you dated an actress, a client?"

He frowned. "There have been…erm…propositions. I've never taken anyone up on them."

"Have you dated an actress though? You know, one who wasn't your client?" Fiona said slyly.

"Is that a proposition?"

"No," Fiona said, feeling less bold than she had been a second ago.

"How about we grab a coffee? It doesn't look like you're drinking."

"No, I don't drink a lot." Fiona's mind returned to the last time she had a drink — with Danny at the bar. Her heart constricted, and she stuck out her chest in defiance of her thoughts. No, she had been successful in freeing her mind from him. She wasn't going to succumb now, especially when she was about to have a sort-of date with the charming man in front of her. "Come on. Let's find the kitchen."

*

Terry was charming. Terry was loving and giving. Terry was everything a woman could hope for, and as she walked down the aisle, only Terry was in her mind. Some called it a rushed wedding, and some even wondered if it was a shotgun wedding. But Fiona didn't care to explain to anyone why she felt the need to grab this man and hold on to him with everything she had. No one, not Danny, especially not Danny, had ever made her feel so secure, so loved, like the only person that existed in his eyes.

So when they had gone out on their third date, and she had invited him into her apartment for a nightcap, he accepted. And when she pulled him to her as soon as she shut the door of the apartment and allowed him to make love to her for the first time, so tender, yet so passionate, so generous and yet so careful, she knew she wanted to be with him and was already in love with him, not more than two weeks after their meeting on the yacht.

When they had lain on the living room rug, his arms wrapped around her, she wanted to hold him there forever. "Is it too early to tell you I love you?" she asked.

"I think I loved you when I saw you on that boat," he replied. "Maybe even ten years ago," he said and snickered.

She turned to face him, and he smoothed the hair away from her face. "Then I think you should marry me."

His eyes narrowed, but there was a glint of excitement in them. "What?"

Fiona lowered her eyes. "Sorry, I don't know where that came from…"

"No, that's not what I meant." He sat up. "I know we haven't talked about it, and…" He rubbed the back of his neck with his palm. "Well, let's face it, this is the first time, we've even…"

"Terry, it's okay," Fiona said, realising how silly and impulsive she must have sounded. "It was just in the moment…"

He turned to her again. "No. I mean, yes. I mean, no, it's not in the moment. Yes, it's impulsive, but so what? I mean, yes. I want to marry you. Let's do it."

Fiona raised herself and threw her arms around him. "Really? It doesn't have to be tomorrow. We can wait a few years or something…"

"Heck no! I'm not letting you get away! Let's do it. This summer."

Fiona thought for a moment. At the beginning of summer, less than six months away, she was to film on a set in Italy. She would be away for nearly two months. "Can't, not this summer. But why wait that long anyway?"

Terry narrowed his eyes again. "Is there a reason you want to marry me so badly?"

"Yes. Because the quicker we do it, the more I can do this with you every night," she said and rolled atop him, pinning him down and planting little kisses all over his chest.

And now, as she walked down the aisle less than three months later, she knew she had made the right decision to grab this guy. It was a small wedding made up of her parents, who had deigned to fly in from Italy, her brother and his family, and a few friends, which included Victoria and Henry and their families. On Terry's side was his brother, a few friends, and his mother, whom Fiona had met just the week before. The woman, so tall and stately, had to look down, literally, on Fiona and bent her neck to allow Fiona to kiss her cheek, but she had a sly smile that Fiona warmed to immediately.

But, walking up the aisle, it was as if no one else in the world existed except for her and Terry, and she banished the image of Danny that tried to push through the barrier she put up for him.

Terry moved into Fiona's apartment after the wedding, and now, three days later, after spending most of their time in bed, they were determined to sort it all out and figure out the lives that stretched before them.

"What about children Terry?" Fiona had put a box of Terry's things into the spare room and now looked at it as more than just an extra room. Perhaps a space for a third member of their family.

"What about them?" Terry asked, taking her in his arms.

"Okay, so I guess it's been pretty full-on for the last couple of months, but maybe we haven't talked about the important things."

"Like children?" A glint crossed his eyes.

"I guess so. Yeah."

"Do you want to start trying now?" He moved her to the bedroom, and she let him throw little kisses over her neck, closing her eyes and smiling at how loved he made her feel.

"We've been at it for the last few days. You're going to get sick of me already."

"Sorry, baby. You're stuck with me for life now," he said, wiggling his ring finger at her. "And I thought you would want to start making a baby…"

The tinkle of the phone on Fiona's bedside table interrupted his sentence, and he threw his head on the pillow beside her and groaned. "Don't answer it," he grumbled into the pillow.

"I have to. People will think you've kidnapped me."

"Fine, I'll make that coffee."

Fiona pushed him off the bed, and he rolled off, groaning. She picked up the phone, still laughing. "Hello. Wife of Terry Parker here."

"Hello Fi," came the voice of Danny, soft, hesitant.

"Danny?" Fiona took a second to comprehend it was him on the line.

"I just found out about your wedding. I just wanted to call to congratulate you and…Terry."

Fiona found her throat constricting and pulled at the skin on her chin. "Oh, erm, thank you. How did you know?" Stupid question.

"I read about it. Made the news even down here."

"Oh, okay…" Fiona's mind was blank, and she had no idea what to say to Danny. A movement caught her eye, and she looked up to see Terry in the doorway, his brows knitted. She must have sounded odd, unlike herself. He was mouthing, *is everything okay?* She nodded, cleared her throat, and gave him a reassuring smile. He ambled back towards the kitchen, a cheerful whistle following him.

"Fi, are you there?"

"Yep. Sorry. Yep."

"Anyway, that's all I called about. Congratulations, and I wish you all the happiness in the world."

"Thank you," she replied in a stilted voice.

"Okay. Well…"

"How are you, Danny?"

She heard him expel a breath. "I'm well, Fi. Business is going well. Finally opened that new branch in Sydney, so busy. Kane is beautiful but a handful."

"And how's Leah?"

"Yeah, Leah's good."

There was an extended silence, and as much as she wanted to talk to him, hear about his life, and tell him about hers, Fiona knew it was best that they stuck to pleasantries and said goodbye. "I have to go, Danny, but thank you for calling."

"Sure, keep in touch, okay?"

"Uh-huh," she replied, wishing he hadn't said that. "Bye Danny. Give my love to Leah."

She hung up before he could say anything more, grabbed the pillow, and hugged it to her, trying to keep the threatening tears at bay. She had managed to keep him out of her mind and even her heart, and she swore softly, angry that he had called.

"Out of milk," Terry called from the kitchen, and Fiona immediately felt her heart lighten at the sound of his voice. She threw the pillow aside and sprung off the bed. Danny wouldn't rob her of her joy with this man, who she knew would make her happy. She found him in the kitchen rummaging in the drawers. He turned at the sound of her footsteps. "I think I finished the long-life milk last time," he said, grinning sheepishly.

"Forget the milk," she said and dropped the sleeve of her top, revealing her shoulder. "Come and make love to your wife. Let's work on those babies."

Chapter Twenty-seven

2014

Fiona prepared the icing for the cake, her hips moving to the music drumming from the speakers. It was icky, and she was trying to get it as smooth as possible. She grinned. Terry certainly hadn't married her for her prowess in the kitchen, and he would assume the icing would have little dry blobs that would burst in his mouth. He would expect nothing less. The cake she had made with a pre-made mix turned out lopsided, but it tasted good. At least the batter had, before she had put it in the oven.

Seven years. She had to make it special but didn't want to have a big do. A quiet candle-lit dinner was what they wanted, what they needed. She frowned. Could they get back to what they had once? She paused, the spatula in mid-air. She didn't know if they would make it. Maybe it was the seven-year itch. But something was gone, missing, and had been for the last couple of years. The spark had dimmed. Perhaps it had been the absence of a child.

She thought of the conversation three years before when they knew it was probably not on the cards for them to be parents. When they had been for tests, they'd tried IVF, which Fiona couldn't go through again.

She had just been to the toilet and had come out of it trying to hold back tears. Terry had been reading a magazine and, looking up, saw the distress on her face. He dropped the magazine and ran to her.

"I'm sorry!" he had said, clutching her hand earnestly and shoving his handkerchief into her hand.

"Why are you sorry?" Fiona whimpered and held on to Terry's handkerchief, wetting it with tears and snot.

"Because it's my fault."

"No, it's not your fault. It's just not meant to happen."

He drew her to him again and led her to the sofa, where Fiona flopped, and they both sobbed together. "Then we adopt." He rubbed her back.

"I don't know if I have the strength after all this," she said. "I'm nearly forty. No kid wants a grandmother for a mother."

Terry managed a chuckle. "For one, there are still a couple of years before you are, and two, this is when most people have their children. No one has a child at twenty anymore."

"I don't know, Terry. I have all I ever wanted. A great career and a magnificent husband. I think I'm too greedy, wanting more than this."

"Your career—"

"Is the thing that has made this all fall apart. It's me, Terry. I was the one who wanted to wait. I talked you out of it. It was my selfishness."

"No, no, don't say that," he said softly, pulling her into his arms and stroking her hair. "We can do it now.

We have everything. Our house on the beach and our apartment in the city. We can give a child everything."

"Maybe we think about it for a bit," Fiona said, wriggling out of his grip. She pushed past him to the bathroom, leaving him alone on the sofa.

She closed the door behind her and turned on the shower. She stripped off her clothes and let the hot needles of water spike at her. Then she cried, wept, and thought of Danny. Danny, with his family, Danny with his growing business, Danny who had everything — without her. She did resent Terry for not pushing her to have a child all those years ago. She just wanted him to urge her in the direction of motherhood. Why was she the one who had to make the decisions? It was always, *it's okay honey, whenever you're ready*, and *no problem, all the time in the world*. She couldn't stand his indecision, his willingness to give her the final say in everything. For once, she wanted to be led and told what she should do.

She had kept putting it off, a film opportunity arose every time she considered it, and knowing that her time on the silver screen was limited, she took the opportunities, and Terry, so considerate and loving, didn't argue — to the point that she thought that maybe he wasn't that keen on children. But now she knew he just didn't want to make her unhappy, so he acquiesced to whatever she wanted. Sometimes she wished he had more of a backbone.

And a fresh bout of tears hit, rolling down her face, mixing with the soothing pins of the water.

Fiona sighed now. It could be just them. They could be happy again, just the two of them. Marriage was not meant to be easy, but it wasn't just stale, something was lacking, and as much as they both tried to spice things up, it just didn't work. She thought of Danny as she allowed herself to now and then. If they had made it, would the same thing have happened? Maybe. She took a deep breath—no point in thinking about whether or not it would have happened. Danny had been a free man for more than five years, or that was what Victoria had told her, and she hadn't wanted to hear anymore. The temptation to see him had been overwhelming lately, but she knew she was also tempting fate when her marriage was not in a good place.

No, she loved Terry, maybe not with the passion with which she loved Danny, but then, she reasoned, all teenage romances stuck in one's head. But it wasn't just a teenage romance. It was love, real love.

The tinkle of her mobile phone interrupted her thoughts, and she frowned when she saw Victoria's number. She had spoken to Victoria a few days before, so she grabbed at her phone, her heart beating fast.

"Hey Vic, what's up?"

"Fi. How are you?"

"Not much has changed since last Tuesday. Why?" The hairs on her arm were beginning to stand on end. Something was wrong. She could sense it.

"What's that blasted sound?"

"Hang on," Fiona said, running over to turn off the stereo. "What's going on?"

"Er, well…erm…"

Fiona's heart was beating faster with every pause. "Spit it out, Vic!"

"It's Danny."

Fiona felt her knees weaken, and the blood rushed to her face. "What about him?"

"He's, er..."

"Just tell me, Vic!" she screamed into the phone. "Is he okay?"

"He's fine. Oh God, I'm sorry. No, no, he's fine, physically."

Fiona moved to a chair and let herself down on it, breathing loudly. "Okay. Don't ever fucking scare me like that again."

"Sorry. No. I don't know if you know. But he's been arrested."

"What?" Fiona didn't quite understand.

"Something about tax evasion. Some weird shit I don't even understand."

"Where is he?"

"He was in Sydney. But he's back in Melbourne now."

"Have you spoken to him?"

"No. Jeff called to let me know."

"Why?" Fiona knew it was an odd question. She should have been asking about the crime, about Danny and how he was, not how Victoria came upon the information, but it was a diversionary tactic. She needed to process it.

"Because he wanted you to know. Jeff, that is."

Fiona's breath caught. "Why me?"

"I don't know, Fi."

"Did he want to see me?" She felt her heart thump harder now.

"No. He specifically said that Danny didn't want you to find out, but you were going to anyway, so it should come from me."

"Is he okay?"

"It's not maximum-security prison, Fi."

"That's not what I meant."

"Sorry, trying to lighten the mood."

"What do I do?"

"Not much, I guess. But there will be a trial I suppose. Sorry girl. I know you want nothing to do with him," Victoria said with a hint of sarcasm. Fiona could never fool her friend.

"No, I guess not."

*

Fiona didn't quite know how to tell Terry her plan. Dinner had gone well. Even the casserole she cooked had turned out edible, and they sat together and made conversation about work. Fiona hadn't much to tell regarding work lately, and she was sure he was sick of her complaining about film sets, actors, directors, and locations. She'd been on a break for a couple of months, her next film role to begin in over two months. It would give her enough time…

She took a sip of her wine. "So, I wanted to run something by you."

"Sure," Terry said. "What's up?"

"I was thinking of taking a trip to Melbourne." She didn't tell him she'd already booked her flight for the following day.

"Why? We went last year. Don't you have a film to prepare for?"

"Yeah. I can do that while I'm gone. Besides, I've enough time."

Terry narrowed his eyes. "What's the emergency?"

"Well, do you remember Danny? I told you about him, a friend from high school."

"You mean your high school sweetheart?" He chuckled, and Fiona wished she hadn't been so forthcoming about her previous relationships. But then she had vowed never to see Danny again, so she didn't think it would ever matter. Terry had never been the jealous type anyway, he couldn't be, not as the husband of Fiona McAllen.

"Yeah, well. Anyway," she said quickly. "He's in some trouble, and I thought maybe I could go over and see if he could use a hand, you know, financially, or some moral support…"

"For a guy you haven't seen in how many years?"

"Well, isn't that when friendship matters? When someone needs you?" Fiona felt the bristles on her neck stand on end. This had been happening way too often lately—a slight irritation that turned to utter annoyance.

"He told you he needs you?"

"No, he didn't. Vic told me he was in trouble, and since I had some time, I thought I may fly down."

Terry picked at the cake icing, and Fiona tried not to frown. He usually ate whatever was before him and pretended to enjoy it. Now he was peeling the scabby bits off the side. "Do you want me to come with you?"

Fiona shook her head slowly. She was hoping he wouldn't offer. He wouldn't understand their relationship. She wasn't sure that she did. "No. I think it's better if I go on my own. I can stay with Vic and Bobby." She looked up at Terry, who was still frowning into his cake. "Besides, I may not be more than a couple of days. I will just check on things, visit with Alfie, and come back."

"Sure," Terry said and, putting all the dry bits of the cake together, stuck it on his spoon and shoved it into his mouth. "Yum," he said, smiling, and a wave of guilt swept through Fiona.

*

"What am I doing here?" Fiona asked Victoria as she waited for her luggage. She smiled at the few people who recognised her and stopped to let her photograph be taken. Even at her age, she was still a star, a recognisable face in a country across the world. She sometimes enjoyed the recognition, and she remembered a time when she hadn't been so nice, as temporary as it was, and no matter how tired or irritated, she always stopped for a handshake or a photograph with fans.

"You've come to see an old friend," Victoria said. "Anyway, an update. He's posted bail, so he's not in the lock-up. I checked in with him, and he tried to sound all *yeah, everything's okay*, but he didn't sound okay."

"Does he know I'm coming down?"

"Um."

Fiona looked at Victoria, who was looking a little sheepish. "What?"

"He asked if you knew, and when I told him I told you, he was pretty shitty."

"He doesn't want to see me?"

"I didn't tell him you were coming. I thought maybe if you surprised him…"

"Vic!" Fiona pulled her suitcase from the baggage carousel, and they began to walk to the car park.

"Well, you could have called him, emailed him, whatever you guys used to do before," Victoria said defensively.

Fiona shook her head. "No, not a good idea to start that up again. That whole friendship thing…"

"Look, I think right now he could use a friend."

"What do you mean?"

"He's lost pretty much everyone. Leah doesn't even speak to him, not really. Just when she drops off Kane. From what Jeff said, his friends have all but disappeared, except for well, Jeff." Fiona smiled at that. He was the only one of his friends that she had truly liked. "And honestly, I'm not that close to Danny. Or else I would try to be there for him."

"What's going on with the case?" Fiona could only gather so much information from the Internet.

"Goes to court in about two months, I think, unless something happens earlier. Or later. I don't know. It's all legal mumbo-jumbo to me. But he said something about trying to find his tax guy or something. I think that's what they're hoping for."

"Oh. Weird."

They stepped out into the cool August Melbourne evening, and Fiona stopped and closed her eyes, taking a deep breath of her home. Victoria laughed. "It's not that great when you live here in this cold every day."

But Fiona was already feeling the magic that her home could bring. A thought that had lodged in her brain for a couple of years now came spilling from her mouth. "I want to come back," she blurted. "To live."

"Really?"

"Yeah, I think it's time." They continued to walk to the car.

"Why? How? You have a career there. You have an American husband."

"And yet, I would give it up in a heartbeat."

"What? Terry?"

"No," Fiona said quickly, not quite sure that was what she meant. "I mean the film stuff. Maybe I just want to go back to the theatre. I thought I could get over it, but I keep returning to that thought."

"Like other obsessions you have," Victoria said lightly.

"No, not like that," Fiona said, bristling, even though she knew the feeling was similar, the want of something she gave away even if it was beyond her control. "Hey, can we go to a show? What's on here?"

"Don't you get enough of that where you are?"

"I guess, but it's not the same."

"Then, if you're here long enough, we can find something," Victoria said and grabbed Fiona's hand and squeezed it, which only furthered her hankering for home. It had been nearly twenty years since she lived in Melbourne, and she only now realised how much it meant to her. She vowed she was going to come back. She just had to convince Terry.

Chapter Twenty-eight

"Fi!" Danny was unshaven, his hair overgrown, and he wore a blue shirt that seemed about ten sizes too big for him. The spark that used to light up his eyes came through as a little glimmer at the sight of Fiona standing at his door, which he had only opened a fraction.

"Hey you," she said, pushing the door aside, letting herself in. He allowed her to pass and watched as she walked into the apartment, large, airy. She eyed the empty bottles of whiskey, opened packets of chips, and an array of empty food containers strewn around the tables — basically, the place was a mess. "You are a fricken cliché," she said as she put her purse on the only stool in the dining room that didn't have clothes and papers on it "You need a cleaner."

"If you haven't heard yet, I can't afford one," he replied, moving past her to pick up things off the couch. "Here, sit. Give me a minute."

Fiona sat, and Danny disappeared into what she assumed was the bedroom. She looked around again. The place was well furnished, with paintings on the wall, the leather she sat on plush, and a sculpture of who knows what on a pedestal in the corner of the room. Expansive glass windows looked over the city skyline, and Fiona walked over to them. She could see the whole of Melbourne from here. Nice digs, she thought in admiration.

Coffee. She needed coffee. And by the look of Danny, so did he. She wandered back to the kitchen area and looked around. She couldn't make head nor tail of the machine on the bench, and she called to him, but there was no response. She could hear the water running from where he went, in what she assumed was an ensuite. She sighed and remembered that she saw a café downstairs. She grabbed her purse and went in search of coffee – good Melbourne coffee. The thought of it made her mouth water. She hadn't gone to a café this morning. She had just drunk the instant that Victoria offered her, which made her feel like she was home.

"Back in a minute," she called out, letting herself out of the apartment.

*

When she knocked on the door for a second time, two cups of steaming coffee in her hands, the Danny that answered the door this time was a completely different man, the one she recognised. He was still unshaven but in a loose shirt and slacks, his hair slicked back carelessly. But the major difference was the look on his face, pure relief, wonder, and fear, and Fiona gaped at him from the doorway. He lifted the coffee from her hands without a word, and she followed him into the kitchen. He placed the cups on the kitchen counter and then turned around and pulled her into his arms, burying his head in her hair.

"Thought you had gone," he said and she felt his breath on her neck.

Fiona stiffened but allowed herself to feel the familiarity of his arms again, and she slowly relaxed in his embrace, putting her arms around him and holding him tight. They remained glued to each other for a moment, Fiona listening to his heartbeat, feeling hers mirror it. She stepped back and, by instinct, reached her lips to his. But before his could touch hers, they both paused and caught each other's eyes. At the same time, they laughed.

"Okay, first coffee." Fiona broke away from him and gave him a cup from the cardboard holder. "Black strong, no sugar? I'm assuming your tastes haven't changed."

"No," he said with a wink, and she blushed. "Thanks."

"Second, I wish I had a change of clothes." She looked down at her fitted green skirt and cream blouse and put out her long leg at the end of which was a beige stiletto. "What was I thinking wearing this get-up?"

"That you wanted to impress me?" He chuckled.

"Yeah, I guess so. Like an *eat-your-heart-out* costume," she said and threw her head back in a laugh. "But I can't wear this to tidy this...this place where you live."

"I don't want you to," he said indignantly.

"Someone has to. You can't afford a maid, remember."

"Fi really..."

"Stop it. You will help me. I can't sit and have a conversation with you in this mess. I'm no clean freak, Danny, but this is ridiculous."

"Okay," he said with a sigh. "I'll get you some clothes."

She followed him into the bedroom, which was even worse, with clothes scattered over the bed, the armchair, and the floor. "Ugh…"

"Are you just going to keep insulting me?" He pulled out a pair of tracksuit pants from a drawer and a clean t-shirt with *Whitesnake* written on the front.

"Yep. Until this is done." She held up the t-shirt and rolled her eyes. "You haven't grown up, have you?"

"I guess not." He walked out of the room, and Fiona got into his clothes, inhaling the scent of him on his shirt as it came down around her neck, and then taking a deep breath, trying not to think about what she was doing, she headed out to him. She found him attempting to tidy up, and she sat on the stool. "Coffee first," she said, and he stood on the other side of the counter and sipped at his. There was an awkward silence at first. "How's Kane?"

He scoffed. "The only thing left in my life that's any good," he said.

"Really?" she said dryly. "You're going to do this *poor-me* thing."

"You don't know what's going on, Fi."

"Then tell me."

Her phone rang, and she pulled it out of her purse. *Terry.* She considered answering it, but it wasn't the right time. She had already spoken to Terry when she arrived at Victoria's house. She'd call him back when she left here. She didn't plan on staying very long. She put the phone back in her bag, and when she looked at Danny, he was frowning.

"Your husband?"

"Yeah. I'll call him back later. Not urgent." She leaned her chin in her palms. "So, tell me."

"I know it sounds like a cop-out, but I had no clue. My accountant, Edgar P Wallace," he spat out the name, "who I have known for over twenty years, pretty much not just buggered me with the tax office but swindled me."

"Swindled?" Fiona tried not to laugh. "That's a word from the 1940s, I hear."

He smiled. "Yeah, there are a lot of new words I've heard lately. Arraignment, attorney, larceny..." Fiona chuckled despite herself. "I wish I had been smarter," he continued. "That I had checked and rechecked things, but I was a bit full of myself, thinking I was building this empire, and who would want to go up against me? Certainly not my friend." He chortled out a cynical laugh.

"What's the bottom line, though?"

"If they find him, it will be good for me, but if they don't, who knows? Up to seven years..."

Fiona gasped. "Wow."

"Yep. I hope that explains my apartment."

Fiona spun around on the stool to survey the damage. "Okay, enough talk. More of that later. Let's get to work." She hopped off the seat and put her hands on her hips. "But where to start?"

"Fi, you don't have to. Let's just drink our coffee. Chat. We haven't talked to each other in, I don't know, seven, eight years."

"Yeah, I guess. So a couple more hours won't hurt, will it?" She looked back at him. "Garbage bags?"

It took more than a couple of hours, but the music that she insisted on and the cool light of winter that filtered through the windows created an enjoyable atmosphere, and Fiona was energised by the sounds that permeated the air and the proximity to Danny, feeling so far removed and yet so oddly close to him. They worked together, beginning in the lounge room, moving to the bedroom, the bathroom and dining and finishing with the kitchen. They dusted, they collected rubbish, and she scrubbed tables and furniture while he vacuumed. She mopped while he cleaned the windows, and when the place seemed to sparkle at them in appreciation, it was well past three in the afternoon.

Three huge garbage bags stood at the door, and Danny made to take them downstairs. "You hungry?" he asked.

"Yeah, now I think about it, I'm bloody starved."

"You want to go out, get something to eat?"

"Yeah, maybe," Fiona said, wondering whether it was a good idea.

"Well, I'll put out the rubbish, and you can decide then."

He closed the door behind him, and Fiona sat on the stool and pulled out her phone again. She knew it would be too early in LA at this time. There was no point waking Terry up. She'd call in the evening when she returned to Victoria's place. She dialled Victoria.

"Hey lady," came Victoria's chirpy voice. "You coming for dinner? I finish in an hour, and I was wondering if you want anything in particular."

"Really Vic. I eat anything. But anyway. I may have dinner with Danny. Is that okay?" She felt bad that it was her first full day in Melbourne, and she'd spent most of it with Danny. Well, she had come back to Melbourne for him…

"Yeah, sure." Victoria paused for a moment. "Everything all good there, I presume?"

"Yeah. I just helped him with some stuff, and I'm hungry."

"Hmmm, that sounds fishy."

"No, nothing like that," Fiona replied. "But we might go out to catch up."

"I thought that's what you were doing all this time."

"Fine, Mrs Nosy. If you really want to know, I spent the afternoon helping him tidy the shambles that is his apartment."

"Hey Fi?"

"Yeah…" Fiona knew what was coming.

"Be careful, yeah? You have a lot to lose now."

"I am, Vic. I'm not going to do anything to make things worse for Danny or stuff up what I have." Fiona wondered just how much she had to lose and what was worth losing in reality.

"Okay, if you get back too late, don't worry. Bobby is a night owl. Has the TV on all night. Keeps me awake."

"Thanks Vic."

Fiona hung up the phone and went in search of her clothes. She found them on a hanger on the bed, and she smiled that Danny had no care for things of his own but made sure he laid out her things neatly. She sat on the bed and looked at his nightstand. A photograph of a boy, maybe five at the time, sat on it. Kane, she presumed. She lifted the picture and looked at the smiling child, with eyes like his father and dark straight hair like his mother. She ran her fingers over the glass, and a tear pricked at her eye. She would never have her own. How she wished she had Danny's child. The thought that had come unbidden to her mind shocked her, and she quickly replaced the picture. She heard the front door open and promptly began to undress. "Getting changed," she called out.

"Okay," came his reply.

She neatly folded his clothes and placed them on the bed, patting them before she walked to the door and opened it. He stopped and stared at her.

"You're stunning. You know that?"

"Stop it," she replied, embarrassed.

"But you looked so much better in my clothes," he said with a chuckle.

"Not for where I'm taking you for dinner."

"And where is that?"

"*Fresias.*"

"Fi, I don't think so."

"Why not?"

"Because it's not where I can go out lately."

"My treat, Danny."

He looked at his shoes. "I..."

Fiona realised she was making him feel bad about his situation. "Okay then. How about a pub meal? Besides, the restaurants don't open until later, and I'm hungry now."

His face lit up. "Yep. Give me a minute to get dressed." He frowned. "Do I have time for a quick shower?"

"Fine, fine!"

*

The place was buzzing, even for a Tuesday afternoon, but Fiona felt like she was sitting alone with Danny. The busyness of the morning had set them at ease, but now, after they had ordered beers and sat at a booth overlooking the bustling street, an uneasy silence fell between them. Fiona ran her fingers along the length of the bottle, wiping off the condensation on the glass, and Danny picked at the label on his.

"Thanks," Danny started. "For today."

"No problem." She smiled. "But if I see that place like that again, I'm going to walk out of there."

He chuckled. "Yeah, it was pretty bad, wasn't it?"

"How long have you been holed up there?"

"For a week."

"And you caused that much damage?" she said, incredulous.

"I've been in and out."

"Do you want to talk about what's going on?"

"Just have to wait and see, Fi. It's a waiting game, but time is short. The courts are not going to wait to get this guy. They need someone to pin it on."

"But Danny…"

"Wait a sec." He narrowed his eyes, piercing them straight into Fiona's. "Do you think I…"

"Gosh no Danny!" Fiona instinctively put her hand on his. "Not for a minute." She knew he couldn't have done anything stupid. He was one of the most honest people she knew, sometimes to a fault, which she knew from personal experience too. He could not have done the things they said he did.

"What really hurts Fi," he said, stroking the hand that was still on his with his thumb. "Is that anyone I ever trusted, save for Jeff, pretty much has disappeared. My business associates, friends, and people who hung all over me when I was taking them out, shouting them dinners at the *Hilton*, were all gone. No calls. No, *how are you doing?* Victoria checked on me. *Your* friend." He laughed cynically.

"I guess that's when you know who your friends are."

"Are we friends?" He looked down at their hands, and Fiona wasn't sure whether she should retrieve hers from his grasp.

"We never could be before. Maybe now we can. Enough time has gone by." Fiona sounded more certain than she felt, but Danny needed her, needed people he could count on. She would have to put everything else aside, including their past. "How's Leah?"

"Leah and I were done a long time ago. Let's face it, even Kane, who I adore with everything I possess," he said with a raise of his eyebrows, "which is not much now, for sure. But Kane was a band-aid baby. Oh, I love him more than life, but it is what it is."

"You seemed...happy."

"Did I? Even against the wall of a bar?" Fiona swallowed and pursed her lips. "Sorry," he continued. "I didn't mean to go there. I just thought, you know, if we are really trying this friend thing again, then let's just get everything out in the open."

"I guess so. But after that night, I knew we couldn't see or talk to each other anymore. I knew I had to move on from you. It wasn't healthy. It took a toll on every relationship I had."

"I'm sorry." He really did look sorry.

"No, in that case, I'm sorry too. But then you had Leah, and you guys seemed so happy, and I just thought, you know, I want that. Why does Danny get to find happiness despite me?"

"I didn't, though..."

"But you did, even for a while..."

"You are a happily married woman, so what you did obviously worked."

Fiona nodded. Sure, she was trying to be Danny's friend, but discussing her problems with Terry with him would be disloyal to her husband, who had been nothing but loyal and wonderful to her. She just wished that she was able to have a child with him. Maybe things would be better now...a band-aid baby like Danny's. No, she guessed that perhaps that wouldn't have been a good idea after all. "Yeah. After that night, I put you out of my head. A hard thing to do as I hadn't much practice. But it worked." She wanted to add *for a while*, but that wouldn't have been right. What she was feeling right now wasn't right. But apart from their indiscretion at the bar, they had been faithful to their partners.

"Well, to friendship," he said, lifting his bottle, and Fiona clinked hers on it.

"For real this time," she replied, just as the server put their food on the table.

* * * *

"I want to be on the stage again, Danny."

"Why don't you?" It took every inch of him to stop from leaning over and touching her face. "You should do it. If there's anything I've realised, it's the mistake of chasing money. When I had the one business, I was having fun, but then I got greedy and having so much didn't make me happy. In some ways, I'm not sorry I lost it all." He snickered. "I will be unhappy to go to jail, though, especially for the crime of stupidity."

"Oh Danny. It will work out. It just has to."

"Enough about that. What about you though? Why can't you go back to what you want to do?"

"Because…I don't know. Because I've invested so much time in film, and yeah, in some ways, it's satisfying, but my heart has always yearned for the stage."

"Like back at high school."

"Yeah, I guess that's where I found my love of it."

"Then why did you change, move from what you loved doing?"

She smiled slyly. "Would you believe you were part of my decision, and maybe I wasn't completely aware of it?"

He leaned back and considered this, a little taken aback. "Really? Do go on."

"Well, of course, there were other things, the money, the fame, the lost chances, the regrets I may have had, but in the back of my mind, I think I wanted revenge." She laughed, and he admired those perfect teeth, the way they slid against her lips as she spoke.

"How was it revenge?"

"Well, now thinking about it, it sounds stupid, but when I hated you," she said, pointing her finger at him. "And I did, Danny. I really hated you at one time." He nodded calmly, even though her words pierced his heart, and she didn't realise the effect she was having. "I just thought, you know, he fucked me up, and I'll never let him forget me. Clearly you are not a theatregoer, though, so that backfired..."

"So you followed me to New York? Stalker!" His heart warmed at the thought.

"Well no." She crinkled her eyes in thought. "At that time, it was the best career move. Remember, I went from the theatre to the theatre. I was in the same city as you were for two years. Can you believe that, Danny? Two years and we never bumped into each other."

"I wish I had known," he said ruefully. He did wish it, but would it have been different for them? He went there to escape her. How would their being together in New York be any different than it was in Melbourne?

"Well, I think I expected it to be like in Melbourne, and then Henry kept pushing for the movies, and I thought maybe that was my path, which I guess it eventually became." She was babbling, and Danny grinned in amusement.

"Get to the point."

"What was my point?" She screwed her mouth to one side.

"That I was part of the reason you are in a job you hate."

"Oh no," she said. "I don't hate it, per se. But I just prefer the stage. But anyway, as I was saying, a little part of me wanted you to eat your heart out. I wanted to make sure you wouldn't forget me." She giggled with guilt. "I mean, how could you with all those posters everywhere…"

He leaned over and took her hand. "Posters didn't remind me of you."

"Oh." She looked disappointed.

"Nothing would have made me forget you," he said. "I meant, I didn't need posters to remind me that you were in the same world as me." He could see her eyelids flutter, and she looked at her hands. "Hey, don't be scared by what I say to you. It's just the truth. It's not meant to make you upset."

"No, it's okay. I'm fine," she said. She looked at her watch. "I have to go, or else Vic will think I've run away with you."

Danny wished she could run away with him. He wanted her to stay, had been talking to make her forget the time, and here she was, had spent the entire day with him. But he kept his thoughts to himself. She finally had found love, and who was he to get in the middle of her life again? He envied Terry and wished he could have given her everything Terry had. Love, security…There was no security in his life, and it was too late for them anyway. "Yeah, maybe you'd better get back. I'll drive you."

"You don't have to. The station is down the road. Things may have changed a lot since I lived here, but I can still find my way around."

"Fi, I may be accused of many things, but I'm not an arsehole. There's no way I'm sending you off by yourself. Come on. I'll grab the car."

They returned to his apartment and got into the car together. There was an uncomfortable silence, an awkwardness in the small compartment of his car, and Fiona reached out to turn on the music. The night was cloudy, and the streets were busy. They always were in the middle of the city, but as they moved towards the suburb where Victoria lived, the traffic died down, and the passing lights shone through the windscreen. Danny looked towards Fiona, who was staring straight ahead, biting her bottom lip. On impulse, he reached out and put his hand on hers. He felt her start, but she turned hers over and entwined her fingers in his. They drove in silence for another ten minutes until they pulled up at Victoria's house.

He pulled his hand away, but she clutched at it and looked at him. The same look he remembered, the same expression of want that he knew covered his own. "Will I see you again before you leave?" he asked.

"Probably not, Danny. I'm only staying for a few days. I have to see Alfie and Petra and spend some time with my niece and nephew. I'm staying with Vic. We're going to try to see a show while I'm here. Maybe I will check in with Anne, my old director at La Flora. We still keep in touch." She was babbling nervously.

"Okay, I understand."

She smiled broadly now, trying to mask her sadness, but he knew she didn't want to go as much as he wanted her to stay. "Now, don't let me return and find that place a mess again." She pulled at the door handle, and it was all Danny could do to keep from wrenching her away from the door and pulling her to him. She leaned over and kissed him lightly on the cheek. He could smell the light perfume that still hung off her neck. "Bye Danny. Let me know what's happening, okay? And remember, LA is only fifteen hours away."

"Bye Fi," he replied and watched as she left the car, turning to wave to him as she got to the door. Victoria opened the door and gave him a wave, and he slowly let the car roll away from her.

Chapter Twenty-nine

Fiona flew back to LA after spending a little over a week in Melbourne. She had managed to see her brother, go to a show, spend time with Victoria and her family, and even catch up with a few friends from her theatre days, including Anne, who was still plodding away at La Flora and loving every second of it. It made Fiona envious, making her heart yearn for what she gave up even more. She didn't want to return to LA so quickly, but she knew there were things to do, a movie to prepare for, some outlandish Western, a damsel in distress role. Fiona, a forty-year-old, was playing a much younger woman. Sure, it was flattering, but really? After having drinks with her theatre friends, Anne, Frank and Tammy, people she had trodden the boards with back in the day, those same people who were now firmly entrenched in the theatre scene, Fiona found herself somewhat jealous. Maybe it was because she had gone and gotten what she thought she wanted, but was it really what she wanted? Was she happy in film?

She looked out at the clouds that floated below her and felt a knot in the pit of her stomach. She didn't even want to return to LA. She didn't want to do this movie. Why was she? It wasn't like she wasn't financially set up for life. She could come back to Melbourne and do the hard yards again if she had to.

She could feel the saliva in her mouth, a taste of building excitement.

"Your drink," the steward said softly, and she took her *Coke*, thanked him, and resumed her train of thought.

Did she want to go back to Melbourne because Danny was there? She shook her head absently. *No, I'm just homesick. I've left everyone behind to pursue my career. I shouldn't have regrets.* Could she come back here? What about Terry? She was not about to uproot his life. He had never suggested having the slightest inclination to move to Australia. The conversation had never come up, but when he visited Melbourne with her some two years earlier, he seemed happy to leave the cold weather to return to sunny California. It would be unfair to ask him to leave behind his life because of what she wanted.

And what did she want, really? She didn't know anymore. But the idea of working on stage again had begun to take root. She felt a longing for it. Maybe it was because it had been so long—it was a romantic notion of her early adulthood when it had been tough. Everything back then seemed so magical, so energising.

Yes, she would talk to her husband, he would understand, and they would work something out. She frowned. Maybe two years ago, he would have dropped the world for her and what she wanted, and she would have for him too. But now she wasn't so sure. She couldn't pinpoint the problem exactly, but she suspected it was after her miscarriage when the doc told her she couldn't have children. She sighed. It probably had more to do with her retreating from Terry rather than the other way around. She felt a little relieved that their problems had nothing to do with Danny. But she loved Terry. She owed it to him to try to make a go of it. She needed to talk to him, make a plan for their future.

When she got back to her apartment, she was optimistic. Things had to work out. They just did.

"Hey baby," she said, dropping her suitcase and enveloping him in a hug. She'd missed him.

"Feels like you've been gone forever," he replied, and she felt his big bear arms pull her closer.

For some reason that she couldn't understand, Fiona felt defensive and stepped out of his arms. "It's only been a week."

"I know, but I've missed you."

"Me too," she said and held him again, but she couldn't scratch the face of Danny's floating in front of her face.

"Shall we go out to lunch?" she asked.

"Don't you have jet lag or something?"

"No, not yet, but I'm hungry."

"I've just made noodles. Want to share instead?"

"Yes, yum."

"Well, you go unpack, and I'll set the table for us."

"You're the best." Fiona wheeled her suitcase into her room. But she sat on her bed and looked about her. She felt alone, a little lost, and she hated herself for feeling that way. She resolved to begin discussions on returning home. She felt stale, not like someone who had been apart from her husband for a week. She should have been rushing into his arms, kissing him, holding him tight, vowing never to leave his side again. It used to be like that when they were first married, when she had to go on location, or he had a job that took him away from home. But not now. Now she didn't know anything anymore.

They had nearly finished their meal, and Fiona talked about her trip, Victoria, her brother, and her friends.

"And what about the man you went to see?"

"Danny," she replied, her throat tightening. She took a sip of *Coke*. "Yeah, it's a bit of a mess, but it was good to see him, for him to know he still has friends."

"Did you spend much time with him?"

"No, we went out for lunch the first day when I went to see him." She felt uneasy telling Terry this even though she had lunched with other males numerous times, but this seemed sordid because it was Danny. "He's in a situation. His accountant messed him up. He was doing really well. Had a franchise, three, in different cities, and now, he's got nothing."

"Some people just don't know how to manage…"

"It wasn't him," Fiona said, feeling the hackles on her neck rise. "He just trusted someone he shouldn't have."

"Well, you don't know the whole story…"

"I do. He told me."

Terry shrugged. "People tell you what they want to tell you. How do you know that he is not guilty?"

"Because I know. That's how I know." Fiona snapped out the words much more harshly than she intended to.

"Sorry baby, I didn't mean to offend you or your friend, but you just never know the whole truth."

"Well, anyway," Fiona said, trying to see it from Terry's point of view. "It's still a couple of months before it goes to trial, and they are hoping to find the guy, so they can clear his name. In the meantime, he just waits, I guess."

"At least he's not in jail."

"No, not for now," Fiona said thoughtfully.

"And did you go to a show like you messaged me?"

Fiona beamed at the thought of it. "Yes, it was amazing! The atmosphere, the actors, the stage, the lights—oh Terry, I know we go to shows here, and you know how much I love them, but this was different. I wanted to be back up there...on the stage...in my hometown."

"Okay," he said, smiling, clearly tickled with her enthusiasm. "Well, we'll try to get there as much as possible then."

"No," she said carefully. "I know I'm not a stage actor anymore, but that's what I want to do again. You know, be on stage, not in front of a camera."

"Sure, but it sounds like you just want it for the sake of it."

"How do you figure that?" This conversation wasn't what she expected. Danny had told her to dream, to take the world. But Danny had nothing to lose from her doing that. Terry was her husband, and everything would change for them. The circles they both moved in would change. She scratched at her chin. She had to bring up Melbourne somehow.

"You have a successful career," he said. "Let's face it, and not to sound negative, but at this stage of your life, you have to try harder to get roles." Fiona frowned, and he quickly continued. "No, I don't mean that. I meant that if you suddenly decide to pick up and do something on a whim, and it doesn't work out, and you want to come back, well, it will be hard."

"A whim?" Fiona leaned back in her chair and surveyed him. He was right, of course. He had enough experience in the industry to know these things, but a *whim*?

"Sorry Fiona, this is not coming out right. I meant, have you thought about it, really? It's not something you've discussed with me before."

"Then you haven't been listening," she replied. "I've been wanting to go back to the theatre since, well, since I left it, really."

"So why did you leave it?"

"Because, at the time, I was young and stupid. I thought I wanted fame and money and…"

"And now?"

"Now I know I never wanted those things, not really." She knew that was never it. "I think I just wanted to know that I wasn't missing out on something. And now I know."

"Twenty years, it took you?" He widened his eyes in derision. Fiona narrowed hers in irritation. But it was hard to explain, even to her husband. "Well, let's talk about it more tomorrow." He rose from the table. "I have an evening run in a couple of hours. Lady Janet," he said, rolling his eyes.

"You're working tonight?"

"Yes."

Fiona yawned. She was tired. "Okay, maybe I'll call it an evening. Watch TV in bed maybe."

After Terry had left, Fiona lay on the bed, drowsily watching the screen, but suddenly she wasn't tired anymore. She picked up a book and tried to read it, but her mind was buzzing. She looked at the clock. *Ten pm.* It would be afternoon in Melbourne. She picked up her phone and scrolled through her email. Her heart thumped when she saw Danny's name in her inbox.

Hope you got back safely. Thanks for everything. I mean it, Fi, x.

She hit the reply button, and her fingers shook above the keys. *I'm back safe. I hope you're okay. Let me know if I can do anything.*

She stared at the screen, and another message came through. *Good. I miss you already. As friends, okay?*

As friends, yeah, I miss you, too, lol.

Shouldn't you be in bed? Jet lag?

Why is everyone so worried about my jet lag? I'm in bed.

Oh. Okay. Well, have a good night, x.

You too. Well, a good day anyway, xx.

She put her phone on her bedside table and turned over. But she couldn't shake the thought of Danny from her mind. She hated that she still thought about him after all this time, but now she let herself. It was harmless. He was a million miles away from her. And she felt so lonely with that thought.

Chapter Thirty

2015

Fiona was going home. It should have made her excited, elated, but what it cost her made her wonder whether it was worth it. For one, she didn't know if the timing was right for her career. She needed to know something was there for her in Melbourne, and although she had put out the word that she may be returning, there were no offers. Against her better judgement, she declined all film scripts sent her way, not even looking at them for fear of being tempted back when she had made her mind up. She needed to make a complete break. Having finished her last film over three months earlier, she couldn't get her mind off returning home. And it had all tumbled down from there.

The arguments with Terry had already been escalating before that, but now they were a constant when they were together. Not full-blown yelling matches, just a slow game of tennis, a back and forth of words, words slowly tearing them apart. Fiona knew she was being unreasonable for wanting to return to Melbourne, a place Terry had no intention of going to—nothing drew him there. He was happy with how things were and where they lived, and couldn't understand why Fiona wasn't anymore.

"Because I want more," she pleaded, trying to make him understand.

"Am I not enough?"

"Not you, Terry. This," she said, looking around her. "All this is not enough. I want to go home."

"And does *he* have anything to do with this turnaround?"

"This is not a turnaround," she said. "I've been wanting to —"

"You set your mind to it eight months ago when you returned from there. When you saw him."

"Get it through your head! He is my friend." Fiona gritted her teeth to stop from saying more. She never wanted to be angry with her husband but these days it was getting harder and harder.

Terry raised his eyebrows and looked away. "The way you talk about him…"

"Yes, I'm glad things worked out for him. I'm happy he didn't get locked up. It doesn't mean I'm running back to him."

"Maybe he should have," Terry said, raising his eyes to meet Fiona's. "Locked up, I mean."

"How can you say that?" She reared back in shock.

For the first time since she met him, Fiona saw a fire burn behind Terry's eyes. "Because you are going to him. You went to him all those months ago. Came back different, changed. Wanting more. From your career, from your life. And you haven't been happy since."

"I hadn't been for a long time," Fiona said, sitting down and putting her hands over her face. She couldn't believe that had come out of her mouth. She'd played the part of a good and happy wife well for the last three years. Maybe too well. But she'd been trying to believe it, too. She already had one failed marriage behind her, and she hadn't wanted to give up on this one as easily.

"You could have fooled me," Terry said quietly.

"What do we do from here?" Fiona said, resignedly. They were at an impasse.

"You are not going to change your mind Fiona. And honestly, neither am I." He sighed. "Go back if you need to. See how things go. I will wait for you." He paused. "Until you tell me not to."

She was at his feet in a moment. "Oh Terry, I love you. That hasn't changed. But sometimes that's not enough. And if I stay for you, I will resent you. I know me. I will. I already do. And you've been everything to me."

He took her in his arms. "I will always love you. But something has to give. And this is it."

Now, as she sat in her seat, looking out the jet's window again, she had already begun questioning her decision. She hadn't tried hard enough with Terry. Maybe if she insisted, pushed, he would have come with her. And then what would he do in Melbourne? There were no young starlets to escort or protect, unlike in LA. No, it was unfair to have done that.

Her mind wandered to Danny now. Terry had every right to question his existence in her life. They had kept in touch via email and phone. He updated her on his case, which was dismissed once the culprit was found, but he'd lost everything. He had moved to a house in the little town of Wood Hills, more than two hundred kilometres from Melbourne, and she'd lost contact some months earlier. But she was worried about him. She could see his demeanour had already been changing, his outlook growing sour, angry. Victoria had tried to keep in contact, visiting him on the odd occasion, but he didn't want to see her, or anyone else, save for Kane, who he drove to Melbourne to see every couple of weeks. At least, that was what she heard from her friend.

Fiona knew she had to see what was going on. To try to get through to him. She also needed to try to get a job. And in that order. Alfie picked her up from the airport and drove her to his house. She was to stay there for a few weeks until she found a suitable place.

"How was the trip?"

"Banal question Alfie," she said, hugging him. "I am glad to be home."

"Have you figured for how long?"

"Hmm. I'm expecting to stay. But who knows? Maybe this place isn't what it used to be."

"Nothing ever is, Fiona. I just hope you didn't give it all up for…"

"I didn't give this up for *him*," she snapped.

"Okay. But I just hope you've thought about it."

"Alfie. I have enough money to live twenty lives over. Even if I didn't, I need to be happy. In a place I love, with people who are my ilk. I've been there for so long that I no longer know who I am and what I want. I want to be on the stage. And if I don't get to do the big shows, then so be it. I'm sure I can get a gig in a local theatre. And I will be happy."

"Okay Fiona. I know you never gave a crap about that stuff anyway, but if you change your mind, you can go on that has-been show, *I'm a Celebrity…*"

Fiona grimaced. But there were options, and she knew it. "Yeah, I guess." She laughed.

"What about Terry? How did you leave him?"

"He's okay. "Fiona frowned at the thought of her husband, alone, waiting for her to come back. Or at least make a decision. How could she have done that to him?

"Are you together?"

"I don't know. I think we were trying to be realistic. If I stay, which I know I will, and let's face it, so does he, then it is over."

"Do you want it to be?"

"Things were…weird. Have been for a while. Even before I came back the last time. So maybe it was already done."

"Typical celebrity. Two divorces tucked nicely under your belt."

Fiona slapped him on the arm. "Stop it."

"Are you going to see Danny?"

"Yeah. I think I will. When I find out exactly where he lives."

"I know. I tried to see him too, when no one could contact him, and Vic was trying to find him. She even called me."

"You've seen him?"

"Once, a couple of months ago. A long drive," he said sheepishly. "But prepare yourself. He's not in a good way. I know I never really kept in touch, but when I bumped into him a few times through the years, he was happy, looked good, successful. This is a different man."

"Then I must go to him immediately," Fiona said almost to herself, ignoring the look of satisfaction Alfie was throwing her way. "Do you have a car I could borrow?"

Chapter Thirty-one

Fiona looked at the GPS and back at the road, a dirt track that seemed to lead to nowhere. The little arrow on the GPS was pointed to nothing but a green patch on her screen, and Fiona took a deep breath, hoping that the five minutes left of the drive time that blinked on the screen was correct. When she saw a letterbox on the side of the road, she breathed a sigh of relief. At least there were other houses on this street. She kept driving, a little more confidently now, until the GPS told her she had reached her destination when she came upon a brown and green letterbox with the number 415 on it. A gate stood closed, and she hoped there wasn't a lock on it. She couldn't even see the house from where the letterbox stood.

She opened the car door, and the most wonderful of sounds struck her ears—birds, the steady chirp of sparrows, intermittently interrupted by the call of a kookaburra. She stood still for a moment, taking it in, letting the atmosphere take hold of her. It was cool, but on an autumn day, it was not unusual. However, it would be dark soon, and she wished she'd taken Alfie's advice to leave early in the morning. She'd underestimated the time it would take to drive out here, but she had been exhausted after her flight. Now she would have to drive back by night, something she didn't relish, especially when she was driving on the wrong side of the road.

She opened the gate, drove her car through and closed the gate behind her, cursing Danny. What normal person didn't have a phone? Or at least one with a number that people knew? She could have organised a better visit. But she was also excited to surprise him. She couldn't wait to see the look on his face when he saw her standing at his door.

She drove about a hundred metres and rolled her car up to the front of the house. She got out and looked at it. A wooden cottage, not unlike those on a postcard, surrounded by shrubbery and miles and miles of brown and green land. It was beautiful in a sort of run-down way. A large shed stood to one side, and a *Ute* was next to it.

She balled her fists in readiness and took a deep breath. She knocked. Nothing. She knocked again and started to move her feet around. It was getting cold, and she realised she was utterly unprepared. She was wearing a cashmere sweater, jeans and leather boots. No jacket, not on her or in the car, unless Alfie kept one in the boot. She considered going to look when the door opened, and the smile that began to spread on her face faded. If she had seen him from afar, she would not have recognised this man, and her gaze treaded from his head to his feet in slow motion, overgrown beard, baggy sweater, track-suit pants, black socks, a hole in one of them.

"Danny?" she said, almost as if she were willing it not to be him.

"What are you doing here?" His face registered surprise but no joy.

"Danny, it's me," she said and moved towards him, reaching out her arms. He stood there and let her put her arms around him, unmoving, and Fiona almost recoiled from the smell of whiskey that emanated from him. She stepped back to survey him again, but he turned and walked into the house. Fiona followed, bewildered. "Danny," she called to him, but he kept walking and motioned her to an armchair, a comfy one albeit strewn with clothes. He didn't bother to remove them, and Fiona gingerly lifted the shirt and looked around for somewhere to place it. Danny held out his hand, and she gave it to him. He promptly dumped it on the centre table atop half-eaten plates of food.

"Why are you here?" he asked, still standing, looking down at her with an expression of distaste.

"To see you," Fiona replied, wondering what answer he was expecting.

"You shouldn't have," he said and moved back to place himself on the sofa, grabbing at an empty glass that sat beside him on the table. He lifted it to his lips, and when nothing poured into his mouth, he shrugged and put it back on the table. He looked at Fiona in question.

Fiona cleared her throat, not knowing what to say at this point. He didn't seem to want her there, but he clearly needed her there. "I see we're back to cleaning," she said with an uncertain smile, which he didn't return. She hoped humour might lighten the tension.

"I'm fine just the way things are," he said, averting his gaze now.

"I think you are not. What's going on?" Fiona knew she needed to get stuck right into it — no point circling around the issue.

"Why are you here?" he asked again, his eyes now narrowed in her direction.

Fiona got off the armchair and went to him. She sat beside him and took his hand, and he let her hold it. "I'm here for you."

"I don't need any help if that's what you're offering. I'm doing just fine."

"No, I don't think you are. I'm not here to rescue you, Danny. I'm here because I want to see you. I've missed you."

"Well, you've seen me." He removed his hand from hers and got off the sofa. "Anything else?"

"Yes, actually," she said, rising from her seat. "I've had a long drive, and I want coffee, and if you're not going to make me any, I will just do it myself." He shrugged, but Fiona noticed the slight smile that graced his face for a split second. "Where's your kitchen?"

He gestured for her to follow down a hallway that opened into a vast space, floors made of mahogany, countertops of the same and a stone dining table. It was as much a mess as the lounge room, but Fiona saw it was a beautiful area, open windows that reflected the space in the dark of the evening, and she set about getting coffee ready, and whenever she needed something, Danny gestured to where it was. Most of the crockery and cutlery were in a heap in the sink, and while the kettle boiled, Fiona rolled up her sleeves and began to wash.

"I don't need you to do that," he said, pursing his lips.

"Then you should have damn well done it yourself," she said without emotion. "Besides, I need something to do while I wait, since you're not offering up any conversation."

He moved around to where she stood at the sink and began to tidy the area around it while she did the dishes, and when the kettle hissed, he let her continue and made them coffee, taking them to the dining table and setting them down. He moved over to stoke the dwindling fire.

"This is a beautiful place," Fiona said, wiping her hands on the dishcloth when she was done, and sat at the table, warming her hands on the hot cup of coffee.

"Yeah, it is," he replied.

"So, do you want to talk about it?"

"About what? I'm happy here."

"Danny, stop it."

"No, Fiona. I am." He wasn't smiling, and she raised her eyebrows at his use of her full name. He rarely, if ever called her Fiona. It was always Fi.

She didn't want to argue with him, and really, this place was beautiful. She even wondered why she never had the urge to live in the wilderness before, but he was hiding away from the world. He didn't even look happy to see her. "Why did you move here?"

"I just saw this place, and I needed to have it. So I did."

"Danny, stop with the crap. This is me." Fiona leaned forward, getting irritated now.

"Fiona, I told you. You don't have to be here if you don't want to. I'm fine."

"Fine!" Fiona slammed down her cup, returned to the lounge room, picked up her purse, and headed for the door. "See ya, Danny," she called out, tears beginning to fall. She opened the front door and hurried to her car, fumbling with the keys. She could hear him follow her and felt his hand on the small of her back. She turned around and let him envelop her in his arms.

"Don't go," he whispered, and she let her tears smudge into his shirt.

Chapter Thirty-two

They walked slowly back to the house and sat back at the table, Fiona cupping the mug of coffee, glad to have her hands warm again. How cold it was! How did he live in this frozen house? Fiona had told Danny about wanting to return to Melbourne for good and that she was here to see if she could do that. He didn't ask about Terry, and she didn't offer any information.

"I just…this is my home," she said.

"It hasn't been for a while," he replied.

"I think it always had been. I left for my career, and I think I've done what I wanted to do. Or maybe I just did what I thought I needed to do."

"You didn't enjoy what you were doing?"

Fiona cocked her head. "I did at times. I enjoyed it when there was a good director or when I was pushing myself, but it was…mundane…I don't know if that's the right word. It just didn't excite me like being on stage did."

"I loved watching you on stage, even when you were a teenager."

"That's because you just liked watching me, full stop," she said, laughing.

"Well, there was that," he said, rolling his eyes, a little smile appearing on his lips.

"I don't know. Maybe I'm just never going to be completely satisfied with anything I do."

"But the stage…"

Fiona smiled at the thought. "Yeah," she said. "I don't ever remember not enjoying that. I don't even know what it was. The live action, the immediacy of it. I used to be so nervous, even after so many performances, but once I was up there, I was just in another world." She looked at Danny, who was grinning.

"Why didn't you just go back to it? You were a hit on Broadway."

"Because I don't want to be on Broadway, as stupid as that sounds. I want to be here, in Melbourne. I want it to come back full circle." She stopped, knowing how it sounded. No, she hadn't meant *him*, but it felt like it had.

"Well, you are here. So what's the holdup?"

"I got back yesterday Danny," she said with a chuckle.

"And you're here, with me, wasting your time with me."

"Well, I needed a bit of time to regain my balance. And you stopped emailing me! I am here to tell you off!"

"I'm sorry," he said.

"And here I thought we were successful in becoming friends."

"We were," he said.

Fiona cleared her throat, not wanting to continue the way this conversation was going. "I'm hungry. Can I stay for dinner?"

"Honestly Fi, I don't think there's much going on in the pantry. I survive on eggs and bacon." She was glad he had reverted back to *Fi*. He was thawing.

"That will do," she said.

"But I think I'm out. I was going to head out in the morning to replenish."

"What will you eat tonight?"

"Nothing. Maybe some biscuits. I think there's some left." He chuckled.

"There isn't a restaurant for a thousand miles around here." Fiona groaned, thinking about the long drive of nothingness.

"No, but there is a pub twenty minutes away. I know how much you love your pub meals."

"Really?" Fiona sat up.

"Yeah, you want to?"

"Yes!"

"Okay, okay. Let me clean myself up."

"Yeah, you need it," she replied with a grin.

*

They drove in Danny's car to a quaint little bar, sat down together and enjoyed their meal. Danny nodded his head to people, fellow diners and drinkers who seemed to know him. Fiona was glad she was here, in the middle of nowhere, where no one knew who she was. By the time they returned to Danny's house, it was past nine-thirty, and Fiona came in to grab her keys. She wasn't looking forward to the drive home.

"Why don't you just spend the night?" Danny asked when Fiona headed to the door.

"Hmmm." She pondered. "Firstly, I don't think it's a good idea."

"I don't think it's a good idea that you drive for two hours in the dark."

"I don't have any clothes anyway…"

"You can wear mine. You've done that before."

"But do you have any clean clothes?" She asked with a laugh.

"I'm not as grotty as I look," he said, smirking.

"I'm kidding," she said. "But I don't think…"

"Well, how about I drive you back?"

"Logistically, that is silly. You have to drive back to get your car…"

"Then just stay. Call Alfie and let him know. I promise I will behave myself."

"Oh, I know you will because *I* will!" She laughed. "Okay, only if you're really okay with it."

"Really, Fi?"

Fiona called Alfie and explained the situation, apologising for keeping his car longer than she thought. He was okay with it; he didn't need it anyway.

"Nightcap?" Danny asked, bringing over a bottle of whiskey.

"Don't really drink much. Do you have, I don't know, Irish coffee?"

"No, sorry," he said. "But a dollop of this in some real coffee will probably do the trick."

Fiona screwed up her nose. "Just a shot of that, maybe." She wasn't fond of alcohol, but she wanted to sit with him for a while, and he didn't seem to have any other drinks in the house. Hot chocolate would go down really well right now, she thought.

"Do you want to get changed? Get a bit more comfortable?"

"Yeah, I guess," she said, looking down at her boots, and she followed him to the bedroom, which compared to the rest of the house, was pretty tidy. Only the bed was unmade.

"Do you have a spare room?"

"Yeah, but it's empty," he replied sheepishly. "No bed, no couch, I just use it as storage."

"Well, what about when you have guests stay over?"

"You're my first stayover," he said with a smile.

"But where will I stay?"

He was already removing the bed linen. "Here," he said. "I'm taking the couch. Comfier than this bed anyway. Clothes are in that drawer over there," he said, pointing to a chest of drawers. He turned on the night lamp.

After Fiona put on his t-shirt and night pants, as well as a pair of warm socks, she returned to the lounge room, where Danny was sitting on the sofa, which was now devoid of the things that had been on it before. She sat beside him, crossing her legs, and they reminisced about their youth until Fiona found her head drooping.

"Time for bed?" he asked, and she nodded.

"Jet lag still playing with me," she said.

"But it's bedtime here anyway," he said, laughing.

"Goodnight Danny," she said, putting her arms around him.

"Goodnight Fi," he replied and kissed her softly on her cheek.

She closed the bedroom door behind her and sat on the edge of the bed. She looked across at the glass doors and saw herself reflected in them, the lamp casting an eerie glow across the room, Fiona sitting alone on Danny's bed. It seemed surreal that she was here, in the middle of nowhere, with Danny in the other room, when she was saying goodbye to her husband, who was on the other side of the world, not so long ago. She pulled out her phone and scrolled to his number, her fingers hovering over the keys. No, she couldn't call him. They both needed space, time. It was over as they had left it. But she did miss Terry, his gentleness, his presence. And being with Danny today was different. Sure, they were *friends,* but she could see they were still so much more. That was never going to go away.

She walked to the window and closed the curtain. She hopped into bed and pulled the blankets up tight around her chin. It was cold, but she really wanted to feel the things he slept in, the sheets he snuggled into every night, the scent of his nightshirt, and she took a deep breath. He was so close and so far. Again.

Chapter Thirty-three

Fiona slept well, much better than she thought she would, and when she opened her eyes, the light from the large windows shone through the room, even through the curtains, and she could hear the soft rush of a stream somewhere close by. She squeezed her eyes shut for a long moment and tried to work out how she had ended up in Danny's bed. This was not what she had intended, even if he wasn't in it with her. She stretched and looked at the time on her phone that was being charged on the side table. *11.42 AM.* Her eyes flew open. Where was Danny? She went to the en-suite and realised it only contained a toilet. She needed a shower. She couldn't function in the morning without one. She tamed her mussed hair with her hands, realising she had nothing with her, no toiletries, no fresh clothes, no make-up. She came out of the bedroom and looked about for Danny. She found him in the kitchen, putting away groceries from a bunch of bags atop the counter. The smell of bacon hit her, and she inhaled hungrily. The place was spotless, and her eyes widened in surprise.

"Morning," he said, looking up. "Or afternoon," he said, looking at the clock on the wall.

"Slept in big time," she said, yawning. "What the hell happened here?"

He shrugged. "Need a shower?" Fiona nodded. "Through there," he said, pointing down the hall.

She nodded again, followed his direction, and entered the bathroom, where she saw clean, folded towels sitting on the edge of the bath. She turned on the shower and stepped into it, the naughty part of her wishing he would join her, knowing he wouldn't. When she returned to the kitchen, having changed into her clothes, she noticed the look of disappointment on his face.

"Are you leaving already?"

"I have to go home," she said.

"Home? Back to LA?"

"No, back to Alfie's."

"Yeah, okay."

"Why don't you come back to Melbourne with me? You know, stay with me for a while."

"At Alfie's?"

"No, I meant when I get my own place."

"I'm fine here, Fi."

"You have to get back to life, Danny."

"I like this life."

"You're running away."

"Have your breakfast," he said, sliding the plate of bacon and eggs towards her. He grabbed a full bottle of bourbon that sat on a shelf, turned and strode out the back door.

Fiona stared at the plate and felt the old irritation towards him begin to attack. She didn't want to leave him in the state he was in. She knew he was going through something and wanted him to talk to her about it. Even if he didn't return to life, and to be sure, this was the most beautiful place in the world, this wasn't the Danny she knew. He was escaping reality. He couldn't do that forever.

But who was she to save him? Some girl he knew or loved once? She shook her head. She knew she was more than that, but what could she do? No, as irritated with him as she was, she couldn't run away from him. Not again. They had to work together. Something kept bringing them back together, this time friendship, and she couldn't abandon him. She had to swallow her feelings, had to tame them, for him. She could see he had so many demons right now, things she couldn't understand. She couldn't leave him like this. Fiona knew she had to help him with whatever he was going through. She had to go to him. She knew it was why she hadn't searched out any jobs yet. She needed time before she could begin to do that. She knew she had to work things out with Danny first and help him return to who he was, even if it wasn't her place anymore.

She poured herself orange juice that she found in the fridge and sat in silence, eating her breakfast. She then followed in the direction he had left and found herself in a large open room, glass on all sides, facing a sea of brush as far as the eye could see. She opened one of the doors, stepped out into the sun, and searched for him.

She found him behind a shed, sitting on a bench, a drink in his hand. "A bit early for that, isn't it?" She crossed her arms.

"What are you, my mother?" he replied, not amused.

"Well, if your mother were here, she'd be asking the same thing." Fiona glared at him in defiance. "Do you even see her?"

"It's one drink," he said and slyly eyed the bottle beside him. It was more than one drink.

Fiona sat beside him. "Don't be mad at me," she said. "I just want you to be okay."

"I'm okay, Fi," he said more gently. "Go home, go back to Alfie's. Visit your family, see Victoria, and get yourself that job you want. I'm really okay."

"I can see you're not."

"I'm better now that I've seen you," he said, trying a lopsided grin that didn't quite work.

"Do you want me to stay a while?"

"No." He reached forward and kissed her hair. "I will be fine."

"Okay," she said. "Then I'd better get going, or else it will get late again, and you'll be stuck with me."

"That wouldn't be a bad thing, though."

She laughed. "Make up your mind, Mister."

"Come on. I'll walk you to your car."

Fiona reluctantly rose, and they walked hand in hand through the house out the front door.

"Thanks for coming," he said and hugged her. She held him tight, breathing his scent again, returning to the first night she told him she loved him. Things were simpler then, but they had seemed so much more complicated. She wished she could have gone back to that day, to change what happened, be a more mature person, and stop the arguments when they couldn't help themselves.

"When do you come to Melbourne? To see Kane?"

"The following weekend. Maybe we can catch up then."

"Sure," she said, already looking forward to it. She tore herself away from him and got into her car, and he walked towards the gate, opening it for her and closing it behind her as she drove out. She felt the tears sting her eyes as she watched him in the rear-view mirror, a forlorn figure, his arm raised in goodbye.

She got to the end of the track and pulled over, rustling around in the glove box in search of tissues. She couldn't find any and leaned her head on the steering wheel, letting herself cry freely. Why she was crying, she didn't know, but she felt like she was losing him again. Losing him? When she didn't really have him. But it was different this time. There was no expectation of anything else. Their pact to remain friends had been kept, and in that, she found a different Danny and a different Fiona, two adults who accepted that they could never be more than friends. And her friend needed her. As much as he denied it, he was not just alone. He was lonely, drinking himself into a stupor. She couldn't leave him like that.

She turned the car around and drove back.

Chapter Thirty-four

Danny watched her drive away and felt the glimmer of hope that had kept him afloat this morning fade. He was angry with himself. She was not his. She was a married woman. How could he have gotten his hopes up? They were friends, and she had been a good friend. There weren't many of them left. Jeff stuck around. He thought back to when he thought that Jeff had designs on Fiona and when his heart had constricted as he watched them talk on that log, a lifetime ago.

What went wrong? His stupidity. That was it. Alice! He still couldn't understand what possessed him to take up with her. But he knew it stemmed from his insecurity in himself and his jealousy with Fiona. Alice knew when to pounce. But he couldn't blame Alice. The fault was his. Anyway, they tried after that. It just didn't work. They were too different. It always came down to that. And jealousy. That was something that he still felt, especially now when he thought about her in the arms of another man. He sighed. That man was her husband.

He walked back to the house and looked at the place, clean, sparkling. He did it for her. What would he do now? He grabbed his bottle and returned to the shed, his favourite place to sit and enjoy the view of the river — his favourite place to think. He had to go back to the land of the living. He didn't want to leave this place, but he couldn't live a solitary existence here. As much as he loved it, he knew it wasn't who he was. Maybe he would keep it. He would rent somewhere around Melbourne, get a job, and come back here for the weekends, maybe bring Kane with him on holidays. He wasn't going to sell this place, the only thing he had left that was his.

He would call his mother tonight. He needed to speak to her and let her know he was okay. His last call to her had ended badly. She agreed with Fiona. "Get back to the land of the living. Stop hiding away." He had stopped answering her calls, and she'd come up to see him, banging on the door until he opened it. She had taken him in her arms and let him sob like a baby.

"You need time," she'd said.

"I don't ever want to go back."

"Well, you need to work. To live again."

"I've lost everything, Mum. My son..."

"You haven't lost anything. You've thrown those things away."

"Mum, you don't understand..."

"I understand that things haven't turned out the way you wanted. Soccer didn't happen for you. It could have, and you gave up. You tried with your father's career. Something you did because you are good at it. You let your marriage go. That was too hard. You even gave up on..." Danny knew what was coming, and he frowned. Grace saw his expression and looked away. Then she looked back at him.

"Everything doesn't revolve around *her*," he retorted.

"But doesn't it? You two were crazy about each other, tried again even. You nearly asked her to marry you. But you wanted it to be easy—both of you. And now you're holed up here, wishing things were different? Grow up Danny. It's time to."

Danny was shaking his head in anger, in denial. His mother rose from the sofa with a deep sigh, walked over to him and placed a kiss on his head. "And don't expect me to clean up after you," she said, looking around. "I may be your mother, but I taught you better."

He had sat in that chair contemplating what his mother had said. She hadn't minced words to save his feelings anymore, and he smiled. He had let her down but would make it up to her.

Fiona. He had let her down too, again. He would also make it up to her and show her he was worth it. He hoped she'd stay in Melbourne but didn't know if that was on the cards for her. This was a trial, she'd said. To see if she could live here again. He hoped to Heaven she would.

He took another swig of his drink and looked at the bottle. Yes, he would have to stop this little habit too. This was one friend he could afford to live without. He lifted it to his lips.

"Danny!"

He almost choked at the sound of her voice.

* * * *

It had been a week, and Fiona hadn't left Danny's side. When she returned that day, she had knocked and knocked, and he hadn't answered, so she let herself in when she found the door unlocked and searched for him. Back to the shed, and she found him again, swigging the bottle, and he looked up in surprise when she came into sight.

"Danny," she said, stunned.

"What are you doing here?" he asked, clearly irritable that he had been caught drinking again.

"I've come to stay. I'm not leaving."

"Why?" He narrowed his eyes.

"Because you need me," she said.

"I don't..."

"And I need you too. One day was not nearly enough. And by the time I leave, you will not be guzzling that shit to make you happy. Enough," she said.

"Go home, Fi. I don't need you."

"I'm not going anywhere," she said. "Come on, show me around." She saw a slight smile cross his face, and he put down the bottle and put out his hand, which she took.

"How long?"

"I was thinking maybe a week?"

"But what will you wear?"

"Your clothes, dummy. They fit me so well," she said and laughed.

They spent the days walking together, went out in the evenings some nights, cooked together other nights, and when Fiona saw Danny brooding, she let him, not asking questions. She figured when he was ready, he would talk.

"I feel weak," he said one evening as they sat on the porch enjoying the sun's setting, the purple sky streaked with trailing white clouds. "I had everything. I let it all go. And no one stayed. My mother, I barely see. I know, it's my fault. My friends," he said, snickering. "Well, you know what they say. Only Jeff stuck around. Good old Jeff. Leah. I thought Leah would back me and stay by my side, but when my reputation was destroyed and when the money went, she went too. I know we were not together, but the divorce was civil when she was getting the perks of being my ex-wife. Now she can barely look at me. And my son. I hardly see him. Once a fortnight…"

"But can't you see him more often?"

"No, she won't allow it, and she won't let me bring Kane up here, not even for the weekend. It's a mess."

"Well, get yourself together and fight for him."

"I have no fight left, Fi."

"No, you never did," she replied thoughtfully. "You didn't fight for me either."

"You! I loved you with every inch of me."

"And yet you let me go."

"And yet, here you are."

Fiona moved her gaze from him. After spending a week with him, she thought they were successful in being what they needed to be to each other. At night she felt a compulsion to go to him, lie in his arms, make love to him, but she knew that everything would change, that they would go back to fighting, arguing, and she had rather they remain as they were now, close but friends. It was safe. "I'll always be here. Even when I wasn't with you, you were with me."

Danny nodded. "Have you spoken to Terry?"

"Yeah, I called him the day before yesterday. He's okay."

"Does he know where you are?"

Fiona shook her head. She couldn't tell Terry where she was, as innocent as it all was. He wouldn't understand, and she didn't want to hurt him more than she had already by leaving him. She assured him she was fine, and they talked about inane things before she realised there wasn't that much to talk to him about anymore. "Time for bed," Fiona said.

"How long will you stay?"

"Are you ready to get rid of me?"

"No, I want you to stay forever."

"And as much as I want to, I have to go get myself a job. You should, too."

"Don't start, Fi."

"I know, I know. I'm a nag. Imagine being married to me," she said and laughed as she kissed him on the forehead.

"I do," she heard him mutter as she entered the bedroom.

*

Fiona left the next day, this time making it back to Melbourne, and as much as she hated leaving Danny, especially by himself again, she knew she had to. She couldn't save him, but she could help. And she intended to.

Chapter Thirty-five

It was her first gig, a secondary role in a major production. At first, they had clamoured for Fiona — as soon as they knew she was on the market. She hadn't even gotten an agent yet, but she'd visited Anne, the first person who had faith in her, and it wasn't long before the offers flowed in. Fiona knew it was because of her name, a big calling card, but she couldn't restart her career on the stage as the show's star. For one, it wasn't right that she came waltzing in and took someone else's place, people who had struggled to get to the stage, just as she had when she began. Secondly, she was nervous. What if she couldn't do this anymore? What if working in film had changed how she acted on stage? It was acting, sure, but it was different. If she got it wrong, there was no second cut.

She played the part of the best friend in the show, and when rehearsals began, her confidence grew. She could feel the familiarity, yet the difference of what she had done in the last twenty years. But it was something she knew was in her blood. She woke every morning excited and ended a long day exhausted but exhilarated.

She had found a place on the city's outskirts, a three-bedroom house, bought it outright and set about making it her home with the help of Alfie and Victoria. When Danny came down to Melbourne on a weekend every fortnight, they had dinner together before he left. And when she had a couple of days off, she went to stay with him.

Three months after she had arrived, she returned to LA to say goodbye to Terry. By now, she knew it was over, and so did he. They talked once a week, and with each conversation, they knew it was ending.

"Hey Terry," she said when he opened their apartment door.

"Hi stranger," he said, giving her a warm hug. "How's my wife?" Fiona pursed her lips. "I'm kidding, Fiona."

When he had made her a cup of coffee, they sat together on the lounge suite, Fiona not feeling quite comfortable and Terry fidgeting.

"How's the stage?"

"Play begins in a month. I'm terrified."

"You are going to be great," he said, looking at her. "You know you could have done it here, on Broadway. They would have taken you in a heartbeat."

"Maybe," she said thoughtfully. "But that's not where I wanted to be."

"You lived here most of your adult life Fiona. This was your home."

"No, I don't think it ever was." He looked hurt. "No, Terry, that's not what I meant. Not you. You were my life for all the time we were together."

"Not all of it," he said.

"I loved you with all of me."

"And now?" He didn't wait for her to reply. "It's okay, Fiona. I know we're done."

Fiona nodded slowly. She knew it was never going to work for them. She knew it was never going to work with anyone except...

"How's Danny?" he asked as if reading her mind.

"He's okay. He's getting better. Getting out more."

"Are you two..."

"No. We're friends."

"Okay," he said, but Fiona was not convinced he believed that.

"I will get in touch with the lawyers. I don't want anything from you, so it should be pretty straightforward. Did you want anything in particular?"

Fiona shook her head, a tear beginning to fall. She knew this had to end, but it still felt sad. She had some wonderful years with this man who had restored her faith in love. "I didn't deserve you," she said.

"Don't Fiona," Terry said, putting his arm around her. "It was a blast while it lasted. I'll always love you, and I know you love me. Things don't work out sometimes, I guess. Maybe one day we can be friends too."

It's Just Chemistry

Chapter Thirty-six

Opening night was terrifying for Fiona. She had been on pins and needles for the past week, Victoria dropping into the theatre almost every evening to calm her nerves when she had called her in a panic. Now here was her friend again, trying to settle her.

"Here's my opening night gift," Victoria announced as she walked into Fiona's dressing room, which two other actresses shared. She handed her a pink steel bucket with her name embossed on the side.

Fiona managed a laugh. "I don't think I can do this," she said. "What was I thinking?"

"That this is what you were born to do," Victoria replied.

"Vic! Stop being so calm."

"No, you stop being so calm. Just throw up already. Get it out of you, go out on that stage, and perform your little heart out."

"What if I fall on my face?"

"Then you get up, wipe the blood off your nose, and continue."

"Stop being so...so..." Fiona swallowed. "Is Danny here yet?"

"He couldn't make it, Fi." Victoria looked at her shoes. "Trouble with Leah. It was his night tonight."

"But I spoke to him yesterday. He said he might be able to try..."

"Well, I don't think so. Look, maybe it's best if he wasn't here anyway. You would just be a bigger bag of nerves."

Fiona nodded. Victoria was right. She would be a bundle of craziness if she knew Danny was out there in the audience, watching her on her first night, where she might well fall on her face. But she couldn't shake the disappointment she felt. As much as she wanted him to be there, she knew it was best he wasn't. Maybe he could come to one of the other performances. It was to be a four-week run, so there was plenty of time, but she already knew the show was sold-out. She had a hard enough time getting tickets for her friends for this show.

He had been amazing. In the last few months, he had gotten himself a job in an advertising firm, one of his competitors, and he was faring well, getting his zest for life back, becoming the Danny Fiona once knew. He fought for his son, rented a flat close to his ex-wife's house and began to get out more frequently. They caught up often and went out together to a show or dinner, and sometimes she went with him to Wood Hills on the weekend. He now had the spare bedroom set up, and he didn't have to sleep on the couch, which she realised was quite uncomfortable. But they were comfortable with each other, talking about their problems, working out what they had done wrong, and never making a move that strayed from their agreed friendship.

Oh, she wanted him. She knew that would never change, but it just worked so well the way it was, and she couldn't bear for it to fall apart and be left without him in her life again. When she caught him looking at her with that expression of want and love, she just blushed and looked away. She wished now that he had come tonight. She would have loved him to see her again, back on that stage as he did more than twenty-five years earlier.

"Last call," she heard at the door, and Victoria gave her a quick kiss and hurried to her seat.

It was wonderful. What Fiona felt when she had finally thrown up in her pink bucket and stepped on stage was nothing she had felt for the past decade or more. It was terrifying, exhilarating, and the most satisfying thing she had done in a long time. And the applause at the end was the icing on the cake. The whole cast left the stage to *Bravos,* and there was a frenzied atmosphere of delirium when the curtain closed.

Fiona came back to her dressing room and closed her eyes, taking it all in, knowing she had done a good job, knowing she had done the right thing in coming back. And when the cast were called in to debrief, there were congratulations all around.

Fiona left backstage and went into the foyer after removing her make-up and saw Victoria and her family, and Alfie and his family, and she threw herself into their arms all at once. "What did you think?"

"Fantastic, great, etc. etc.," Alfie said, punching her lightly on the arm.

She looked around. "He didn't come?"

Victoria nodded and smiled, gesturing behind Fiona, and she turned to see Danny, a big bunch of roses in his hands. "From my backyard," he said, and Fiona felt herself weaken with relief. She took them from him, and he planted a kiss on her cheek.

"Thank you for these. Thank you for coming, and thank you for making me believe you didn't." She turned back to the others, who were slowly moving to the door, waving sheepishly at her. "Where are they going?" she asked and turned back to him. "And why do you get to stay?"

"Because I want you to myself, and those guys are old and tired and need to go home to bed."

"And you?"

"Well, there's a pub open around the corner. I thought you might be hungry after all that hard work."

"I can't think of food right now," she said.

"Can you think of me, though?"

"Danny," she said, her heart beating faster. "Remember that we're supposed to be..."

"Oh, bugger friendship, Fiona. We were never going to ever be just friends."

"But Danny..."

He put his arms around her and kissed her. "My first," he said, kissing her again. "And my last. No one on this earth I want to love like I love you. No one I *can* love, even if I tried." He reared his head back and surveyed her face. "And I've tried."

"But what about...it will just go back to all that crap." She wanted him to convince her it was going to work this time.

"Then we don't give up so easily. We fight. For us."

Fiona put her arms around his neck and leaned into his chest, feeling his heartbeat, one that echoed hers.

She looked up at him again. "I think I am hungry now," she said. "Let's do this."

The End.

About the Author

Rita H Rowe is a teacher and author with a Bachelor of Arts, a Diploma of Education, and a Masters in Writing. Her journey into writing began as a lifelong dream that she was finally able to pursue at the age of forty-seven, resulting in her first novel, *Never the Moon*. Rita pours her heart and soul into her writing, incorporating her personal experiences with love, romance, hurt, and abuse. To Rita, writing is both a form of therapy and a way to connect with like-minded readers on a deeper level. As an author, Rita hopes to be remembered as someone who created worlds that readers could lose themselves in, even just for a little while. When she isn't writing, Rita enjoys playing pool, painting, going on motorbike rides, and spending time with her children and mother.

OTHER NOVELS BY RITA H ROWE

NEVER THE MOON

https://www.amazon.com/dp/B085RMBS4W

Perfect for fans of Nicolas Sparks' *Dreamland* and Dobyn Carr's *Shelter Mountain*, Rita Rowe's *Never the Moon* is a moving and emotionally charged contemporary romance about overcoming abuse and finding a second chance at love.

Jennifer's life is a labyrinth of pain and turmoil as she finds herself trapped in a marriage with her abusive and controlling husband, Jack. But her heart still beats for her first love, David, whose engagement to Jack's ill sister shattered their chance at a future together.

Years later, fate brings Jennifer and David back together, reigniting their passionate love affair and the hope for the life they always dreamed of. However, with Jack's hold on her growing stronger with each passing day, Jennifer must find the courage to break free from his grasp and reclaim her life with David. Torn between the man she loves and her commitment to the life she has already built, can Jennifer finally escape her abuse and rekindle the happiness she once had in her own life?

Equally heartwarming as it is heart-wrenching, *Never the Moon* brilliantly captures both the tragedy of domestic abuse and the beautiful hope of finding peace, escape, and love.

'Inspired and emotive, a great romance and heart-string tugger of a story...well done to a new voice of romance...' Debra, Indiebook reviewer.

THE BAD SEED

https://www.amazon.com/dp/B093X1Z2RP

In the small town of Treville, love, betrayal, and murder intertwine in a gripping tale of redemption and survival. Joey, the new kid with a troubled past, finds unlikely solace in the arms of Jenna, the only one who sees the good in him. But with enemies lurking in the shadows, including the ruthless thug, Tommy, and Jenna's mysterious mother, their love is put to the ultimate test. Only Tim, the compassionate police officer, offers a glimmer of hope in their desperate situation. But as their enemies close in, will their forbidden love be enough to overcome the odds stacked against them?

As secrets unravel and dark truths come to light, Joey and Jenna must navigate a dangerous web of deceit and danger.

Full of twists and turns, "The Bad Seed" is a gripping tale of young love fighting against the odds. Can they escape the fate that seems all but certain, or will they be torn apart by the forces conspiring against them?

Journey into a world where love is a rare and precious commodity, and discover if Joey and Jenna can defy the odds in this captivating thriller.

'A thrilling, heartbreaking read. I finished this book four days ago and I still can't get it out of my mind.' Tina MK, Amazon reviewer.

BECOMING RUTHLESS
https://www.amazon.com/dp/B09K6J9BBB

Embark on a thrilling journey with Ruth as she discovers the harsh reality of love's deceptive nature.

Betrayed and shattered, she must embrace her inner strength and cunning to survive in a cutthroat world. As she battles her inner demons and navigates treacherous waters, Ruth must decide if she will succumb to darkness or rise as a fierce, unapologetically ruthless force. With twists and turns at every corner, this gripping tale of love, deceit, and self-discovery will leave you hooked until the final page. Join Ruth as she transforms into a woman unstoppable in her quest for survival and redemption.

'When I tell you I was excited for this book, I'm not kidding! I read it in one sitting, and absolutely could not put it down.' Rebecca, Amazon reviewer.

DANCING WITH GHOSTS

https://www.amazon.com/dp/B09W1FZPG3

Alex's world shattered in one tragic moment, leaving her unable to dance or believe in love again. Fleeing to the quiet town of Chernut, she finds solace at Lovelet Manor, where the troubled family residing there mirror her own pain. Amidst the enchanting gardens, Alex meets Edward, igniting a spark of hope in her heart. But as she grapples with her haunting past and uncertain future, she's left wondering if she's truly losing her mind. Will Alex confront her demons and embrace love once more, or will the ghosts of her past continue to haunt her?

Dive into this captivating tale of redemption, love, and self-discovery in "Dancing With Ghosts" and embark on a journey of healing and second chances.

'Binge worthy. This is a ghost story with romance and characters so very real they are believable. I loved it.' Amazon reviewer.

THE IMPOSSIBLE CHOICE

https://www.amazon.com/dp/B0B81PF2R6

In the quaint seaside town of Righteous Creek, Mary thought she had found peace after the devastating loss of her husband. Running a boarding house and focussing on her two teenage daughters were her only priorities until Lawrence arrives, stirring up emotions she thought were long buried. As Mary grapples with her growing feelings for the younger man, she soon realises that their love may come at a price too steep to pay. When faced with an impossible choice that threatens to shatter her world once again, Mary must summon the courage to make a decision that will change everything.

With complex characters, emotional depth, and a gripping plot, 'The Impossible Choice' is a poignant tale of heartbreak, sacrifice, and the power of love in the face of adversity.

'The rollercoaster of emotions that Ms Rowe manages to evoke in each one of her books is astounding and this novel is no exception. A little gem of a book with a conclusion that you will never see coming.' Amazon Reviewer.

DOUBLE DECEPTION – A NOVELLA

In a world of Double Deception, Tess finds herself caught in a web of love, lies, and betrayal. With the perfect life on the surface, Tess craves a love that ignites passion and fills the void in her heart. When she meets Brian, she's swept away by a love that defies all boundaries. But Brian is entangled in a loveless marriage, leaving Tess to question how far she will go to make him hers and hers alone. As their forbidden romance deepens, Tess finds herself consumed by an obsession that threatens to shatter the lives of all involved. Will she risk it all for a love that could cost everything she holds dear? Double Deception is a gripping tale of love, desire, and the dangerous game of deceit that can unravel even the most perfect facades.

'Double Deception is a thrilling, twisted tale that hooked me from the first page. If you enjoy a well-written story with some non-explicit spice, you will not be disappointed. Highly recommend.' Amazon Reviewer.

ALMOST HAPPY

https://www.amazon.com/dp/B0CDTMCB23

In "Almost Happy," embark on a poignant journey with Beverley, a timid woman with health struggles who finds solace in the small blessings life offers. When her controlling childhood sweetheart, Troy, leaves her, Beverley discovers a new love in Jay, only to have her world shattered once again when he abandons her. As Troy resurfaces and proposes, offering the illusion of stability, Jay returns with secrets that threaten to undo everything Beverley holds dear. Torn between past and present, betrayal and forgiveness, Beverley must choose between being almost happy or chasing true joy. Dive into this heart-wrenching tale of love, loss, and self-discovery that will leave you questioning what it truly means to find happiness.

'Oh wow what can I say? This novel is strikingly sad if you look deeply into it but comes across as only tinged with sadness. The theme of emotional abuse and threatening behaviour may be hard for some to read but I felt it was handled well and made for an enjoyable read. For me it had vibes of "Never the Moon" by the same author so if you enjoyed that, I feel you would love this too.'
Amazon Reviewer.

EVERYBODY'S GOT A BILLY

https://www.amazon.com/dp/B0CKMWBB49

Delve into the intricacies of love through a collection of heartwarming and heartbreaking stories that will tug at your heartstrings.

From chance encounters that turn into lifelong love affairs to the bittersweet memories of first loves that still linger, this book explores the various facets of romance and the lasting impact that love leaves on our lives. Whether it's a tale of betrayal, manipulation, or unwavering devotion, each story is a testament to the power of love and the profound effect it has on our hearts. Get ready to be swept away by these intimate accounts that showcase the beauty and complexity of human relationships.

Embark on a journey through the highs and lows of love with "Everybody's Got A Billy" and discover the enduring power of love in all its forms.

'From the tingling highs of love, to the titanic lows, this collection of stories had me reading a few every night. Short and sweet and sometimes sour, each one was more heartfelt than the last. Highly recommend for any short story lover and collector of poetic works in the journey of love, heartbreak and fate.' Amazon reviewer.

GIN AND TOXIC
https://www.amazon.com/dp/B0DC6PK97B

A tumultuous journey through love, betrayal, and self-destruction. Elizabeth, a spirited woman living in the sixties, falls in love with Mike, a charming officer who introduces her to the world of gin and passion. But as their relationship deepens, Mike's dark side emerges, and Elizabeth finds herself trapped in a cycle of abuse and dependency. When Mike's infidelity pushes her to the edge, Elizabeth turns to gin for solace, spiralling into a destructive obsession that costs her everything. Can Elizabeth reclaim her children, her sanity, and her independence, or is she destined to drown in toxic love?

A gripping tale of resilience, redemption, and the power of self-discovery, "Gin and Toxic" will leave you breathless and longing for more.

'Rowe's writing mixes the edge-of-your-seat feeling of a thriller with the deep thinking of serious literature. She brings Elizabeth's world to life in a detailed, moving, touching, sometimes sensory, and even synesthetic way, creating a story that feels both personal and universal.' Julia Kalman, Editor in Chief, New Literary Society.

THE THING WE DON'T TALK ABOUT

Three friends. One secret. But it's a big one. Grace, strong, caring and broken. Her love for Sean is immeasurable but her fear of commitment is greater. Darla, fierce, independent and ambitious. Her whole life has been about getting to the top, but is it worth what she has to pay? Charli, the glue that holds them all together. But at   what   cost?

On one fateful night, their friendship is torn apart, a night they have tried to forget but one that keeps coming back to haunt them. A secret that they have tried to keep hidden for years threatens to pull apart the fabric of their fragile   lives.

The Thing We Don't Talk About – a story of friendship, of hatred, and of love.

Visit Rita H Rowe's website or follow her on her socials. Leave a review or drop her a line. She loves to hear from her readers.

Rita H Rowe - www.ritahrowe.com

Amazon - https://www.amazon.com/stores/Rita-H-Rowe/author/B085WNQCHG?ref=ap_rdr&isDramInt egrated=true&shoppingPortalEnabled=true

Facebook - https://www.facebook.com/ritahrowe

Instagram – www.instagram.com/ritahrowe

www.ingramcontent.com/pod-product-compliance
Lightning Source LLC
Chambersburg PA
CBHW020905200626
46814CB00001BA/189